A Case of Bier

ALSO BY MARY DAHEIM

Here Comes the Bribe

Clam Wake

Gone with the Win

The Wurst Is Yet to Come

All the Pretty Hearses

Loco Motive

Vi Agra Falls

Scots on the Rocks

Saks & Violins

Dead Man Docking

This Old Souse

Hocus Croakus

Silver Scream

Suture Self

A Streetcar Named Expire

Creeps Suzette

Legs Benedict

Snow Place to Die

Wed and Buried

September Mourn

Nutty as a Fruitcake

Auntie Mayhem

Murder, My Suite

Major Vices

A Fit of Tempera

Bantam of the Opera

Dune to Death

Holy Terrors

Fowl Prey

Just Desserts

A Case of Bier

A Bed-and-Breakfast Mystery

Mary Daheim

An Imprint of HarperCollins*Publishers*

A CASE OF BIER. Copyright © 2019 by Mary Daheim. All rights reserved. Printed in the United States of America. No part of this book may be used or reproduced in any manner whatsoever without written permission except in the case of brief quotations embodied in critical articles and reviews. For information address HarperCollins Publishers, 195 Broadway, New York, NY 10007.

HarperCollins books may be purchased for educational, business, or sales promotional use. For information please e-mail the Special Markets Department at SPsales@harpercollins.com.

FIRST HARPERLUXE EDITION

ISBN: 978-0-06-268795-1

HarperLuxe™ is a trademark of HarperCollins Publishers.

Library of Congress Cataloging-in-Publication Data is available upon request.

19 20 21 22 23   ID/LSC   10 9 8 7 6 5 4 3 2 1

Author's Note

The story takes place in August 2006.

Chapter 1

Judith McMonigle Flynn checked the mailbox, noticed it was empty, and hurried down the front porch steps. "Arlene!" she called to her neighbor. "I hear you on the other side of the hedge. Has your mail come yet?"

There was no answer. Judith kept walking to the end of the Rankerses' giant hedge. Arlene suddenly appeared, looking vexed.

"The mailman has come," she replied. "In a way."

"What do you mean?" Judith asked, wishing it wasn't so hot under the late-afternoon sun.

"Charles is new," Arlene replied, her blue eyes darting off to one side. "Carl started trimming our hedge this morning, but it got too warm after lunch, so he quit. Charles thought he could take a shortcut through the hedge where part of it had been removed. He's stuck."

"I thought his name was Chad," Judith said, following Arlene onto the Rankerses' lawn.

"It is," Arlene replied, "but it doesn't suit him. That's why I won't call him Chad. What were his parents thinking? Yoo-hoo, Charles! Are you still in there?"

Judith heard a muffled, fretful voice call out something that sounded like "My bad."

"No, no!" Arlene shouted. "It's not your fault. That is, the blame is on Carl. He didn't need to prune the hedge just because I insisted he should do it before—" A yelp and a thud interrupted her. "Oh dear," she murmured. "That doesn't sound good."

"You're right," Judith agreed, starting for the Flynns' side of the hedge. "If he fell, he must've landed in our yard."

By the time she and Arlene went around the hedge and down the walk next to Hillside Manor, they saw Chad—or Charles—struggling to get to his feet. Judith winced as she noticed that some of her peonies were being trampled underfoot.

"Are you okay?" she asked.

After the fair-haired young man brushed off leaves, twigs, and dirt, he stepped tentatively onto the grass. "I guess so. I don't think I tore my uniform. It'd be awful if I damaged U.S. Postal Service property." He looked at Arlene. "Did I take the wrong route? Through the hedge, I mean."

"Well . . ." Arlene paused, pondering the question. "Not *all* wrong. You did a fine job of *going into* the hedge, but you didn't do as well *coming out.*"

"I guess not," he said, swiping at a twig in his cowlick. "I'd better be on my way. I'm running kind of late." He trotted off down the walk.

"Such a good sport," Arlene remarked. "I must dash to go through our mail. I want to make sure there are no loose ends when we take over at the B&B."

"It's so good of you to fill in while we're on vacation . . ." Judith stopped. Arlene was greeting their daughter, Cathy, who had just pulled into the Rankerses' driveway.

With a shrug, Judith turned toward the porch—and saw Chad rushing toward her. "My mailbag!" he cried. "Have you seen it?"

"No," Judith replied. "Did you leave it in the hedge?"

Chad's sparse eyebrows raised up. "I . . . Right! That's how I got so tangled up. The strap, you know." He disappeared on the other side of the hedge.

Judith shook her head and realized she was sweating under the hot summer sun. Even her shoulder-length gray hair felt damp. But she might as well wait for Chad to come back so she could collect the mail in person. He was new to the route, new to the postal service, and new to the city. As a recent bridegroom whose Pacific Northwest–born wife wanted to remain on her native turf, Chad had left his small Midwestern town and followed her home like a lost pup.

He returned with the Flynns' mail in hand. "Mrs. Rankers says you're taking a trip somewhere," he said. "Do you want the mail stopped?"

Judith shook her head. "Mr. and Mrs. Rankers are going to go back and forth between the houses so that I can keep the B&B open during August's peak travel time. We're just going for about a week. But thanks for inquiring."

"Sure," Chad said with a chipper smile. "Have a good one." He limped off across the cul-de-sac.

Relieved to get out of the sun, Judith went inside. Except for the public utilities bill, the mail was junk. She was tossing the unwanted pieces into the recycling bin under the kitchen sink when Joe Flynn entered the back door.

"Your gruesome mother may be dead," he announced in a cheerful tone, pausing to kiss his wife's cheek. "Where should I put the Spot's fish-and-chips?"

"In the fridge," Judith replied. "It's not even five. What do you mean about Mother?"

Joe's ruddy complexion darkened. "She was letting Sweetums into her hovel when I came out of the garage. She talked to the cat but not to me. Hey, I'm not complaining, but the old bat must be sick. You know she never misses a chance to give me a bad time."

Judith checked the fridge to make sure Joe had remembered to get coleslaw. He had. "It's the weather. She hates the heat as much as I do."

Joe feigned surprise. "She hates the heat more than she hates me?"

"She doesn't hate you," Judith declared. "She didn't even hate Dan when I was married to him. Mother simply doesn't like to share me with anybody. I think that's because my father died so young."

Joe looked skeptical. "Are you sure your father didn't run away from home?"

"You know he didn't. He was born with an enlarged heart. He knew he'd never reach an old age. He was only in his forties. What should've been the rest of his life was stolen from him."

"By your mother?" Joe retorted. "How old is she now? A hundred and ten?"

Judith's usual good nature was ruffled. "Stop. I have to make the appetizers for the guests. Go away and leave me in peace."

"I'll make the appetizers," Joe said. "Why don't you

build us a couple of Scotches and take yours outside? It's cooler under the fruit trees."

Judith smiled wanly. "Maybe I will. You do know your way around a kitchen. And around me."

"We waited a long time to get to this point," Joe said, putting his arm around her. "Which, unfortunately, reminds me that Herself e-mailed me this afternoon."

Judith went rigid at the mention of the first Mrs. Flynn. "What does she want now? Is she tired of being chased by crocodiles in Florida?"

"I think they're gators up around the gulf where she's got her condo," Joe said, still holding on to Judith. "Frankly, she sounds bored. I wonder if she's quit drinking."

"Ha! Maybe she's bored with the brands she's been buying. Why doesn't she switch? Or has she run out of kept men to make a trip to the liquor store?"

Joe finally removed his arm from his wife's waist. "Cut her some slack. Vivian," he went on, using Herself's real name, "is in her eighties. She's not as spry as she used to be. She's talking about going on a cruise."

"Alone?" Judith asked, dark eyes snapping. "Or has she gotten married? Again?"

"No clue," Joe replied, going to the refrigerator. "Go outside, take a seat, and I'll bring your drink. Just make sure your gruesome mother doesn't leave the toolshed."

Judith didn't argue. She wasn't really annoyed with Joe; she was just uneasy about leaving Hillside Manor during the height of the tourist season. It wasn't that she didn't have confidence in the Rankerses' ability to run the B&B. They'd done it on several other occasions. Furthermore, Arlene and Carl doted on Judith's mother. That was no mean feat, given that Gertrude Grover wasn't easy to please.

As if to prove the point, the old lady opened the door to the converted toolshed and called out in her raspy if still-strong voice, "Are you sick or did Lunkhead throw you out of your own house?"

"Joe's making the hors d'oeuvres," Judith replied. "He thought I needed to rest. And in case you've forgotten, the house still belongs to you, Mother."

Gertrude had advanced to the top step. "You think I've lost my marbles? Guess again, kiddo. I'd still be living in *my* house if you hadn't married that jackass. What's for supper? You know I like to eat at five."

Judith could hardly forget the old bone of contention between them.

"Spot's fish-and-chips with coleslaw. I'm not cooking in this weather."

Gertrude curled her lip. "That doesn't sound like supper to me."

"Then call it what we do—dinner," Judith said, brushing perspiration off her high forehead and wishing her mother wouldn't compete with the weather to annoy her. "In fact, you can have it now. I'll heat it in the microwave."

"That's not cooking, that's voodoo," Gertrude retorted. "Faster isn't better. Is your oven broken?"

"Of course not," Judith shot back. "But I don't want to heat up the kitchen. You're older, your circulation isn't as efficient."

"As efficient as what?"

Judith managed a feeble smile. "As it used to be?"

"Look who's talking. Except for some of my teeth, I've got all my original parts. You've got a phony hip."

"It works just fine." Inwardly, Judith winced. During winter nights when the thermometer dropped down into the low thirties, she felt some twinges. But not now, with the mercury edging toward ninety.

Gertrude seemed to read her mind, not an uncommon occurrence. "You won't feel so frisky when you go gallivanting off to the Rockies. You'll probably get frostbite."

"The average temperature in August at Banff and Lake Louise is in the seventies. The weather should be lovely," Judith declared. "Joe and Bill made all of the arrangements this time around. Renie had a big graphic design project to finish by mid-August and I'm always busy with the B&B full up this time of year."

"How does my niece get paid for drawing what looks like squiggles?" Gertrude muttered. "Why doesn't she draw *people*?"

"She does what her clients ask of her," Judith explained for the umpteenth time.

Gertrude made a dismissive gesture. "Dumb. Not as dumb as you and my niece letting the idiots you married arrange your trip. You'll be lucky you don't end up staying in a wigwam."

"We'll be at the historic hotel in Banff," Judith responded. "You remember it from when we went there with Renie's folks back in the fifties."

"Which century?" Gertrude snapped.

"Never mind." Tired of standing in the sun and even more tired of arguing with her mother, she headed back to the house to get Gertrude's so-called supper.

Joe was putting the finishing touches on the appetizers. His green eyes glinted when he saw his wife's sour expression. "The old bat nailed you, right?"

"Mother's had enough practice," Judith said, leaning against a kitchen chair. "You know she really doesn't mean half of what she says. It's her way of teasing."

"Not when she's dumping on me." Joe handed Judith the Scotch he'd poured for her. "Hey, relax. It's just two more days before we take off. Oh—Renie called to say the car rental will be ready for us Thursday morning at eight o'clock. She's in a snit, of course."

"You know my cousin hates mornings," Judith said. "Bill may have to carry her out of the house in her bathrobe. What kind did they rent?"

"A Lexus GX470," Joe replied after taking a sip from his own drink. "Very roomy."

"Very expensive," Judith murmured. "Why didn't they get something cheaper?"

Joe sighed. "If we wanted cheap, we could've taken one of our cars. But we agreed your Honda and the Joneses' Camry would be too cramped. What next? You want to make the trip in my MG with Renie and Bill in the boot?"

Judith couldn't help but smile at Joe's referring to the trunk of his classic red sports car as its boot. He'd had the car when they first met over forty years earlier and still kept it in almost mint condition. "I'm not sure which one I fell in love with first—you or your car."

"That's not very flattering," Joe said in his low, mellow voice. "Hey, are the current guests checking out tomorrow?"

Judith nodded. "By chance, they all stayed through

the weekend. But we'll be full again tomorrow. As I've mentioned, we're booked until after the Labor Day weekend."

"Good." Joe picked up the hors d'oeuvre tray and carried it out to the living room.

Judith sipped from her Scotch before putting Gertrude's dinner in the microwave. When she carried the "supper" out to the toolshed, Sweetums leaped from behind the birdbath, his orange-and-white furry body almost causing her to drop the plate.

"You . . . cat!" she cried. "You're too old to cause problems. Why don't *you* need a hip replacement? Four of them, in fact." With an indignant swish of his plume-like tail, Sweetums ascended the two steps to Gertrude's door.

"Don't bother me," the old lady said. "I'm watching the news. It's all bad." Making the announcement seemed to please her.

"Here's your dinner." Judith set the plate down on the cluttered card table.

Gertrude stared at the food. "That's it?"

"It's the same thing Joe and I are having."

"Where's the dessert?"

"You don't need dessert. Joe and I don't need it either. It's not good to overeat in hot weather."

Gertrude's faded blue eyes pinioned her daughter.

"Hot? I should be wearing two sweaters, not just one. Go away. I want to find out what's happening in Angioplastystan or wherever some jackasses are blowing up other jackasses."

Judith complied. She realized her mother was probably even crabbier than usual because the Flynns were going on vacation. But she also knew that Carl and Arlene would pamper the old lady to pieces. Their own parents had been dead for years. If nothing else, it made Judith feel less guilty about leaving her mother for any length of time. Deep down, she would miss the old girl and Gertrude would probably miss her.

Maybe.

Chapter 2

The next two days flew by. Guests in, guests out. Packing had taken up almost all of a full day. With their departure set for 8 A.M. Thursday, Judith had gotten up at the usual early hour to start the guests' breakfasts. She'd insisted that Joe sleep in—a relative term at six in the morning—since he and Bill Jones would share the driving. Carl and Arlene arrived at seven thirty to take over the kitchen. Judith took Gertrude's breakfast to the toolshed and kissed her mother good-bye.

"Don't take any wooden nickels," the old lady cautioned. It was her standard unsentimental farewell.

At seven forty, a Yellow Cab pulled up in front of the B&B. Judith could see only one passenger—Bill Jones.

When Joe opened the front door to sit by the driver, he asked where Renie was.

"Back here on the floor," Bill replied. "She's asleep. Watch it, Judith. Try not to step on her."

Judith edged her way onto the leather seat. Renie was curled up in a lump-like fashion, but at least she was dressed for travel. "How come she's not in her bathrobe?" Judith whispered to Bill.

"She got dressed last night," he replied in his normal voice. "Renie couldn't cope with the concept of getting ready before ten o'clock. I'm used to it," he said in the manner of a martyr being led out into the Roman Colosseum.

In retrospect, Judith remembered the next hour only in a hazy, disjointed way. A family with three noisy young children at the car rental agency had briefly disturbed Renie's rest. Judith recalled something about "birth control" and "openings at an orphanage" before her cousin went back to sleep. Then they were in the Lexus SUV, where Renie flopped onto one of the two spare second-row seats and nodded off again.

That was just as well. The Flynns and the Joneses were stuck in the tail end of downtown morning traffic. Joe frequently swore under his breath. Bill offered an occasional word of wry consolation. Renie slept on. Finally, at nine thirty-eight, the Lexus turned onto

I-90 and headed east. Joe expelled a sigh of relief; Judith patted his arm.

"We're on our way," she said softly.

Joe smiled.

Fifteen minutes later, they heard a rustling sound behind them. Judith turned around. Bill was staring straight ahead, his expression stoic, his arms folded. Suddenly Renie's tousled head popped up behind her cousin's seat. "Where am I? What happened?" she asked in a foggy voice.

"We're heading for the pass," Judith informed her.

"The pass? What pass?" Renie scrunched her eyes together before struggling to get onto the seat next to Bill. "Oh. I know where we are. Banff, right? Has anybody been murdered yet?"

"Why," Judith said in exasperation, "are you saying that?"

Renie looked puzzled—and sleepy. "Because that's happened before when we went on a trip."

"Not this time," Judith declared with fervor. She was about to tell her cousin not to even think about coming across a corpse, but Renie's head fell on Bill's shoulder and she immediately went back to sleep.

Despite the rocky start, the trip went well. Joe and Bill had taken turns driving, but they both balked at covering over six hundred miles in a single day. Besides, there was no point in reaching the Banff Springs Hotel until the afternoon check-in time. They'd spent Thursday night at a Best Western motel in Cranbrook, British Columbia, before making the short drive to the province of Alberta and their luxurious accommodations. On Friday morning, the farther east they traveled, the more spectacular they found the scenery. Lush forests, rugged mountains, and an occasional placid lake dazzled Judith.

"Moose!" Renie shouted as they passed an alpine meadow. "Hey, everybody, give me a dollar."

Judith twisted her neck to look at her cousin. "Are you crazy? We aren't playing that old travel game."

"We did when we were kids and made this trip the first time," Renie responded with a pout that looked like it belonged to the era of the earlier vacation. "The winner got quarters back then. My father won and he did all the driving. You came in last because you were reading a book about juvenile delinquents. I don't think you saw any bears or deer, let alone a moose. The only thing you spotted was some roadkill. A beaver, I think."

"*Ten Million Delinquents*," Judith asserted. "That book was pretty far-out stuff back then. Raunchy, as we used to say. And Mother almost got kissed by a bear on that trip, but she rolled up the car window really fast."

Joe, who was driving, darted a glance at his wife. "That bear must've needed glasses."

"Grandeur!" Renie exclaimed. "That's the word to describe the scenery. The majestic, verdant evergreen trees, the austere, craggy mountains, the glittering, jewel-like lakes! That's the kind of language I'll use when I design T-Nubile's new brochures. They'll foam at the mouth."

Bill, who had been napping, stared at his wife. "What has any of that got to do with telephone networks? I don't see the rationale for your emotionally overwrought approach."

Renie stared back. "Who cares? I don't aim for relevance, I aim for mood. If their mood is good, they pay me. Don't use your psychobabble on me, Dr. Jones. I know it's rubbish."

"My patients don't," Bill said, taking off his glasses and rubbing his eyes. "Hey, we must be almost to Banff. I'm glad I finished my nap in time."

Judith leaned forward. "I can see the hotel. It really does look like a Scottish castle. We're in time for lunch."

"Yay!" Renie cried. "They have a fabulous restaurant. I'm starving."

"You usually are, coz," Judith said good-naturedly. "I'm kind of hungry, too. It's going on one."

Less than five minutes later they had turned off the Trans-Canada Highway and were on Banff Avenue. The Banff Springs Hotel was on the edge of town, benignly looming over the residents and the tourists who crowded the main street. Judith checked the map, giving Joe directions on how to get to the main entrance.

As they approached their destination, Renie was bouncing in her seat. "I remember when we came here as kids, I wished we could've stayed at the hotel. All we got was a peek into the lobby."

"Watch it," Bill said dryly. "You're going to break the seat belt."

Renie ignored him. "We're going to go through the porte cochere. I love a porte cochere!"

Judith turned to smile at her cousin. "Maybe I *was* too much into that juvenile delinquent book. I don't even remember seeing the hotel."

"Serves you right," Renie said, but she was still grinning like a chimp.

Joe turned off the engine. "Hey, Bill, come with me and we'll check in, then figure out where we park, okay?"

Bill craned his neck, looking around outside. "They

should have somebody here to—ow!" He winced. "My damned neck's going out on me again. Okay, let's go. I need to get settled in and do my exercises."

The men exited the car. Renie had turned serious. "Bill and his chronic neck problems! I hope they've got a chiropractor on the hotel payroll."

"They might," Judith said. "Judging from the brochures, they've got just about everything including a world-class spa. A massage sounds good about now, after all this sitting. I'm not used to that at the B&B."

"I'll settle for a lavish lunch," Renie said, rolling down the window. "Mmmm. The air smells wonderful. It reminds me of the summers we spent at the family cabins."

"A wonderful way to grow up," Judith murmured, nostalgia washing over her. "So what if we didn't have electricity or running water? It made us hardy."

"It did," Renie agreed. "I was really kind of sorry when they finally hooked us up to the county public utility district. It took away some of the rustic . . . Oh, here come the husbands." She paused. "They look grim. Does that mean nobody's going to help with our luggage?"

Joe opened the driver's door; Bill opened the rear passenger door. Both of their faces had turned quite ruddy.

"There's been a mistake," Joe stated solemnly. "Our reservations were . . ." He appealed to Bill. "How would *you* put it?"

"I wouldn't," Bill said. "I told you, we should've sneaked out the back way."

Judith was confused. "We didn't get a big suite?"

Joe gulped. "We didn't get any of their suites. We . . . we didn't even get rooms."

"*What?*" the cousins shrieked in unison.

The husbands looked as if they were about to run away. But being of mature mind and aging bodies, they reconsidered.

"Okay," Joe said, finally getting behind the wheel as Bill semi-collapsed in the backseat next to Renie. "We made a little mistake and got the name of this place mixed up. It's being changed to the Fairmont Banff Springs hotel."

"You mean we have nowhere to stay?" a flabbergasted Judith demanded.

"No!" Bill bellowed. "We have reservations, but they're at the Banff Springs *Motel.* Ow! There goes my neck again!"

"A good thing," Renie snarled, "or I might break your neck. And why aren't we having lunch at the hotel?"

Joe was pulling out from under the porte cochere.

"Not only are they full up, but they're hosting a big convention that takes a break at one o'clock. We *do* have directions for the place with the reservations we did make. The woman at the desk told us it's very nice."

"It better be," Judith muttered. Maybe she and Renie should have retained their longtime roles as the travel planners. But, Judith reminded herself, at least they were in beautiful Banff. What could possibly go wrong?

Chapter 3

"Hey!" Renie cried. "How'd we get on Squirrel Street? I hate squirrels. They're the most subversive of all terrorists. They should be nuked in their cozy little nests."

"I'm following directions, damn it," Joe snapped. "The motel is by the Bow River."

Judith's dark eyes were darker than ever. "It'd better not be *in* the river."

After a few more turns and what seemed like at least a couple of miles, they finally espied the Banff Springs Motel in a fairly secluded area. Its two cedar-shake stories looked well maintained and the landscaping featured what looked like native plantings. Judith recognized the bright yellow of Gaillardia and goldenrod, but the pale lavender asters seemed to be past their prime. More importantly, she noted a sign that read SUITES AVAILABLE.

"This time," she said in an almost normal voice, "Renie and I will do the checking in."

The husbands remained silent.

The lobby was small but tasteful. There were several paintings by what appeared to be local artists, mostly of the area's scenery, judging from the variety of geographical features represented. Judith thought they added a homey touch. A bald, burly older man stood at the rear of the reception area. He nodded at the cousins before opening a door and disappearing from view. Mindful of her status as guest and not innkeeper, she gave the young ponytailed desk clerk a friendly smile, identified herself, and told him they had reservations.

"I have reservations about a lot of things," Renie whispered to Judith as the clerk checked his computer. "Especially our husbands. Can a nonresident file for a quickie divorce in Canada?"

"Dubious," Judith murmured.

"Here you are, the Rose and the Yew Suites," the clerk said, reaching for the key cards. "How many?"

Judith asked for two of each, noting that the clerk's name tag read NIALL MCPHERSON. "Is that older man the motel owner?" she asked in her friendliest voice.

Niall nodded. "George Barnes had the motel built four, maybe five years ago."

"It looks very nice," she said. "Where do we park?"

"On the river side," he replied. "Great view. Your suites adjoin, just to the right as you get out of the elevator."

The cousins headed for the car. "It seems like a decent place," Judith remarked.

But Renie wasn't yet mollified. "They don't have a restaurant. If I don't eat something soon, you'd better cover your arms. I might start gnawing on one of them."

"The mosquitoes are already doing that," Judith responded, waving a couple of them away before getting into the car.

"Well?" Joe said doubtfully.

"We're registered," Judith replied in an unenthusiastic tone. "We'd better stow our stuff and head for a restaurant."

"Stuff the stowing," Renie yipped. "I'm about to pass out from hunger. It's going on two."

Bill agreed. "She's right. My ulcer's acting up. Let's hit it. Boppin'!"

Judith and Joe had no choice but to keep up with the Joneses.

The Maple Leaf Café was able to seat them at once. The decor was deemed rustically elegant by Renie, who ordered the smoked salmon bagel and practically swooned when she saw the size of the portion. Joe and Bill both opted for portobello burgers, while Judith chose the smoked turkey sandwich. By the end of the meal, the wives' good humor was partially restored. At least they'd stopped threatening to kill their mates.

But after they parked the car behind the motel and went up to the second floor, they discovered that the word *suite* had been lost in the Canadian translation.

"It's just a big room!" Renie exclaimed after Bill opened the door.

Joe was still fiddling with the key card. "Go inside. Maybe you're only looking at part of it." He felt the lock click open and ushered Judith inside. "Well?" he said, sounding a little unsure of himself.

Judith studied the large room with its reasonably tasteful appointments. The bathroom was fairly spacious and there was a roomy closet. "That other door must open into the rest of the suite."

"I doubt it could . . ." Joe began, but Judith was reaching for the knob.

The door opened. "Coz!" Renie cried. "I thought this was part of our suite!"

Joe rubbed at his high forehead. "Forget it. Apparently, it's the motel's version of a suite, okay? Bill and I screwed up." He looked at Judith and then at Renie. "If you two want to keep bitching about the accommodations and ruin our vacation, fine. But where we stay isn't as big a deal as what else this area has to offer. Bill and I still plan to go fishing, so if you two are going to sulk, we won't be around to let it drive us nuts."

The cousins exchanged quick glances. "Joe's right," Judith admitted. "This is our big getaway. We probably won't spend much time in the motel. There are other things to do around here. We might even spend a day at Lake Louise's chateau."

Renie finally stopped scowling and sighed. "You're right. We've been bratty. Let's have fun instead."

Judith took Joe's hand. "What would you like to do?"

He winced. "Honestly? Take a nap. All that driving wore me out."

In the other room, Bill was already plumping up a pillow. "You read my mind. Everybody pipe down. I need at least an hour to recover. My morning stretch at the wheel was rugged."

Renie looked at Judith. "I think we need to go away."

"Yes. Yes," she agreed as Joe started removing the

counterpane on their bed. "We'll explore our surroundings."

The cousins headed to the elevator and went outside.
"I keep forgetting," Judith said, "we're not as young as
we used to be."

"We're still alive," Renie noted as they walked to
the river's edge, where a slight breeze made the riffles
sparkle under the late-afternoon sun. "That's a start."
She paused. "What's that weird rig up ahead by the
bend? It looks like a platform, but it's got wheels. And
there's a big tent. Are we by a campground?"

"Could be," Judith allowed, batting at a couple of
mosquitoes. "They do have them in Banff."

Ever curious, they followed the river's curve and
saw a half-dozen people standing between an aging
VW bus and a wooden picnic table. "That bunch seems
to have the clearing to themselves," Renie said. "I don't
see any sign of other campers nearby. It looks like a
private gathering. Maybe we shouldn't butt in."

"This isn't private property, it's part of the town,"
Judith said, waving at a wooden sign pointing in various directions, to the golf course, the ski lifts, and the
town center. Or centre, as it was spelled in Canada.
"Should we turn around?"

Renie shrugged. "We're almost there. Maybe
they're Gypsies. We could get our fortunes told."

The cousins kept walking. Within twenty yards of the little group, a rawboned young man with dark slicked-back hair called out to them. "You from the funeral home?"

Judith wasn't sure she'd heard right, but waited until she got closer to respond. "We're from the motel," she finally said. "Are you camping here?"

"In a way," the man replied, putting out a suntanned hand. "I'm Teddy Stokes. How-de-do." His grip was so tight that Judith winced. He reached out to Renie, but she backed off.

"I've got spots," she said solemnly. "Very contagious."

Judith noticed two more people emerging from the tent. "You have quite a crew here. Are they all family?"

Teddy nodded. "Yep. But none of the young'uns are here. Not a good idea to bring 'em on a trip like this."

"Well . . . yes, small children don't appreciate scenery," Judith said for lack of anything more cogent.

"I s'pose that's so," Teddy said vaguely as he glanced back at the others in his traveling party. "It's the dying part that we fussed over. Best to leave the kiddies behind with Auntie Sheba. Aw, c'mon. You might as well meet the rest of us Stokes folks while we're all still alive."

"You expect to be dead soon?" Renie blurted. "Won't that spoil your vacation plans?"

"Huh?" Teddy said over his shoulder. "I mean Codger. He's older than dirt and just about gone. Who wants to live to be a hundred? No point when you're feeble. I expect he'll hang in there for an hour, hour and a half, maybe. The ride from Big Stove, Nebraska, plumb tuckered him out."

"Big Stove?" Judith echoed.

"Right," Teddy responded, pausing for a moment. "We saw a sign for somethin' called Radium Hot Springs and kinda wondered if dunkin' Codger there might help, but it was out of our way. Then we spotted another sign for the Cave and Basin National Historic Site with sulfur hot springs. That sounded like the devil hisself, so we figgered it'd do Codger more harm than good. He never was much of a one for messin' with demons and such. He liked to, as he put it, 'live like a rightful man.' Or was it 'a righteous man'? I ferget."

Judith glanced at Renie, but she merely shrugged. They followed Teddy to the picnic table, where the rest of the Stokes family had gathered. One of two younger women looked at the cousins curiously, but the seated middle-aged couple seemed absorbed in a game of cribbage.

"Not right to have such a fine day," Teddy muttered. "Not right at all." But as he drew closer to the picnic table, he changed gears. "Met some nice ladies from the motel," he announced. "Where's Codger? They'd probably like to see him before he takes off."

"We would?" Renie whispered.

"Shhh." Judith nudged her with an elbow.

One of the younger women stepped forward. Her freckled face might have been pretty if she didn't look so worried. "Teddy, honey," she said, putting a hand on his arm, "this is family stuff, private-like. We don't want strangers hangin' out with us."

"You're right," Renie agreed. "We'll be going now. Bye."

"Hold it!" The deep masculine voice came from the older man who'd been playing cribbage. "Are you two from one of those smutty tabloids?"

Renie opened her mouth to say no, but Judith spoke first. "We've heard about Codger. We've come to learn about his . . . plans. They should make fascinating reading." Her cousin's groan was barely audible.

Several sets of eyes grew very round. "Really?" the young woman exclaimed. "That is *too* thrilling!"

Judith ignored what sounded like Renie gnashing her big teeth. "It isn't every day that we come across a story like yours."

The older man took off his hat, which looked to Judith as if it were made out of seed corn. He beckoned for the visitors to join him at the picnic table.

"Take a seat," he said, gesturing at the woman who sat across from him. "This here is Ma Stokes. I'm Pa. I don't shake hands—early arthritis. Danged rough on a farmer."

Judith noticed the reddened, swollen joints of Pa Stokes's big hands. He was probably in his fifties, with shrubby eyebrows, a long jaw, and tanned, sinewy arms. Even sitting down, Ma looked like a butterball. Yet her round face was curiously unlined and her gray eyes seemed unusually penetrating.

"What do you raise?" Judith asked.

Pa's expression was wry. "Corn. What else would us folks raise in Nebraska? Oh, we plant some soybeans, too. Earlier harvest than corn. Every little bit helps, but corn's the main thing. You ever hear of the Cornhuskers football team? That's our big university. Had some real famous players, lot of 'em came off of farms."

"Of course," Judith said with a smile. "Our aunt Ellen and uncle Win live in Beatrice and have season tickets. They inherited them from his father, who owned a farm equipment store."

"Don't know Beatrice that well," Pa murmured. "We don't travel much."

"But you've come all the way to Banff," Judith pointed out. "That's a fairly long trip."

"Necessity," Ma said, speaking for the first time. "Codger rules."

Pa nodded once. "That's my old man." He looked at the young woman. "Where *is* the old coot, Martha Lou? He's too feeble to wander off."

"Teddy and I put him in the tent," she replied. "The bugs were eatin' him alive."

"Dang. He's all but dead anyway. Let me see to it." Pa struggled a bit to get his long legs out from under the table. "Be back shortly. Oh!" Stretching a bit, he looked at Teddy. "You ever get them commodity reports?"

"Not yet, Pa," Teddy said. "The local newspaper don't have 'em. My laptop's batteries are down."

Pa nodded once. "Tell me when you have the dope. I gotta keep up with prices."

Renie was obviously growing restless. Or maybe she was tired of swatting mosquitoes. "Okay, Ma," she addressed the clan matron, "let's hear why you stay-at-homes made the trip to Banff."

Ma heaved a big sigh, making her big bosom bounce. "It's Codger's idea. Back in the fifties, he saw a Marilyn Monroe movie and that actor who always looked as if he was falling asleep. Richard or Ronald or—"

"Robert Mitchum," Renie said. "Was the movie *River of No Return*?"

Ma's gray eyes snapped. "That's right! I forgot what

it was called. Before my time. Anyways, Codger fell in love with Marilyn—and with the Bow River up here. He vowed that when he died, he wanted to be sent off down the Bow. We never could say no to Codger. So here we are. It looks like his time has finally come." The last words sounded jarringly hopeful.

Pa nodded solemnly. "Yep, Delia. I expect so."

Judith's eyes darted to the so-called platform. Now that they were closer, she realized that the wheeled conveyance was an elegant piece of workmanship. "Is that a . . . bier?"

Ma nodded. "We borrowed it from the Big Stove Funeral Home. But," she went on with a frown, "it seems we won't be able to return it unless Codger falls off and it washes up on the bank. Maybe we didn't think that through."

Pa exited the tent. "Not yet," Pa said, shaking his head. "It seems like the old coot has rallied a bit. I can tell he's still breathing. Dang."

Teddy had sidled up next to Pa. "If nothing's gonna happen for a while, why don't Martha Lou and me head into town and rustle up some grub?"

Pa shrugged. "Bring some back for the rest of us. We gotta keep watch. Oh—get your sis some of that foreign taffy or whatever she likes." He craned his neck to look beyond his son. "Where *is* Ada? She didn't wander off again, I hope. She might go into the river, not knowin' it's kinda deep."

"Here she comes," Teddy said. "Ada's keepin' watch on Codger. Fond of him, in her way."

If Ma struck Judith as a butterball, Ada looked like a string bean. The younger woman was almost gaunt, with deep-set eyes and an expressionless face. "Hello, Ada," Judith said, smiling.

Ada walked by the picnic table without making eye contact and sat down in a flimsy striped canvas chair. Pa chuckled. "She don't talk much. Shy, is our Ada."

"That's okay," Renie said. "I don't talk much either when I'm with coz."

Judith resisted giving Renie a dirty look as she struggled a bit to get up from the picnic table. Sitting too long on a hard, wooden surface had caused a few twinges in her artificial hip. "We'll be going, too. It's after hours in New York City, but we should check in with our editor. Have a pleasant evening."

Renie was already ten yards ahead of Judith. Her farewell to the Stokes folks had been one slightly raised hand along with an expression that indicated she hoped she'd never see the Big Stove contingent again. Judith, however, was curious about the corn-raising family and reluctantly admitted to herself that Renie's hope was probably in vain.

Chapter 4

"Why," Renie asked in annoyance, "didn't we make our husbands nap in the same room? We've only been gone for a little over half an hour, so how do we amuse ourselves?"

Judith slowed her step as they reached the motel grounds. "I *think* I saw an arrow pointing to 'Guest Bar.' Let's go through the main entrance and check it out."

They noticed the No Vacancy sign had been lit. "I hope those folks have reservations," Judith said as they walked around a bronze Buick parked in the driveway.

"Not your problem," Renie pointed out, glancing at the front license plate. "They're from Iowa. It's a wonder these mountains don't scare them away."

"Not everybody in Iowa is scared of mountains," Judith said. "They obviously came here to see the real thing."

But judging from what they saw confronting Niall at the desk, the couple from Iowa was irate. "How the hell could you lose our reservations? My wife requested them two weeks ago. We already paid a deposit by traveler's check. Look again. The last name is spelled *O-D-E-L-L*."

"Yes, sir," Niall mumbled. "I'll see if . . ."

Mrs. Odell jabbed her elbow into Mr. Odell's arm. "It's not under our name," she declared, with an annoyed glance at her husband. "The rest of my family is here in Banff, so I used my maiden name—Stokes. Adela Stokes. I assume my relatives have already checked in."

A relieved Niall looked up from his computer. "Yes, I've got it. Two rooms. The other Stokes party hasn't arrived yet."

But the burly, balding man who was Adela's husband wasn't giving in easily. "The second room is for our twins. They're eighteen and of legal age. The rest of the Stokes bunch are on their own." He glanced at Adela. "Unless the reservation is under your cousin's married name."

"That's their problem, Norman," his wife snapped.

"I don't care if they're staying in a cave. They're all idiots. Go tell Win and Winnie to grab their luggage and come inside." With a flip of her blond pageboy, she turned back to Niall. "What's the legal age for drinking in Alberta?"

"Eighteen," Niall replied.

"Good." Adela turned to her husband. "The kids can get tanked while you unpack for us. I need a nap." She practically ripped the key cards out of the clerk's hand and stomped off to the elevator. Norman shrugged and ambled out the door.

Niall offered the cousins a feeble smile. "Kind of a . . . forceful lady, eh?"

Judith smiled. "Not all Americans are like that."

"I know." He sighed. "Most of you Yanks are nice. Maybe their other relatives decided not to join them here. I'm not sure I'd want to spend my holiday with them."

"True," Judith conceded, thinking that neither *holiday* nor *vacation* suited the Stokes folks' reason for the visit. "Is the bar open?"

It was. Judith and Renie went down the hall, where they found a cozy sitting room with an unlit stone fireplace, uninspired-looking but comfortable chairs, and a silver bell by a handprinted sign that said RING FOR SERVICE.

Judith had barely withdrawn her hand when a pert young Asian girl came through what looked like a wall panel behind the mahogany bar. "Hello," she said with a big smile. "I'm Jenny. What would you like?"

"Scotch on the rocks, water back for me," Judith said. "Naughton's, the same way for my cousin."

Jenny smiled and nodded. "I hope you're enjoying your visit," she said, expertly pouring the drinks.

"We only arrived about an hour ago," Judith replied. "But we've been here once before, when we were much younger. It's breathtaking country."

"Changed a bit since then, I'll bet," Jenny said, keeping eye contact with Judith. "It's new to me. I'm working here for the summer to pay for university, but my usual job is in the office. I'm majoring in business, so I help with the accounts."

"Where are you going to school?" Judith asked.

"UBC." Jenny handed Judith her drink. "That is, the University of British Columbia in Vancouver."

Judith nodded. "We live fairly close to the border. I've actually seen the campus on visits to Vancouver."

Jenny finished making the second drink, but looked a little uncertain about putting it down in front of Renie, who was staring straight ahead like a zombie. "Is it all right if . . . ?" She let the rest of the question hang in the air.

"She'll be fine," Judith replied. "She rarely tries to drink out of her hands."

"Um . . . good. Yes. That'll be eighteen dollars Canadian."

Judith grimaced. "We haven't yet changed our money."

"Then it's thirteen," Jenny said. "Are you staying here? I'll put it on your room tab."

Judith assured her that was fine, adding that they were staying in the Rose and the Yew Suites. Forcing another smile, Jenny thanked Judith and disappeared behind the panel.

"Why," Judith demanded, "do you look like a pickle? It drives me crazy when I'm talking to someone new."

Renie's brown eyes snapped. "When we meet strangers you always take over. Yes, you're more outgoing, you're friendlier by nature, but sometimes I like to prove I can actually talk."

"Oh, coz!" Judith exclaimed in dismay. "I'm sorry. Really. I'm so used to chatting up B&B guests that I can't help it."

Renie laughed. "You've always been like that. You're social by nature and you love people. I'm used to it, but sometimes it still gets to me. Especially since our idiot husbands put us in the wrong lodgings." She raised her glass. "Here's to us cousins."

Judith smiled back. They'd just clinked glasses when a young man and a young woman entered the bar. While they didn't actually look alike, Judith guessed they were the Odell twins. Under ordinary circumstances, she would have greeted them, but Renie's reprimand had turned her mute.

"How," the young man asked, "do you get a drink around here?"

"There's a bell, idiot boy," the young woman said. "Give it a shot."

"I'll bet the beer's in that fridge behind the bar, Winnie. Let's check it out. There's more alcohol in Canadian beer than we have in ours."

Winnie eyed the cousins with suspicion. "Maybe not."

"Hey, Win," Renie said. "Go for it. You Iowans have lots of nerve."

The twins looked startled. "How do you know who we are?" Winnie asked. "Do you work here?"

"Does it look like we're working?" Renie nudged Judith. "Your turn. I proved I could talk. You can quiz them about the rest of the Stokes folks."

Win and Winnie exchanged confused looks. "Whoa," Win said under his breath. "What's that supposed to mean?"

Judith put on her greet-the-guests smile. "My cousin

and I met your relatives earlier. They're staying in a big tent by the river not far from here."

"Why?" The word all but flew out of Winnie's mouth. "I mean, that they were supposed to stay here at the motel."

"They seem to prefer camping out," Judith said. She was tempted to mention the twins' dying grandfather, but decided it was a bad idea. "There's quite a group. Maybe they couldn't get accommodations for everybody."

"That bunch is cheap," Win stated. "I'll bet they wouldn't spend the money on a motel. Old Codger's tight as the bark on a butternut hickory when it comes to spending money on what he'd call luxuries."

Winnie made a slashing gesture with her right hand. "Don't bad-mouth Codger. He's been okay with us."

"I guess," Win said. "Oh well. Hey, let's see if there's beer in that fridge. We can leave a couple of bucks and take it outside."

The cousins had finished their drinks. "Good luck," Judith said, moving to the door.

Renie merely smiled and waved.

The rest of the evening passed without a hitch. An excellent dinner at a Bavarian-style restaurant, a twilight stroll past intriguing shops, and the moon rising over the granite mountain peaks made the Flynns and the Joneses feel as if they were really getting away from it all.

But they had no idea what they were getting into.

Joe and Bill had signed on for a two-day fly-fishing adventure on the Bow. They both arose early Saturday morning to be picked up by their guide at eight o'clock. The first half of the day included tips from a local fly-fisherman they had read about before leaving on the trip. Snapper MacDougall was so named because of the graceful, accurate way he could cast his fly-fishing line. Joe and Bill were like little kids waiting to meet Santa Claus. Judith got up to see her husband off; Renie slept in.

Judith had decided to wait for breakfast until her cousin woke up, but by ten o'clock her stomach was growling. She was about to go into the adjoining room when her cell rang. Figuring it was Renie, she asked what had finally awakened her.

"The alarm, of course," Arlene Rankers said in a testy voice. "I had to set it for five A.M. in order to make the guests' breakfasts."

"I usually don't get up until six," Judith blurted—and immediately felt remorse. "I mean, you've taken over the B&B before, so you—"

"Yes, yes," Arlene interrupted. "But I've always

had your cleaning woman to do all the housework. Honestly, I've never considered her flighty—stubborn, complaining, cranky, prone to hypochondria, filled with fundamentalist religious zeal, but not *flighty.*"

"How so?" Judith inquired in a puzzled voice.

"She eloped!" Arlene all but shouted. "Last night. She's on her honeymoon. Can you imagine?"

Judith was speechless. She gulped before responding. "No. No," she repeated. "What is he? I mean, *who* is he?"

"A man from her church," Arlene replied, still sounding out of sorts. "I didn't ask his name. It might be an alias. Besides, Phyliss was giggling so much that it was hard to understand her."

A giddy Phyliss was beyond Judith's imagination. "I'm stunned. But you can't do the housework. Really. Call one of the cleaning services. In fact, I have the name of the outfit that came in after one of the guests set the house on fire. I think it's called Mighty Tidy and Sons."

"I'll do that," Arlene said, with a touch of relief. "I really hated to bother you, but—"

"Never mind," Judith broke in. "It's not your fault. But it *is* unbelievable."

"Yes. I wonder what your mother will think."

Judith didn't want to know.

She'd just hung up when Renie appeared in the doorway of the adjoining room. "You woke me up," she mumbled, her eyes not quite open. "Oh. You're not being attacked. I'm going back to bed. Ni-ni."

"It's after ten!" Judith shouted. "I want to eat breakfast. Don't you?"

"Well . . ." Renie's eyes opened all the way. She blinked twice. "I thought we were on vacation."

"We are," Judith said, trying not to grit her teeth. "You sleep in all the time when you're at home."

Her cousin actually seemed to be considering the statement. "So I do. Okay, I'll make an exception. I am kind of hungry." She staggered back into the other room.

They breakfasted in the same café where they'd had lunch the day before. Except that it was termed *brunch* on the menu after ten o'clock. Judith regaled her cousin with the tale of Phyliss's elopement. Renie insisted she didn't believe it.

"It'd be more like Phyliss to join the circus," she said. "She *is* kind of a freak. Besides, sometimes Arlene gets things mixed up."

Judith allowed that was true. But, she realized, there was no way to find out any details while they were in Banff. She was about to say as much when she saw the

Odell family get out of a booth just after the cousins had filled their plates at the buffet.

"Eat fast," Judith urged Renie. "I'll bet they're going to meet up with the so-called Stokes folks. It could be interesting."

"Not to me." Renie saw Judith's disappointment and sighed. "Okay, why not? We haven't got anything else on the schedule with our mates off and fishing. It'll beat spending a lot of money on overpriced items we can't afford. Except maybe sweaters. No woman can have too many sweaters."

The early cloud cover had lifted, showing off every cleft and crag in the majestic mountains above the town. The air was clear though tinged with the scent of vehicle exhaust and evergreen trees. *The price of a tourist economy,* Judith thought to herself. They didn't encounter any mosquitoes until they got closer to the river.

As they turned toward the Stokes family encampment, Renie asked why Judith wanted another encounter with a bunch of people who were waiting for someone to die.

"Maybe that's why," Judith replied.

"You *are* a ghoul," Renie declared.

"No, I'm not," Judith retorted, pausing on the

pathway. "I can't help it if I have . . . accidental encounters with dead bodies. But this is the first time I've run into having the deceased's demise announced in advance. Humor me."

"Your problem is that you love people, alive or dead. Years ago, someone told me that you'd never met a stranger. It's true." Renie's smile was wry. "We're both only children, but even as a kid, I liked my own company. You always preferred being with as many neighbor kids as you could round up. I wasn't envious, but I admired you for it."

"Oh, coz," Judith said, looking chagrined, "you were two years older and the one I looked up to. You know that I always—"

Renie laughed. "Stop. The mosquitoes are gathering in force. Let's call on your latest clutch of crazies."

Approaching the Stokes encampment, they noticed that most of the family, including the Odells, were gathered around the picnic table. "A family meeting?" Judith mused. "Do you suppose Codger has died?"

"Maybe . . ." Renie hedged. "How could two sides of a family be so different?"

"Let's face it, some of *our* relatives are a bit strange."

"True. I've been trying to forget they're actually our relatives. I confess I always admired Great-Aunt Rosie for fighting off boredom in that little mountain town where she and Great-Uncle Drano lived."

"His name was Duane," Judith pointed out.

"That's not what she called him," Renie countered. "Aunt Rosie joined the Ku Klux Klan and the Communist Party. Remember how one night she got the meetings confused and showed up in her bedsheet to denounce capitalism?"

"No," Judith said, "but I believe it. Rosie was quite a character. Uncle Drano—I mean, Duane—was a gravedigger during the Depression."

Renie laughed. "See? You can't avoid dead bodies, even from the past."

Judith didn't try to defend herself. The cousins slowed their pace as they neared the Stokes family, who seemed rather subdued. In fact, Martha Lou was slumped by the bier with tears running down her cheeks.

"We shouldn't bother them," Judith said. "Let's go back to the motel."

Renie kept going. Judith hurried to catch up with her. "Coz," she whispered, "what are you doing?"

"What you really intend to do," Renie retorted. "You know damned well that you're more curious than I am."

"They're grieving," Judith declared. "We can't intrude. We're strangers."

"I may be, but you're not," Renie said. "What did I tell you? You're never a stranger to anybody."

"Ohhh . . ." Judith sighed. "I suppose they might need help. If Codger has died, they may be emotionally overwrought. It's often difficult for mourners to make decisions at such a time."

"There you go," Renie said cheerfully. "Your usual logic has snapped into place. You offer them comfort while I figure out where we go to lunch."

Judith shot her a dark look. "Fine. You really are the most unsympathetic person . . ."

Before she could get the words out, Teddy Stokes emerged from the family group and hurried toward them. "Guess what?" he cried, but didn't wait for an answer. "Codger croaked!"

Judith nodded solemnly. "That must be a relief to all of you. Will you grant his wish about putting him on the bier to go down the Bow River?"

Teddy blinked several times. "We can't. Not now. Later, maybe."

"Why not?" Judith asked.

Teddy twisted his fingers together. "Because"—he gulped, going pale under his summer tan—"Codger was murdered."

Chapter 5

Judith was stunned. Deep down, she knew the reaction would be normal for most people, but experience should have hardened her. Then, before the usual shocked responses came out of her mouth, she asked Teddy if he was sure that the old man had been a homicide victim.

"Sure?" Teddy gasped. "Heck, yes! He was stabbed twice."

"That'll do it," Renie said. Seeing Teddy look confused, she continued. "His advanced age. His lack of strength. He was dying anyway, right?"

"Well . . ." Teddy took a swipe at his unruly forelock. "Yeah, but why kill him? I mean . . . he was practically a goner."

Judith cleared her throat. "That's what my cousin means. Have you notified the police?"

"I think Aunt Adela's gonna call on her fancy cell phone," Teddy replied, "but we're not legal. I mean, we ain't got no real camping permit."

"I see," Judith murmured. "Is there anything we can do to help?"

The question seemed to puzzle Teddy. "Shucks, I don't know . . ." He turned around to glance at his family members, who now seemed to be facing off with each other. "Everybody's kinda upset. Aunt Adela's doin' her best to shush 'em up, but . . ."

"That's natural," Judith assured him. "But let's see if there's some way we can be of assistance. After all, we Americans should stick together since we're in a foreign country."

"We are?" Teddy responded in an uncertain voice. "I thought we were in Canada. It's North America, ain't it?"

Judith's usual patience was fraying. "Yes, but Canada is a separate country. It's part of the British Commonwealth."

Teddy took some time taking in the information. "Hunh," he finally said. "So that's why they speak English. But some of the signs are in another language. Ma says it's French."

"That's because Canada is bilingual," Judith said. "English is a second language for many of the people to the east, so the country is bilingual to accommodate—"

"Stop!" Renie cried. "You lost him at 'bilingual.' Let's move on and check out the corpse. I know that's what you're dying—excuse the expression—to do."

Judith glanced at Teddy, who was looking even more befuddled. She reached out a hand to him. "Maybe we can help. We've already met your cousins because your aunt and uncle are staying at the same motel as we are."

"Oh." Teddy's face brightened almost imperceptibly. "That's good. I mean, you're not . . . strangers."

"True," Judith said, relieved that at least the statement was credible.

The first person to notice the cousins was Adela Odell, who confronted Teddy. "Who are those women?" She didn't wait for an answer. "Do you work at the Banff Springs Motel?"

"We're guests," Judith replied politely. "We met your twins last night in the bar." Seeing Win and Winnie on the edge of the gathering, she waved. They didn't wave back.

"Why are you here?" Adela demanded. "This is a private family meeting."

Martha Lou waved both hands at her aunt. "Don't be mean to them, Auntie. They're going to write us up and make us famous. Maybe we'll get some big bucks out of it."

Adela eyed the cousins with suspicion. "Is that true?"

"We work freelance," Judith replied. "It depends on you and your family if the story's worth publishing. We understand the elder Mr. Stokes has died. Is there anything interesting about how that happened?"

At least two people uttered short, harsh laughs.

"That also depends," Adela said coldly. "How much is it worth to you?"

"I'm a writer," Judith replied with dignity. "Writers aren't rich. In fact," she went on, figuring it was time to tell at least one truth, "my cousin is a graphic designer. She provides the art."

Adela sighed and moved closer. "Look," she said, lowering her voice, "this is awkward for us. I gather you know why we're all here." She took in Judith's nod. "Then you know Codger was almost dead when the rest of the family arrived yesterday. He died during the night, but . . ." She ran an anxious hand through her platinum pageboy. "Someone apparently couldn't wait for the inevitable. He was stabbed."

Judith decided not to reveal that Teddy had already delivered the gruesome news. "Was he suffering?" she asked in a sympathetic tone.

"I don't know," Adela admitted. "Norman and I didn't come to the camp until this morning. We only found out that Codger was dead about an hour ago. In fact, our twins had never met him and went to his tent."

Judith noticed a much smaller tent closer to the river. "Was he ill?"

"He was very old and very frail," Adela replied. "He wanted his privacy. Win and Winnie came here a few minutes before Norman and I arrived. They'd never met their grandfather, but he's been generous with them since they were very small. I haven't been back to Big Stove in over twenty years."

Renie finally had to speak before she exploded. "How big *is* Big Stove?"

Adela looked surprised by the question—or maybe because she thought Renie really was a puppet. "Well . . . I'm not sure," she replied. "There were fewer than a hundred people when I grew up there, but so many of them were related to each other. It was a peculiar community."

Renie nodded. "Any extra arms or legs? Ears in the wrong places? How about noses? I've always felt they could easily go astray."

"Not *that* peculiar," Adela said with a touch of umbrage. "It's more of an environmental or educational deficiency. Oh, come along, you might be able to convince the rest of the family that they should contact the police. They won't listen to Norm and me. In fact, they're talking about sending Codger down the river on that stupid bier they brought along. That can't be legal, even in Canada."

"Probably not," Judith agreed.

The group had simmered down and was looking appropriately mournful. Pa Stokes was the first to speak.

"You two got a real hot story now," he said in a dismal tone. "But can you keep it to yerselves for now? We don't want no trouble with the law."

Judith decided to take a soft approach and smiled kindly. "Don't you want justice to be done? If you think he was murdered, his killer must be caught."

Pa shrugged. "Codger was half dead anyways. We can pack up now and head on back to the farm. Ain't no reason to tarry here."

"But," Judith persisted, "don't you want to know who stabbed him?"

"Some hobo," Pa said dismissively. "Besides, we're furriners in these parts. They won't care if one of us got done in. Back home, we've got corn growin'. And those soybeans. They need tendin' to." He turned away.

Judith looked at Adela. "You can't let your relatives flee the scene of an apparent crime. You know the Royal Canadian Mounted Police will track them down."

Adela sighed. "I hate to do it, but Norm and I will have to go in person to tell the RCMP what happened. We'd better do it now before they put Codger on that stupid bier." She gestured at her husband to join her. "Poor Norm! I don't think he realized until now what kind of a family he married into." Shaking her head, Adela hurried to join her husband.

Renie was looking unusually concerned. "Can we stop the Stokeses from doing such a stupid—and illegal—stunt?"

"When," Judith asked incredulously, "did you get so softhearted?"

"It's not that," Renie asserted. "It's common sense, my mother's favorite virtue. The whole thing is no doubt not only against the law, but gruesome."

Judith didn't respond right away. "Maybe we'd better make sure Codger is dead."

"What?" Renie shrieked, keeping up with her cousin's pace. "You plan to stick pins in the old duffer?"

"If necessary," Judith replied grimly.

"Ghoul," Renie muttered.

Adela was conferring with her husband and Teddy

had separated himself from the herd. He was now wearing a cap with a jutting visor in the shape of a corncob. Judith approached him with a kindly smile.

"I'm sorry about your family's loss," she said. "I hate to trouble you, but could I see Codger?"

Teddy's tanned visage was puzzled. "Why?"

"For verification," Judith replied, realizing the word seemed to puzzle Teddy. "That is, we writers have to make certain our facts are right."

"Oh. Sure, why not?" He beckoned for them to follow him past the big tent. "Codger liked to be alone. Couldn't stand noise. Kinda odd, since he was deaf as a fence post."

As they passed the gathering at the picnic table, only the Odell twins seemed to notice. Adela had taken Norman aside, apparently conferring with him about calling in the police. Pa was peeling an apple while Ma laid out a game of solitaire. Martha Lou was flipping through a stack of what looked like celebrity magazines. Ada sat in the same canvas chair where she had been the previous day. She still stared straight ahead.

Going by the big tent, Judith glimpsed rumpled sleeping bags, empty beer and soda cans, assorted items of clothing, more magazines, and a black top hat.

"I'll bet that hat belonged to Codger," Renie said.

"I can't see anybody else in this bunch wearing one of those."

"True," Judith agreed. "There's something tawdry about the Stokes folks, but I'm not sure what it is."

"You're comparing them to the Nebraskans you know—Aunt Ellen and Uncle Win. They'd never wear a Cornhusker hat like Teddy's to a Nebraska football game. They're educated and classy, like all of us Grovers."

"*We're* classy?" Judith said sarcastically. "We just have better grammar."

"You know what I mean," Renie mumbled as they approached the smaller tent. "Oh, drat. This is ghoulish. Why didn't I stay back at the motel? I hate gore. And I just got bit by another mosquito."

"Quit griping." Judith lifted the tent flap. "After you."

"No thanks," Renie shot back. "I'm not going in there."

"Fine." Judith sighed and ducked inside the tent.

Apparently, Codger slept in his overalls. They were well worn, as was his frayed denim shirt. The clothing fell loosely about him, as if what had once been a larger frame had been wasted by illness. He wore heavy work boots and there was a straw hat on the tent's floor. His wrinkled, veined hands were big but callused, evidence of hard work growing his corn. She couldn't see his face and didn't want to for fear he'd died in agony. Judith said a prayer that the old man had finally found eternal rest.

Then she studied the two wounds in his back. One was slightly deeper than the other, as if the killer had wanted to make sure the victim was dead. The blood on his shirt and the blue blanket he'd slept on had dried. From her previous encounters with dead bodies, Judith realized that rigor had set in three or four hours earlier. There was no sign of a struggle. Codger had probably been asleep when he was killed.

"You done in there yet?" Renie called.

"Yes." Judith backpedaled out of the tent. "Poor old guy. I figure he never knew what happened."

Renie was solemn. "The problem is why it happened."

Judith's dark eyes flashed. "Yes. But before we find out *why*, we have to find out *who*."

"I knew you'd want to know that," Renie said. "After all, what's a vacation for if we can't find a corpse?"

Judith didn't answer.

Chapter 6

The surviving immediate members of the Stokes family were now seated around the picnic table in deep conversation. All four Odells, however, apparently had gone off to contact the RCMP.

"Let's not bother them," Judith said. "They need time to collect themselves."

"Are you kidding?" Renie retorted. "They need time to collect their wits. They could be anywhere."

"Adela and Norman seem smart," Judith pointed out.

"That's because they're the Odells," Renie shot back. "Adela escaped before she could become contaminated."

"She probably went to college." Judith thrummed her fingers against her cheek. "Where's the weapon?"

Renie frowned. "You're asking *me*? I didn't do it."

Judith checked her watch. "It's after noon, but even you can't be hungry after that big brunch."

"You're right. Give me another hour. What do you want to do in the meantime?"

Judith considered. "I really wouldn't mind looking at sweaters. They always have nice ones in Canada. The good Scottish woolens and all that."

Renie laughed. "Why not? It seems wrong not to buy a souvenir. A wearable one, at that. And we've got the car."

Fearing that Arlene might have called with another crisis, Judith insisted on checking for messages at the motel desk. There weren't any. Relieved, she joined Renie, who was already sitting in the rental's passenger seat.

"You drive better than I do," she said. "I never had to hold down two jobs to make ends meet. It's a wonder you didn't meet yourself coming and going between the library and bartending at Dan's café."

"You were lucky," Judith murmured.

"I have a husband who worked for a living as a shrink," Renie said. "If that's luck, I'll take it."

Following the river, Judith kept her eyes on the road, but her mind went back almost forty years to when she and Joe had become engaged. She'd been so happy with her fun-loving policeman and his magic Irish green eyes. And then, after a rough night on the job, he'd stopped for a drink—or two or three or . . . Judith winced at the memory.

"What's wrong?" Renie asked.

"I was time-traveling backward," Judith replied, turning off from the river. "To the fateful night that Joe got drunk after dealing with a gruesome homicide case and ran into Herself at a bar by the downtown precinct. The next thing he knew, he was on a plane headed for Vegas."

Renie nodded. "When Joe sobered up, he discovered he was married to Vivian instead of you."

"And I was pregnant with Mike." Judith's smile was melancholy. "Dan didn't mind. I guess he'd always had a thing for me. He played the gallant and asked me to marry him. So I did."

"You always were too easygoing," Renie said, but not without sympathy. "I was amazed that Joe stayed married to Vivian for so long. Wasn't he Husband Number Four?"

"At least." Judith slowed down. "Check that street sign. Does it say Lynx?"

"Links?" Renie frowned. "We already passed the golf course. Since when did you take up golf?"

"*L-Y-N-X*," Judith spelled out, looking for a parking space. "Yes, I took the turn that Trixie told me about."

"Trixie? Who's she?"

"The girl who sometimes fills in when Niall is away. Very sweet."

"Good for her," Renie said vaguely. "Hey, why are we stopping here?" She paused. "The Mounties! This is the police station! I should've guessed."

"I want to make sure the Odells reported what happened to Codger," Judith said, easing into an open spot near the entrance. "I'm not certain I trust any of those people, including the ones with good grammar."

"No argument here," Renie said. "So why aren't we getting out of the car?"

"Because the Buick with the Iowa plates is parked two cars back. It's a good thing this rental has tinted windows, so the Odells can't see us."

"Oh, lordy!" Renie cried. "Now I feel like a spy in a bad B movie. Where's my beat-up trench coat and slouch hat?"

Judith ignored the comment. Five minutes passed, but there was still no sign of the Odells. Renie was growing restless.

"Maybe they confessed," she said hopefully.

"How would you like to explain the Stokeses' plan for Codger's send-off? It'd take some time. Although,"

Judith went on more slowly, "they might leave out the zany part."

"That'd spoil all the fun," Renie asserted. "Not to mention the novelty. Even you haven't come across a homicide like this one. It's occurred to me that you've gotten a bit blasé the last two, three times you found a dead body."

Judith glared at her. "That's a terrible thing to say! I'm never blasé when some poor soul meets a violent end. You're always telling me I'm too sympathetic, even too softhearted."

Renie was unmoved. "You omitted my earlier remark—too easygoing."

Judith opened her mouth to respond but saw the Odells come out of the police station with two uniformed officers. Adela, Norman, and the twins went to their Buick; the officers got into a cruiser.

"Do we follow them?" Renie asked.

"No. At least not yet. We know where they're going. Let's see if we can find a bakery," Judith said as she pulled into traffic on Lynx Street. "We can get a little something there. Or are you starving?"

Renie thought about it. "Starving's at least an hour away. Doughnuts will do."

At the next corner, Judith spotted a bakery sign to her left. "Two bakeries. We're in luck."

"Wild Flour!" Renie exclaimed, practically bouncing in her seat. "I like the name. Let's go there."

The cousins also liked the coffee and the ambience. Judith ate a brownie and Renie devoured a chocolate croissant, a cinnamon twist, and a sugar doughnut. Half an hour later, they were back in the car.

"This," said Judith, pulling away from the curb, "is when I could hate you. I have to watch my weight while Little Pig gobbles up everything in sight and never gains an ounce."

"So you've mentioned," Renie replied wearily. "It's metabolism. Some pigs got it, some would-be pigs don't. Get over it."

"I try to," Judith said. "It's still galling."

"Then resume sleuthing. You're very good at that."

"I intend to. The police should have gone over the crime scene by now. But they probably haven't taken the body away. I assume they're questioning the suspects. I prefer not to get involved, but merely observe."

"Oh, good grief!" Renie cried. "You *are* involved. Did you touch anything when you got a look at Codger's body?"

"No. Do you think I'm crazy?"

"The family saw you go to the tent and Teddy went partway with you," Renie reminded her.

Judith thought back to the scene. "True, but I'm not a suspect. Codger was already dead."

"Okay," Renie said. But she looked worried. That wasn't like her usually blasé cousin.

It made Judith worry, too.

When they approached the campsite, the first thing they noticed was that the family members were behaving in an uncharacteristic manner. Unlike the relatively calm scene Judith and Renie had witnessed earlier, most of them seemed agitated or at least upset. Except Ada, of course. She simply sat and stared.

The taller, dark-haired RCMP officer was focused on Ma and Pa Stokes, while his red-haired, freckled companion seemed to be searching the ground.

"They're looking for something," Judith murmured. "More blood? Footprints?"

Renie shrugged. "Don't ask me. I'm just here to enable you."

"Don't say that," Judith scolded. "You make me sound like a . . . ghoul." She looked more closely at the scene in front of her. "Something's missing. What is it?"

"Party hats?" Renie shot back.

"Get serious. Think what we saw the first time we came here."

"There was a big—"

"Bier!" Judith cried—and quickly put her hand over her mouth. Fortunately, no one seemed to have heard her. "I wonder."

"So do I," Renie agreed. "Go get 'em, coz."

They approached the picnic table. Judith addressed Pa Stokes. "Excuse me, but what's going on? What are the police looking for?"

Pa shook his head and looked away. Ma glared at Adela, who was standing off to one side with Norman.

"Busybody," Ma hissed. "She thinks she's so smart just because she got a college degree. Adela never could keep her mouth shut. We told her to leave well enough alone, but oh no! She had to call in the police!"

Judith was taken aback. "I'm confused. Don't you want to find out who stabbed Codger?"

Pa took a corncob pipe out of his shirt pocket. "Don't matter. He was a goner anyhow. And now he's . . . gone."

"You mean . . . on the bier?"

Narrowing his eyes, Pa stared at Judith. "Not exactly. We ditched the bier. We heard them cops were getting curious-like. Now they're asking a bunch of questions about things that are none of their beeswax."

For once, Judith was at a loss for words. Renie,

however, was looking impatient. "Come on, coz," she said. "There's nothing we can do here. Let's go."

"Fine," Judith muttered.

They'd barely moved when the dark-haired Mountie called to them. "Pardon, ladies, but are you family members?"

"Are you kidding?" Renie retorted. "We don't even belong to the same species."

He nodded faintly. "I'm Sergeant Brewster, RCMP." He gestured toward the younger red-haired Mountie, who was entering the big tent. "That's Constable MacRae. If you're not with this party, then I must ask you to leave. It's a crime scene."

"We've seen too much, if you ask me," Renie blurted as she grabbed Judith's arm. "We're going now. Come on . . ."

Brewster interrupted. "If you've seen so much, ma'am, could you tell us where the alleged victim is? A Mrs. Odell reported a possible homicide, but we can't find a body. If you know, please tell us."

Judith and Renie both looked blank.

Chapter 7

Since Renie had opened her big mouth, Judith decided that it was up to her cousin to explain. Surprisingly, she responded in a reasonable manner.

"As I mentioned, we aren't related to the victim's family, and we hardly know them. Mrs. Odell is a relative, and if she reported a homicide, you should ask her what she thinks happened to the victim. If you have any further questions, we're staying at the Banff Springs Motel. So, in fact, are the Odells."

"Very well," Brewster said. "Give me your names."

The cousins complied. Judith reluctantly followed Renie back toward the motel.

"I'm trying to figure out if you just did us a favor," she said. "I'm also wondering why Codger's body disappeared."

"*Why?*" Renie echoed. "How about *where?*"

"That's the easy part," Judith replied as they neared the motel entrance. "They granted his wishes and sent him down the river on the bier."

Renie laughed. "Of course! I should've realized that."

"I should hope so," Judith agreed. "Let's have a drink at the motel. I could use a Scotch about now."

Renie agreed. In the lobby, they greeted Niall and Trixie, who were both behind the counter. Judith told them they were headed for the bar.

"Changing shifts," Niall said cheerfully. "Trixie usually tends bar at night, but Jenny's working in the office, so Trixie's filling in."

The girl's pert, pretty face lit up. "I'm new at it. Be patient with me."

"We will," Judith assured her. "I tended bar in the evenings when my first husband owned a café." Her mind veered back to those not-so-happy nights when she'd go from her day job at the public library to The Meat & Mingle to help Dan keep the place afloat. But the enterprise was as doomed as the *Titanic,* eventually sinking off the shores of the city's rough and rowdy Thurlow District. Dan had never worked again.

Trixie smiled, revealing perfect teeth. "It's more fun serving cocktails than waiting on tables. People are much more cheerful when they're drinking."

"Not always when they haven't yet been served the first one," Judith said, smiling back.

With a little wave at Niall, Trixie came out from behind the desk and was leading the way down the hall to the bar. "Oh," she said as she opened the door and let the cousins go in first, "Niall and I heard sirens a while ago. We figured it was an accident out on the highway, but they stopped nearby. Do you know what that was all about?"

Judith hesitated, but realized that the news would be all over town soon enough. Still, she decided to soften her response. There was no need to cause un-necessary panic. "An elderly man died at a campsite by the river near here."

Trixie's big blue eyes widened. "An elderly . . . man?" she gasped. "Who?"

Judith was suddenly disconcerted. "He was called Codger. His last name was . . ."

Trixie clapped both hands to her cheeks. "Noooo! My world has . . ." Her knees buckled as she collapsed onto the floor.

Renie rushed off to alert Niall. Judith cautiously leaned over to speak softly to Trixie, whose eyelids were fluttering. "Can I get you some water?" she asked.

Trixie groaned as she opened her eyes. "No. It was . . . death upsets me, no matter who died. I hope Niall doesn't tell Mr. Barnes. I don't want to get fired after such a short time on the job. He's kind of a grump for being someone who deals with guests."

Renie returned alone. "Niall's checking in some newcomers. Is Trixie okay?"

Judith explained while she and Renie helped the young woman to her feet and into a chair.

Trixie looked apologetic. "I worked as an aide in an old folks' home," she said. "I got so fond of those elderly darlings. And then they died. It made me so sad. I finally had to quit before I lost my mind."

"I understand," Judith assured her. "Are you sure you wouldn't like some brandy? You're very pale."

"I'll be fine," Trixie asserted, sounding more angry than distraught. "I can't help overreacting. I'd better tell Niall I'm all right. Then I'll mix your drinks. Or do it yourselves."

As Trixie moved away at a surprisingly fast pace, the cousins exchanged puzzled looks. "Odd," Judith remarked. "She goes from fainting to hard-boiled?"

Renie shrugged. "You realize that people are very complex. Who knows what kind of grim experiences she's had."

"Especially dealing with older people," Judith said,

going to the bar. "I wonder how she'd deal with my mother?"

"Or mine." Renie grimaced. "Damn! I was supposed to call her yesterday to make sure she knew we'd arrived in one piece. You know how she worries. I'd better do that now." She dug her cell out of her big handbag.

"I'll make our drinks," Judith said.

"Good. I'll need a stiff . . . Hi, Mom. I'm still alive . . . Yes, I'm sure. All of us are just fine . . . No, I don't need an extra sweater . . . I didn't bring a woolen cap. I don't own a . . . Yes, it's the Rockies, it's summer, and you were here years ago . . . Climate change didn't turn Banff into a deep freezer . . . It's not global *warning,* it's global . . . No, Mom. I haven't worn supports in my shoes since I was twelve . . . She is? Then you go have a nice visit with her, okay? I'll call you in a couple of . . . Mittens? Honest, it's over seventy degrees here. Bye, Mom." Renie signed off. "Mrs. Grumpus just stopped by. I can't remember a day when Mom didn't have visitors. Unlike Aunt Gert, she actually enjoys people, even the ones like the ever-gloomy Grumpus."

"My mother only likes them if they play cards with her," Judith said, handing over a glass of bourbon and ice. "You want water back, right?"

Renie looked at the ceiling. "I know it's been a

while, but have I changed so much since I talked to Mom? Yes, of course. Just put the glass on the counter. Where are we lunching?"

"Wherever we can find a parking place," Judith replied after taking a sip of Scotch. "We've been lucky so far. The town is full of tourists."

"Not everybody stops in at the police station," Renie pointed out. "Who killed Codger? Your brain must be swirling with suspects."

"That's the problem," Judith said, joining Renie on the settee by the bar. "There are too many of them. One of the Odells could've sneaked out of the motel during the night. It could even be a random thing. But I doubt it."

They sat in silence for a couple of minutes. It was Renie who finally spoke. "Trixie never came back here. Do you think she's still upset?"

"Maybe," Judith allowed. "Never having seen her before today, I have no idea what she's like. Some people are overly emotional by nature."

"True." Renie gulped down the rest of her drink. "It's after two. Will anybody still be serving lunch?"

"Probably. It's a tourist town, remember?"

"Stop saying that," Renie said after they'd left their glasses on the bar and they were going down the hall. "I *am* a tourist. You are not. You're a traveling ghoul."

Judith scowled at her cousin. "That's a terrible thing to say!" She kept going, but paused by the front desk, where Niall had just ended a phone call. "Where's Trixie?"

Niall looked around to see if there was anyone else coming into the lobby. "She didn't feel well," he said, lowering his voice. "Nerves, maybe. This is only her first week on the job."

"Understandable," Judith agreed. "By the way, where's the Catholic church?"

"St. Mary's on Squirrel Street," Niall replied. "A block up from the police station. Do you know where that is?"

Judith said she had a vague idea. The cousins headed outside.

Renie was chortling. "How come we didn't see it? Were you too agog over another murder?"

"No! The streets here go every which way at angles," Judith replied. "It adds charm, but you can't see very far."

"It reminds me even more of Scotland," Renie said. "Uh-oh. Here come the twins. Maybe they're heading for the bar again."

The young people paused to greet the cousins. "Have you been grilled by the cops, too?" Win asked.

"Not really," Judith replied. "They weren't inter-ested because we aren't related to the victim's family."

"We are, though," Winnie said in a glum voice. "They threw all sorts of questions at us. It's been a major bummer of a morning."

"The police have to do their job," Judith pointed out.

"Waste of time," Win declared. "Why would any-body kill Codger? He was *old*."

"How old?" The question fell artlessly from Judith's lips.

The twins looked at each other. Win shrugged. "Who knows? I never asked."

"*Really* old," Winnie put in. "At least seventy." She punched her brother in the upper arm. "Come on, let's get the tennis racquets. I need exercise."

They moved on to the motel entrance.

Renie stared at Judith. "Seventy? That's not so old!"

"Not to us, but it is to them." She frowned. "What if . . . ?" She shook her head and continued walking to the rental car. "Never mind."

"Don't pull that on me," Renie snapped. "Some-thing's flitting around in your brain."

"Get in the car," Judith ordered. "The mosquitoes are doing their flitting and I just got bit again."

"Well?" Renie said after they were headed away from the motel.

"I may be crazy," Judith began, "but I got the impression from what someone said that Codger was really ancient, as in almost a hundred. But what if he wasn't?"

Renie considered the idea. "You saw him, I didn't. What was your reaction?"

Judith sighed. "I never saw his face. He was lying on his stomach. Maybe he slept that way, or having been stabbed in the back, he'd fallen forward. His fingers were gnarled, and his hands callused, too, which indicated he was getting up there." Stopping at an arterial, she glanced at Renie. "Well? Do you think I'm wrong to speculate about his actual age?"

"No, but you like to speculate." Renie grew thoughtful. "The old guy had worked the farm all his life. I'm no expert on agriculture, but I don't think that what we'd call 'modern' farming came along until fairly recent times. Codger probably inherited the acreage, which means he started young. Heck, for all we know, maybe he never converted to high-tech farming."

"Yes, he did," Judith said after a pause. "Pa Stokes has arthritis and his hands are kind of beat up, but Teddy's aren't. I'm guessing from Pa's concern about commodity prices and such that he's up-to-date on modern farming."

Renie smiled. "Your powers of observation have not been dulled by age."

"I can't help it. I study people. I have to, because people are my job at the B&B."

"And they don't stick around long enough for you to get tired of them. Hey, there's a parking place! I see something called Earls a couple of doors down. I'll bet it has edibles."

The café did have food, but at this time of day the cousins had to settle for soup and salad. Judith was relieved that Renie didn't pout. The thought that they wouldn't have to wait so long for dinner kept her in good spirits. Once they were seated, the conversation returned to the murder investigation.

"Think about it," Judith said. "How old is Pa? Fifty or so?" She saw Renie nod after spooning in some chowder. "Adela is his sister and I figure her for not much over forty. I doubt that Codger waited until middle age to get married and have his children."

"So what's the point of saying he was older than dirt?" Renie asked. "An insurance scam?"

"That's possible," Judith said, "but I doubt it. I considered that Codger might have been suffering from an incurable illness, but why not say so? Even if the old guy didn't know, why would the family keep it a secret?"

"I don't think the Stokes folks *could* keep a secret," Renie responded. "I assume Mrs. Codger has already gone to that big corncrib in the sky."

"Probably." Judith nibbled at her salad greens. "I wonder how much money people make raising corn."

"It depends on how big a farm they have," Renie said. "Aunt Ellen once told me that many of those Nebraska farmers are millionaires."

Judith was surprised. "She did? I never heard that."

"You're not her goddaughter. Ha-ha."

"True." Judith paused to study their bill. "We never got our money changed. I suppose the banks are closed. Drat. We'll have to wait until Monday."

Upon paying their bill, the cousins drove back to the motel. "We should check the bulletin board in the lobby," Judith said. "I'll bet St. Mary's has a Saturday Mass. Since we're eating a late dinner, we might as well go this evening. Then you can sleep in tomorrow."

Renie gave her cousin a sideways look. "You think I haven't done that when I'm actually in church?"

"Yes," Judith said primly. "I've been there. At least you don't snore."

"You talk in your sleep."

"So Joe tells me. He doesn't mind."

"You've only been married for fifteen years. Wait until you're together as long as Bill and I have been."

Judith turned into the motel's driveway. "How long has it been now? I forget."

"I don't know. I can't do numbers. I'm a visual person. And I see a cop cruiser by the motel. I'll bet it's for you."

"No!" Judith protested. "It's probably checking on the Odells. Maybe the parents have some more information about the Stokes family."

But she was wrong. Sergeant Brewster got out of the cruiser and motioned for Judith to pull over. Complying, she rolled down the window and asked what he wanted.

"Please get out of the vehicle and come with me," he said, his long, tanned face expressionless. "You can answer questions in the cruiser or at headquarters."

"About what?" Judith blurted.

Brewster's black eyes snapped. "About the victim."

"I never met him when he was alive," Judith protested.

"Maybe not. But you may be the last one to see him dead."

Judith couldn't argue the point.

Chapter 8

The cousins got out of the rental, but Brewster pointed to Renie. "Please remain in your car, ma'am. I want to speak to your friend in private."

"I'm her attorney," Renie declared. "Serena Jones of Jones, Jones and Berfle. I must insist on being present. Or do you want me to call the U.S. consulate in Calgary?"

Still expressionless, Brewster motioned with his hand. "Come along, then, eh?"

They drove in silence, except for an occasional crackling voice coming over the cruiser's radio. Judith and Renie didn't look at each other, but stared out of their respective windows. Brewster pulled into a driveway behind the RCMP building. Obviously, they were going to enter through the rear.

"Perps' entrance," Renie whispered as Brewster got out to open the rear door. "I forget. Have we ever been busted before?"

Judith didn't answer. When they were inside, he led them to what appeared to be an interrogation room and told them to sit down in the two chairs that faced a table and a third chair. Then he left and closed the door with a clicking sound.

"We're locked in," Renie said. "Do you think they serve food? Or at least a beverage?"

Judith looked exasperated and pointed to the near wall. "Why don't you ask? There's a camera in here."

"Oh." Renie smiled and waved. "Hi. My client is innocent."

Brewster returned before Judith could threaten to strangle Renie. After he sat down, he spoke in a formal voice, announcing his name, the time and day of the interview, and then asking the cousins to identify themselves. Judith went first, then tensed for fear that Renie would say something outrageous. But she didn't, only adding that she and Mrs. Flynn were cousins. Brewster directed his first question to Judith, asking if she had seen the body of the victim, Emory Alfred Stokes.

"I did," she replied with a lift of her chin.

"Why did you do such a thing?" Brewster asked, still without expression.

"Because I wasn't sure it was true. That is," she went on, "the Stokes family seem a bit . . . eccentric. I wasn't sure I could take them seriously."

"You've known the family for some time, eh?"

"No. We only arrived in Banff early Friday afternoon. Later on my cousin and I went for a walk and met the Strokes family for the first time. Did you know about their plan to send Mr. Stokes down the Bow River?"

For the first time, Brewster's face showed a reaction, though whether it was surprise or dismay, Judith couldn't tell. "There was some mention of a bier," he replied. "Constable MacRae and I didn't take it seriously."

"You should," Judith declared. "Did you talk to Mr. Stokes's daughter, Mrs. Odell?"

Brewster took umbrage. "I'm asking the questions here, Mrs. Flynn." Apparently, he saw that Judith was very grave and decided to make amends. "Yes, we did, but she wasn't very forthcoming."

"Then talk to her again," Judith said. "I doubt that she approved of their plan for the body disposal. Have you found the weapon?"

The query made the Mountie scowl. "Why do you ask?"

Judith shrugged. "It seems like an obvious question."

He sat back in his chair and fretted his upper lip with his index finger. "Who are you, Mrs. Flynn?"

"I own a B&B," Judith replied. "My husband, Joe Flynn, is a retired police homicide detective. He and Mrs. Jones's husband are on a fishing trip. Naturally, I took an interest in his job over the years." She hoped that Renie was keeping a straight face.

"I see." He shifted in his chair. "If I check with your city's law enforcement personnel, will they confirm that?"

"Of course," Judith said. "In fact, my husband's former partner, Woodrow Price, is now a precinct captain. It's Saturday, so he's probably home. If you want to call Woody, I can give you his unlisted phone number."

Brewster nodded rather absently. "I believe you," he said, but turned to Renie. "Is your law practice also in the city?"

Renie shook her head. "I don't need to practice. I got too good at it after the first few years, so I went pro."

"Coz!" Judith shrieked. "Stop that!" She turned back to Brewster. "She's putting you on, Sergeant. She's really a graphic designer."

"I see." Brewster again looked stoic. "At least I think I do. Dare I ask what your husband does for a living?"

"He's a psychologist," Renie replied.

Brewster stared at her briefly and then nodded. "Yes. Your husband has the right job."

"What," **Renie** demanded after Brewster had dropped them off by the motel, "did he mean by that crack?"

"You know what he meant," Judith said. "I don't know why you came up with the lawyer bit in the first place. You never tell lies."

"Because you do it all the time," Renie asserted, "and for once I wanted to beat you to it."

"I never lie," Judith declared. "I only tell small fibs for a good cause. At least the rest of the interview went well. I think we gave a fairly accurate picture of the Stokes family. I wonder if they really sent Codger down the river on that bier."

Renie grimaced. "If they did, I hope Bill and Joe don't reel him in instead of a trout."

Traffic was even heavier than usual with every kind of conveyance from giant motor homes to bicycles. The late-afternoon sun cast a golden glow on the town, making it sparkle as if beckoning the tourists to come inside the shops and restaurants. In stark contrast, the rugged granite peaks rose up as if shielding the inhabitants from all the bustle of their visitors. The disparity between brash commercialism and raw nature struck Judith as a metaphor for the human condition. Amid so much beauty, there was also menace. Codger's murder struck her as tragic proof of Man's betrayal of Nature's bounty.

"Hey," Renie said, breaking into her cousin's musings, "it's ten to five. We'd better get to church. It's on Squirrel Street, so do you suppose the pastor is Father Rodent?"

"Dubious," Judith said vaguely after they got into the Lexus SUV. "I wonder where they crossed the border."

"The squirrels? They sneak in. Though I once heard that a gang of our gray squirrels stowed away on a ship headed for the U.K. After landing, they drove all the English native red squirrels out of—"

"Stop," Judith interrupted. "I mean the Stokeses."

Renie grew serious. "We don't know what part of Nebraska they came from. Maybe they drove to Montana or entered via Manitoba. What difference does it make?"

"Probably none. But it'd be quite a drive with a dying man if they came from eastern Nebraska." Judith paused. "Brewster never told us if they found the weapon."

"You're right," Renie agreed. "You didn't see it in the tent?"

"I'd have told you if I had. No one else mentioned it

either. That *is* odd." She paused. "Ah! We're almost to St. Mary's."

Both cousins immediately recognized the little granite stone church they'd attended half a century earlier as youthful teenagers. It had been almost new back in the 1950s. The pews were already filling up. Judith scanned the worshippers, but didn't see anyone she recognized.

"No suspects here," she whispered before dipping her fingers into the holy water font and crossing herself.

"No squirrels either," Renie whispered back.

The liturgy was reverent but efficient; the homily mercifully brief. Obviously, Judith thought, the priest realized that his attendees were as anxious to continue their vacations as the merchants were eager for their money. She'd noticed at least two locals from their various stops in town.

"Disappointing, huh?" Renie gibed as they came outside. "No suspects on hand. You should've nailed the priest to see if he'd heard a homicidal confession today."

"You know he wouldn't tell me if he had," Judith said. "When do you want to have dinner? We'll probably need reservations."

"Why not the Banff Springs Hotel?" Renie suggested. "Then we'll be able to say that at least we've been there."

"Good idea. Why don't you call them on your cell?"

Renie was on the phone for so long that they'd reached the motel before she finally clicked off. Judith asked if she'd been put on hold.

"No," Renie replied, rubbing her ear. "They've got so many bars and restaurants and cafés that I can only remember one of them—the 1888 Chop House. Somehow, it seems appropriate for this trip. I was able to key in a nine o'clock reservation. That's all they had left."

Exiting the SUV, they could hear music. "Where's that coming from? It sounds like a hymn," Judith said.

"They've got other churches in town," Renie responded, "though I haven't noticed any nearby. It also sounds like they've got awful voices. Is that a banjo I hear?"

"Yes. I think it's coming from the Stokes folks," Judith said. "Maybe they're doing some kind of informal memorial service for Codger."

"No. No," Renie repeated calmly. "We're not going to join them. Never. Not in my lifetime. I refuse . . ."

But Judith was already headed for the encampment. Renie expelled a big sigh and joined her. They were halfway to their destination along the river when the singing stopped.

"Show's over," Renie stated. "Can we go back now? My feet hurt."

"Stop whining," Judith said. "Somebody's coming in this direction. Two somebodies."

"So?"

The sun was starting its descent over the Rockies. Judith shielded her eyes. "It's Teddy and Martha Lou."

"Hey," Teddy called out. "You seen those snooty twins lately?"

Judith waited to answer until they came closer. "Not for a couple of hours. They were going into the motel."

Martha Lou's freckled face was flushed. "Brats." She spat out the word. "Too good for the rest of us. They wouldn't stick around for tellin' 'bout our memories of poor ol' Codger."

"I understand how you feel," Judith said kindly, "but I don't think they ever met him."

"Ha!" Teddy exclaimed, blue eyes snapping. "Those two gold-diggin' creeps got their claws into Codger from way back. Wouldn't surprise me if they stabbed the poor old duffer."

Martha Lou's auburn curls bounced as she nodded her head. "You betcha! I took a mislikin' to them straight off." Her green eyes swerved as if she feared being overheard by other family members. "The cops told all of us they need Codger's body 'cause they had to do a . . . like an operation on him. Why? I mean he's dead. What's the point?"

"An autopsy?" Judith suggested.

Teddy and Martha Lou looked at each other. "Yeah," he said. "That's the word. But it won't bring him back to life, will it?"

"No," Judith responded. "But it's probably a rule here when the death is suspicious."

"Of what?" Teddy demanded. "He got stabbed by some weirdo. Those cops should spend their time lookin' for that guy instead of buggin' us."

Martha Lou nodded vigorously. "This whole thing's been too weird. Me an' Teddy here are kinda fed up with this mess. We're goin' to find us a tavern and kick back." She put her hand on his arm. "Let's be gone, okay?"

Teddy held his head and groaned. "Might as well. They're singin' another danged hymn. Sounds like a catfight to me. I'm so hungry I could eat a snake." He nodded to the cousins before the couple toddled away, hand in hand.

Judith raised her eyebrows. "A breach in the family unit?"

"They may sound dumb, but they might be savvy," Renie said. "Are you sure you want to join the hymn fest?"

"It's cheap entertainment," Judith replied. "Besides, what else have we got to do?"

"My feet still hurt," Renie said. "Oh well."

"What did you think about the twins apparently making nice with Codger?"

"They sent him valentines? How would I know?"

"That's probably what they did," Judith asserted. "Christmas and Easter cards, letters letting him know about their school grades, what they were doing for fun, pictures, whatever."

"Sucking up," Renie murmured. "It all fits."

The last words of "The Old Rugged Cross" squawked to a merciful finish. The mourners moved apart, leaving only Ada sitting in a camp chair and staring off into space.

Pa gestured at the cousins. "You two see Teddy and Martha Lou go off just now?"

Judith nodded. "They were going to get dinner in town." She saw Pa's thick eyebrows come together in a frown and changed the subject. "I'm curious. How big is your farm?"

"Just a little over fifteen hundred acres," he replied, looking suspicious. "Why are you asking about our farm?"

Judith barely heard the last of his words. "Fifteen hundred acres? Isn't that . . . big?"

"Depends." Pa's expression softened slightly. "The more land you got, the more corn you can plant."

"We understand that," Renie said dryly. "Is it all planted with corn and soybeans?"

Pa nodded. "'Cept for the cows. They need pasture-land. Milk cows, that is. Always good to have some-thin' to tide you over in the winter. 'Course Codger pre-sold the corn most years."

Judith was still a bit dazed by the whole operation. "How many people work the farm?"

"Just me an' Teddy. 'Course I'm kinda buggered up by the arthritis. But with all this modern stuff, you don't need extry hands." Pa glanced at the rest of the family. "Dang. Teddy and Martha Lou shoulda stayed put. We gotta sing another hymn. Martha Lou's got a mighty fine singin' voice. We need her to lead." He trudged away to join the others.

Judith turned to Renie. "Let's go back to the bar."

"You want to get hammered? Are you serious?"

"We could go to our so-called suite, for all I care," Judith shot back, "but I want to call Aunt Ellen. They should still be up. It's only a little after eight in Bea-trice."

"Oh, for . . . Fine. My feet still hurt. Maybe I should buy new shoes while I'm here. And sweaters."

They ended up in the Flynns' half of the suite. Aunt

Ellen answered on the third ring. "Oh, Judith, great to hear your voice, but hold on. I've got jam cooking on the stove and I'm making a fall wreath out of wood shavings for the front door. Or maybe I'll send it to your mother. She'll love it! Or would she rather have the one I just finished that's made from old movie film strips?"

Judith made a face. "Ask her what she'd like." *None of the above,* she mouthed to Renie, who was leaning over her cousin's shoulder to hear their aunt.

"I will," Aunt Ellen said briskly. "You're not calling to tell me somebody died, are you?"

"No," Judith assured her, since she wasn't about to prolong the call by mentioning the latest murder victim. "We're in Banff on vacation with the Joneses. We met some farm people from Big Stove who raise corn. I'm curious. One of them mentioned . . ."

Aunt Ellen was laughing. "You're always curious, Judith! Sometimes you get into trouble. Do be careful. Tell my goddaughter to watch you like a hawk. Hold on, the jam's about to boil over. Win! Let out the dog! He's going to piddle on my clean kitchen floor."

Judith and Renie exchanged beleaguered looks. They heard Uncle Win open the door and speak to Varmint, a mixed breed who'd been abandoned near the Cornhusker stadium. The door closed. Maybe

Uncle Win had gone outside, too. The cousins always wondered if his wife's nonstop activities didn't wear him out. Maybe it was just as well that he was the laid-back type by nature. Otherwise, Judith and Renie figured, Win might have been laid out long ago.

"Where were we?" Aunt Ellen asked. "Oh—the people from here. What about them?"

"The farm has over fifteen hundred acres," Judith said. "Is that as big as it sounds?"

"Not really," Aunt Ellen replied. "If you want to make a living growing corn, you have to have a lot of land, often handed down from generation to generation. Acquiring additional acreage is accomplished by marriage with the son or daughter of a neighboring one. It can be a very profitable—and big—business. Millionaire farmers like the ones you've met aren't uncommon around here."

"Seriously?" Judith exchanged looks with Renie.

"Oh yes!" Aunt Ellen exclaimed. "Your new friends must be rolling in money! Got to hang up. The jam's ready and the mayor's at the front door."

Judith stared at Renie. "The Stokes folks are rich?"

"Sounds like it." She wore an ironic expression. "Lucky you. Aunt Ellen just gave you a very big motive for murder."

Judith nodded. "But not so lucky for Codger."

Chapter 9

Renie wasn't sparing sympathy for anyone. "Unfair," she muttered. "Dumb people don't deserve to be rich."

"They may be dumb about some things," Judith said, "but not about raising corn. They don't need a college education to do what their ancestors have done for generations."

Renie was still muttering. "I knew I shouldn't have slept through Economic Geography at the U. It was the only class I ever took at eight in the morning, and it was so *boring*. Three times during the quarter I didn't wake up until a different prof was lecturing on international econometrics. I thought his subject was foreign poetry."

"Now who's dumb?" Judith asked with a smile.

"Okay, I get your point. But you're right about money always being a good motive. Is it time to go to dinner yet?"

Judith glanced at her watch. "It's almost eight. We've been doing a lot of walking today. Let's relax."

"By doing what?" Renie retorted. "Wondering how much money the Stokes family has? I can answer that. More than we do, put together."

Judith looked a bit sly. "But who really has it? You're the one who mentioned money as a motive. Why do I think Codger kept a tight rein on the finances?"

Renie's answer was cut short by a pounding on the door. She got up from her chair to see who it was.

A harried Adela practically fell into the room. "Have you seen my kids?" she asked in an overwrought tone.

"Not since late this afternoon," Renie replied. "They were coming back here from wherever they'd been, which we gathered was with you at the campsite."

Adela collapsed into the closest chair. "Wherever they are, they got there in our car. It's gone."

Judith's expression was sympathetic. "They're probably at a bar or a restaurant. Come to think of it, they were going to play tennis."

The other woman's eyes snapped. "They wouldn't still be doing that now. How did they seem to you? Upset? Anxious?"

Judith briefly considered the question. "They did seem annoyed about being questioned by the Mounties. Don't get me wrong—just the usual hassle that kids their age resent from dealing with authority figures."

Adela showed no sign of taking comfort from Judith's words. "I don't like not knowing where they are. There's a murderer loose, don't you know? Maybe this homicidal maniac wants to wipe out all of us. Why was Codger killed in the first place when he was dying?"

"That's a good question," Judith said. "Was it old age or did he suffer from an incurable illness?"

"Old age is incurable," Adela declared. "People wear out." She frowned. "Pa—my brother, Cornelius—never actually told me what was wrong with Codger, only that they'd brought him here to carry out his last wishes. Norman and I never asked for specifics. We didn't have time because the rest of the family had already left for Banff and we had to rush to get ready to join them."

Another knock sounded on the door. Renie got up to answer it. Norman Odell burst into the room, breathing heavily and red in the face. He spoke directly to his wife.

"You better come quick, hon. We've got problems with the cops."

"What now?" Adela cried. "Is somebody else dead? Or is it the twins?"

"No, not that," Norman said, putting a hand on her shoulder and warily eyeing the cousins. "I'll tell you on the way back to the camp."

"Tell me now," Adela said, and gestured at Judith and Renie. "I've been dumping all over them. They're totally trustworthy."

Norman looked dubious. "All the same . . ."

Adela put a finger to Norman's lips. "Sergeant Brewster ran a background check and told me that Mrs. Flynn is FASTO."

"What?" Norman's heavy features wadded up like used bubble gum. "What the hell does that mean?"

"It means," Judith said reluctantly, "that I've been—rather accidentally—involved in a few homicide investigations. My husband is a retired police detective and still takes on an occasional private investigative assignment," she added, hoping that would explain everything.

It didn't—at least not to Norman. "So what's with this FASTO moniker?"

Judith sighed impatiently and turned to Renie. "You tell him. I've always thought it was silly."

Renie nodded once. "My cousin has attracted a fan club over the years. People all over the country became intrigued by her ability to help solve crimes. They made up an acronym—Female Amateur Sleuth Tracking Offenders."

Judith was thankful that Renie hadn't added that sometimes the nickname was mistakenly changed to FATSO. Since she had always been self-conscious about her weight, the error drove Judith crazy.

"Hunh," Norman said. "That's kind of wild." He sat down in the only other available chair. "Okay, I might as well open up. The cops—the Mounties, I mean—found that bier thing about a quarter of a mile down in some trees by the river. Your idiot brother told them they'd granted your father his last wish. But they haven't found the body."

Adela regarded her husband with a level gaze. "What a mess." She sighed and stood up. "But it's our kids going off on their own that worries me most. Have you seen anything of them since I came here?"

Norman also got to his feet. "No. Stop fussing. I'm not worried unless they wreck the car. Let's go. Sorry to bother you. Have a good one."

The Odells departed.

Renie ran a hand down her face. "Sheesh. Maybe if we stay here every suspect will eventually show up and we can order from room service."

"They don't have room service here at the motel," Judith reminded her.

"So I forgot. It's close to eight thirty. Let's go to the Banff Springs Hotel and have drinks in one of their bars. We might get called early for our nine o'clock reservation."

"With traffic, it might take us that long to get there," Judith said, standing up. "What do you think about the police finding the bier downstream, but no sign of Codger?"

Renie looked bleak. "Not much. Just for an hour or two, could we pretend we're on a real vacation?"

Judith smiled. "Of course."

Neither the words nor the expression convinced her cousin. After all, Judith was FASTO.

The excellent dinner at the hotel's 1888 Chop House kept Judith from focusing on murder and mayhem. They dined on Caesar salad and filet mignon, prepared over cherrywood. Neither cousin flinched at the expensive total on their tastefully designed bill. Perhaps the two stiff whiskeys they'd had before dinner and the snifters of Drambuie afterward had taken the edge off thinking about thrift. On the other hand, the exchange rate was in their favor.

"I wonder what our husbands are doing," Judith mused in a vague voice. She'd taken a roundabout way to avoid traffic and drove the big Lexus GX470 very carefully.

"Who?" Renie asked with indifference. "Oh, right. Bill and . . . Joe. They're probably sitting around a campfire eating some of the fish I hope they caught. Hey—this isn't the way back to the motel. Are you really loaded?"

"No," Judith said, "but I'm being cautious and taking a back road to come in from a different direction. There's still too much traffic in and around the town. Besides, I think this is the way to that Cave and Basin historic site Teddy mentioned."

Renie looked nonplussed. "We're going to visit a historic site in the dark? Did you bring extra flashlights?"

"Don't worry, I know where I'm—damn!" She hit the brakes to avoid a family of raccoons crossing in front of them.

Renie held her head. The younger raccoons were dawdling. "Kids these days!" she moaned.

"That's odd," Judith murmured. "Mama and Papa Raccoon have stopped by those big trees."

"Maybe the family lives there," Renie said. "Do you want to interrogate them, too?"

"They wouldn't live so close to a road," Judith responded. "Look, the whole lot of them have stopped."

"Maybe they met some friends. Can we go back to the motel now? I'm sleepy."

"At home you go to bed at midnight," Judith said, still staring out the car window. "It's only a little after eleven."

"You're blocking traffic," Renie declared.

"What traffic?" Judith retorted. "I haven't seen anybody on this road since we turned off."

"Raccoon traffic. Don't mess with them. They'll come back to haunt us with their big, doleful eyes and sharp, pointy teeth."

"They've moved on," Judith said, rolling down the window and noting how quiet it was away from the town. The only sound was of the wind ruffling some leaves in a nearby cottonwood tree.

Renie squirmed in her seat. "Well? Are we camping out here or going back to the motel?"

Judith had taken her foot off the brake, steering the SUV to the verge. "I've got a weird feeling about this. You know I have to go with my hunches. I want a look."

"Oh, for . . . !" Renie didn't finish the exclamation. "Fine. But I'm staying in the car."

"Do that," Judith said, turning off the engine. "Oh— see if there's a flashlight in the glove compartment."

There was. Wordlessly, Renie handed it over. Judith turned it on as soon as she stepped onto the ground. The raccoons had made a fairly decent trail on their passage to wherever they lived at night. But she still walked very carefully on the uneven path. The scent of evergreen needles evoked the evenings that she and Renie had spent at the family cabins by Mount Woodchuck. The night air was not only fresh but fragrant, a potpourri of woodsy earth and, from somewhere nearby, ripe berries. It was cooler, Judith thought, and to her surprise, she shivered.

Less than fifteen yards off the verge, she spotted what looked like a large, dark bundle. Sucking in her breath, she moved closer. The fabric covering whatever lay beneath it was an ordinary blue blanket. It was ripped in places, as if torn by animals or birds. Raccoons, she suddenly remembered, were omnivorous.

But through the rents in the blanket, Judith recognized the overalls and denim shirt that covered Codger's corpse.

Chapter 10

Judith fought back a sudden onrush of nausea. Seeing the old man's body in his tent wasn't nearly as upsetting as finding him abandoned in the forest. She tried not to stagger as she made her way back to the car.

"Coz!" Renie yelped when she saw her cousin struggle to get into the driver's seat. "What's wrong?"

"Codger," Judith gasped. "They never sent him down the river. We have to tell the Mounties." She handed over the flashlight, but made no attempt to start the car.

"Now?" Renie finally asked.

"Yes. But give me a minute. That was kind of gruesome." Briefly, she recounted what she'd seen.

"Why," Renie asked, "would they do such a thing?"

"'They'?" Judith said. "Maybe only one of them."

"The killer?"

"Maybe. I don't know. They're peculiar people."

"The Odells seem normal," Renie noted.

"They're still related. Genes don't lie." Judith turned the ignition key. The sighting of Codger's body had sobered her in more ways than one. "Maybe they took him to the Cave and Basin Hot Springs, but the curative waters didn't help. Then they gave up and left him here." She shook herself. "I want to get away from this place. It's just too weird."

For once, Renie didn't comment.

Ten minutes later when they reached RCMP headquarters, the building was dark. Judith rolled down the window and looked out at the sign by the door.

"Drat! They close at eleven and open at seven in the morning. I suppose they have patrol cars on duty, but that's no help."

"Why don't you speed through town and knock over a few pedestrians?" Renie suggested. "Of course, you might have to take a Breathalyzer test and then you'd get a DUI."

"Come up with a helpful idea for a change, okay?"

"I did. I bet the thought crossed your mind."

Judith smiled. "Not quite. But you and I often know what the other one is thinking."

"Propinquity and heredity," Renie allowed. "So

why would anybody hide Codger's body in the woods? Why not follow the old coot's plan to be sent down the river on that bier?"

Judith didn't answer until they were almost in sight of the motel. "The bier was hidden from the police," she finally said, "so maybe they wanted to make it look as if his wish had been granted without the chance of the body being found downriver and being arrested for violating a local law. The answer to your question may be that the body would've been found eventually. But that poses the obvious question of why didn't they want the police to find the body? They knew he'd been murdered. Naturally, they'd all become suspects."

"Now you're the one who's saying 'they,'" Renie pointed out. "How come?"

Judith pulled into the parking area behind the motel. "We have to assume that only one person killed Codger. Maybe all or some of them know who did it. But the body disposal had to involve at least two people because it was done in broad daylight. One to do the deed and one to keep watch. The only thing I know for sure is that the Mounties aren't going to let them leave Canada until they figure out who's *not* guilty."

Renie frowned. "As opposed to who's innocent?"

Judith shrugged. "I'm not sure any of them are

innocent. In fact, I'm not even sure the Stokes folks are really the Stokes folks. They seem unreal to me."

When they got out of the car, Renie pointed to an empty parking place. "No Buick."

"You're right. But the twins may still be partying somewhere. It's not quite midnight."

"True," Renie agreed. "Let's put ourselves to bed, along with all our speculations."

"Good idea," Judith murmured.

But that was easier said than done, even after she'd gone to sleep. Judith had nightmares of a hooded Codger-like creature waving a scythe. But instead of a black robe, he was wearing bloodstained overalls.

It was not a restful night.

When Judith awoke shortly before eight thirty Sunday morning, she was tempted to call Arlene and find out if Mighty Tidy and Sons had shown up to do the housework. But it was only an hour earlier at the B&B and the Rankerses would be preparing the guests' breakfast. Instead, filial devotion overcame her, so she dialed her mother's number.

"What now?" Gertrude rasped. "You need bail money?"

"Of course not," Judith replied. "Renie and I had dinner last night at the big hotel after we went to church. The boys have gone fishing but should be back tonight."

"*The boys?*" Gertrude sounded as if she were sneering. "Haven't those two knuckleheads been draining the Social Security system for almost as many years as I can count on my fingers?"

"Not nearly as long as you have," Judith reminded her mother, and changed the subject. "How are Phyliss's stand-ins doing?"

"What stand-ins?" Gertrude snapped. "Her Royal Religious Loonyness was here yesterday."

"She was?" Maybe Gertrude's memory was slipping.

"Are you sure?"

The old lady chortled. "The crazy fool got jilted. Why not? Who'd be dumb enough to marry Phyliss?"

"They say there's someone for everybody," Judith said. "So who was Phyliss's suitor?"

"A serial bigamist, that's who," Gertrude declared. "Her groom-to-be has at least three other wives. He got the idea that Phyliss owned *my* house. I guess she didn't let on that she doesn't live in the B&B. She met him at her weird church. No surprise there."

"Poor Phyliss." Judith felt sorry for her cleaning woman. "Have you talked to her?"

"She says the devil made her do it. I told her even

Satan wouldn't come up with a crackpot idea like that. He's too busy trying to get everybody to vote for the Republicans. Speaking of which, Aunt Deb and I are playing bridge tonight with Sophie Savery and her sister, Samantha. Sophie lies about her age. I know she voted for Dewey not once but twice—against FDR and then Truman. She swears she only did it in '48."

Judith knew better than to get her mother launched on politics. She'd never stopped insisting that Herbert Hoover had caused the Great Depression all by himself. "I hear Renie stirring in the next room. I'd better see if she's ready to go out to breakfast."

"She better not be stirring up trouble," Gertrude warned. "You two are behaving yourselves, aren't you?"

"Of course! We haven't even been shopping yet."

"Good. Don't. Unless you see a nice cardigan," Gertrude added. "I could use a new one if they don't try to gouge you. Tourists can be treated like saps. I ought to know. I've seen some of your dopey guests."

Judith ignored the remark. "I'll make sure we don't have that problem," she promised before ringing off.

Renie stood in the doorway between the two rooms. "You woke me up," she asserted. "These walls must be made of cardboard. Who were you talking to?"

Judith said she'd called her mother. She'd save the news about Phyliss's broken romance until her cousin was fully alert.

Renie yawned and staggered back into the Joneses' half of the suite. "Give me half an hour to put myself together. Maybe after that I'll wake up."

Judith needed some time, too. It was well after nine when they got into the elevator. A female voice called from the hall to hold the door. A moment later, a breathless Trixie rushed inside and virtually fell against the far wall mumbling something that sounded like "thanks."

Judith noticed that Trixie looked very different from the pretty, cheerful young woman she'd met earlier at the front desk. "Are you okay?" she asked in a concerned voice.

"Yes. No. I mean . . ." Trixie pressed the back of her hand to her forehead. "The last few days have been real bummers."

"Yes," Judith said, "you came to work at the height of the tourist season. Baptism by fire, as they say."

Trixie's reddened eyes narrowed. "More like hell."

The elevator stopped. Judith's smile was sympathetic. "You have a steady job. You should be thankful for that."

"Thankful?" Trixie curled her lip. "A job's the last thing I wanted! What's money compared to love? Men are rotten!" She stomped out of the elevator and disappeared down the hall.

"Gee," Renie said as they walked out into the parking area, "you flunked a personal relations encounter. Isn't that the first time in about five years?"

"Not that long. I wonder why she's so upset?"

"I advise you not to try to find out," Renie responded. "Maybe she's the overly emotional type."

Shaking her head, Judith got behind the SUV's steering wheel. "Trixie's certainly distraught. I can relate to her. She has my sympathy."

"Give yourself a break," Renie advised. "You have enough to do trying to find out who killed Codger."

Judith didn't say anything as they drove away from the motel. When she finally spoke, it was to change the subject. "The RCMP office is open now. We'll stop there first to tell them about finding the body."

"No, we will not," Renie stated firmly. "We'll eat first. I'm starving and Codger's not going anywhere."

Judith knew better than to argue with her cousin when she was hungry. "Okay, how about Wild Flour?"

"They don't have pancakes," Renie said, now sounding cranky. "I want a real breakfast. I checked the guide at the motel and Phil's is supposed to have great pancakes. It's right across the river from the police station. What more could you ask?"

"The address?"

"Jeez," Renie growled, "I'm weak at math, I don't do numbers. It's on Spray Avenue. How hard is *that*?"

Judith decided that finding Phil's would be easier than dealing with her crabby, ravenous cousin. Happily, once she crossed the bridge, the restaurant was only a short distance away. But when they got inside, there was a long line of customers. Apparently, everybody loved Phil's pancakes.

"Curses!" Renie said under her breath. "Do I have to fake my own death to get served before noon?"

"Why don't you try it?" Judith retorted. But she said it softly.

Renie merely growled again. Unless, Judith thought, the sound came from her stomach and not her throat.

Twenty minutes later they were seated. Judith unloaded Phyliss's sad story. Apparently cheered by the prospect of food, Renie was uncharacteristically sympathetic.

"She's led a really dull existence. Oh, I know she was born late in her parents' lives and her father abandoned them and then her mother got sick. Phyliss had to nurse her for years. The only source of comfort she had was the peculiar church she joined. I suppose she doesn't really know any better."

"That's true," Judith agreed. "She complains a lot, but the basic attitude is grounded in her religious beliefs. She may be happier than a lot of people with money and status. Look at the Stokes family. They're apparently rich, but they don't seem very happy. I wonder what's with Ada."

Renie didn't answer right away. Their order had arrived. Lavishly buttering her pancakes and pouring syrup over them, she finally responded. "Mentally disabled, I assume. She's so thin. Maybe she doesn't eat enough." She shoveled in a big bite of pancakes, egg, and sausage.

"You do. And you're still thin." Judith smiled. "It's hard to tell how old Ada is. Probably around thirty unless there's a big gap between her and Teddy." She paused. "Speaking of age, I'd like to know how old Codger was."

Renie looked up from her plate. "Does it matter?"

"Yes. I really doubt he could have been close to a hundred as someone suggested. But why lie about his age? I'd like to see his passport. And the photo on it. We have no idea what he looked like. His face, that is. We never saw it."

"You could go back to have another peek at his corpse," Renie suggested with a puckish expression.

"No thanks." Judith actually shuddered. "That was too grim even for me. But the police may know."

Renie didn't speak until she'd swallowed another mighty mouthful of food. "Speaking of grim, I wonder what Phyliss's no-show looked like."

"That might be grimmer," Judith said. "Let's stick to murder."

Her cousin laughed. "I knew you'd say that."

Half an hour later they arrived at RCMP headquarters. Sergeant Brewster was on duty along with two other officers, and explained that Constable MacRae had Sunday off. If the stalwart Brewster was surprised to see the cousins, he didn't show it, but merely asked how he could help them.

"It's the other way around," Judith said apologetically. "We found Mr. Stokes's body."

Only a tic in Brewster's forehead revealed his surprise. "I see. How and where did you find it?"

"By accident," Judith replied. "We took the long way back to the motel after dinner at the Banff Springs Hotel."

Brewster nodded faintly. "So where was the victim?"

Judith was at a loss when it came to the exact

location. She looked helplessly at Renie, who looked at Brewster. "Do you know where the raccoons live at night?" she asked the Mountie in a guileless voice.

"They live all over the area," Brewster replied with a touch of impatience. "Can you be more precise?"

Fearing that Renie's overly benign expression might rile the sergeant, Judith quickly intervened. "It was late and quite dark, but we could show you the route we took."

"Fine," Brewster said. "We'll go now in my cruiser, eh?" He led the way out back.

After he drove from the parking lot, he asked if they'd gone over a bridge after leaving the hotel. Judith said they hadn't, but she recalled seeing something about a golf course in the vicinity. Brewster nodded once.

After a short distance through town, they did cross a bridge. "You were coming from the hotel, eh?" he said. "For some reason, you went the wrong way."

"It really was quite dark," Judith pointed out, not wanting to admit that she and Renie had been a bit fuzzy at the time. "I guess we got turned around."

Brewster didn't respond at once. When he did, he asked if they remembered any landmarks.

"Only that we could see the trail made by the raccoons," Judith replied. "We'd stopped to let them cross."

"Ah" was the sergeant's only response as he slowed down. Judith took that as a good sign. A minute or so later he signaled to turn off onto the verge. "Is this the spot?"

"It could be," Judith replied. "It really was very dark."

Brewster opened his door. "Come along, show me where you found Mr. Stokes."

Judith got out of the car, but Renie stayed put. "I didn't go with my cousin," she said. "I don't suppose you brought any snacks?"

Brewster's dark eyebrows rose. "Snacks?"

Renie sighed. "Never mind. It was just a thought."

Judith squared her shoulders and led the way. "You can see the trail for yourself. We don't have far to go."

They walked for longer than Judith remembered doing the previous night. She finally stopped by a fallen fir branch and looked at Brewster. "Something's wrong. We've gone too far. I don't recall that branch and there's been very little wind here. Let's go back a few yards."

The nerve in Brewster's forehead ticked again. "If you say so."

Judith moved slower, finally pausing by a tall cedar. "That big whorl in the bark—I remember it. I happened to shine my flashlight on it. The body was right there by this tree. Except," she added after a gulp, "it's not here now."

"I can see that," Brewster said in a controlled voice.

"Look," Judith said, annoyed with herself for feeling defensive, "I didn't invent finding Mr. Stokes here. If you bring in your crime-scene people, I'm sure you'll find evidence that the body was ditched here. He was covered by a dark blue blanket that looked as if it had been torn in places by some of the local wildlife."

Brewster regarded Judith with what she first took for skepticism, but realized was more like curiosity. "You have a reputation as an amateur detective," he said at last. "Why would anyone put the body here in the forest?"

Frustrated, Judith shook her head. "I don't know. But there has to be a reason. As a guess, I'd say it was because they didn't want an autopsy performed on the victim."

"That makes some sense," Brewster allowed. "Then why didn't they bury it, eh?"

"Because they didn't have time?" Judith suggested. "Then again, there's nothing about that family that does make sense, including why he was killed in the first place."

Brewster didn't comment until they returned to the

cruiser. "I'll request a crime-scene team to come from Calgary. Hopefully, they'll get here later today."

Judith nodded faintly. "I have to ask—have you found the weapon?"

"No." The sergeant's face was expressionless. "We suspect it may've been thrown into the river."

"Oh." Judith felt remiss for not considering as much. "I don't suppose it could wash up somewhere."

"We've thought of that," Brewster said, still deadpan. "Of course, a half-dozen knives could fall into the Bow from fishermen or hikers or picnickers. The chances of getting prints from any of them would be slim, eh?"

"Yes," Judith agreed. "But someone in the family might recognize it."

"Maybe." Brewster ushered her into the cruiser. "Meanwhile," he continued, getting into the driver's seat, "we don't have extensive forensic resources in Banff. We'll secure the site here by the tree to keep out trespassers."

"Of course," Judith echoed. She'd settled in next to Renie in the backseat and nudged her cousin in the upper arm. "Are you conscious?"

"No," Renie replied, and closed her eyes in an attempt to prove it. She stayed that way until they'd returned to headquarters, where Brewster told them they were free to go, but to keep in touch.

"Having fun?" Renie asked after they got into the SUV.

"Murder is never fun," Judith declared, and then told her that Codger's corpse had gone missing.

"No kidding," Renie said vaguely. "Why am I not surprised?"

"I was," Judith admitted. "Well . . . maybe not as surprised as I was to find the old guy there in the first place."

Renie fastened her seat belt. "When do we get to the part where we discover that Codger isn't really dead?"

"Don't say things like that!" Judith cried. "Nothing about this crazy case could surprise me."

But to add to her unease, all sorts of weird notions niggled at her brain, including that maybe Codger wasn't Codger. For once, she kept that nutty idea to herself.

Chapter 11

Adela Odell was waiting for them in the motel parking area. She was pacing, wringing her hands, and looked as if she'd been shortchanged on sleep.

"They're not here," she called to the cousins as they got out of the SUV. "Have you seen them?"

"You mean . . . your twins?" Judith asked.

"Yes! They never came back last night," Adela replied, gesturing frantically at the motel's parking slots. "The car's still gone and their beds haven't been slept in."

"Maybe you should alert the police," Judith said.

Adela shook her head. "No! I can't. That would . . . well, it might make the Mounties think Win and Winnie did something . . . foolish."

"Such as what?" Renie inquired. "Ditching Codger's body?"

Adela turned pugnacious. "What do you mean by that?"

Judith had an urge to strangle her cousin. "Serena refers to your father's disappearance. We were told by the Mounties that his body can't be found."

"Then they haven't looked very far," Adela snapped. "As silly as it may seem, Pa and Teddy may've carried out Codger's wishes to be sent down the Bow on that bier. All the police have to do is search the river."

"I take it," Judith said solemnly, "they haven't done that yet?"

"How would I know?" Adela shot back. "The cops here are no different than they are in Iowa. They keep things to themselves. I'm less interested in where Codger is than in where my children have gone. If you hear or see anything about them, leave word at the motel desk. Please?"

"Of course," Judith promised.

"Well?" Renie said after Adela went inside. "What's your take on that? Other than the obvious—that Pa and Teddy lied to Adela and the cops about Codger's body disposal."

"I don't know," Judith confessed. "Being young and

maybe a bit callous, did the twins take off because they didn't want to deal with their family's dilemma?"

"Maybe they were scared," Renie suggested. "Having Grandpa whacked might make them nervous."

Judith didn't respond right away. "Let's go up to the so-called suite. I've got an idea."

"Which is?" Renie asked, shooing away mosquitoes.

"I'd like to find out some background on the Stokeses," Judith replied. "Aunt Ellen's tight with her old pal Mayor Boo Whoozits. You'll recall that our aunt ran her last two successful campaigns."

"Along with about six other jobs Aunt Ellen was juggling at the time. You want the mayor to start an investigation of the Stokes folks?"

"Boo must have access to all sorts of records," Judith said as they got in the elevator. "It's going on noon, so Aunt Ellen and Uncle Win should be back from church. Maybe this is silly, but I'm curious about Codger's actual age."

Renie shrugged. "Why not? Curiosity should be your middle name."

Upon leaving the elevator, Judith noticed that the door to the Flynns' room was open. "Are we being robbed?" she murmured only half facetiously.

The question was answered when the cousins saw

Trixie making up the bed. She gave a start when Judith and Renie entered the room.

"Sorry," she said. "I'm running late this morning. I haven't yet vacuumed."

"Is Mrs. Jones's room finished?" Judith asked with a friendly smile.

Trixie gestured halfheartedly. "You mean next door?" She gave a jerky nod. The cousins moved on to the other half of the so-called suite.

"That girl's a mess," Renie declared after she closed the door. "Is she sick or a head case?"

"Bitter," Judith replied, after taking a moment to consider. "She's had some kind of recent romantic disappointment."

"Got dumped, probably," Renie said. "It happens. She'll get over it. Maybe Niall can help her."

"Whatever it was, she obviously didn't plan on working here at the motel." Judith sat down to call Aunt Ellen. The phone in Beatrice rang four times before going to voice mail. Their aunt's message was terse: "Busy. Will call back ASAP."

Renie, who had leaned in to hear the response, laughed. "Maybe she's become the assistant pastor."

"It wouldn't surprise me," Judith said.

"I suppose it's too early to eat lunch." Renie sounded wistful.

"By at least an hour," Judith replied. "I wonder what time the guys will show up this evening? Maybe they'll call to let us know. If it's not too late, we could wait for them."

"They can always get burgers at a—"

Renie was interrupted by a ring on Judith's cell. Assuming it was Aunt Ellen, she knelt next to the chair to listen in.

"I just got back from the rummage sale after church," their aunt said. "I had to chair it again this year, so I stayed on to supervise the cleanup. Don't tell me you've got more questions. Or would you like me to send you some of the leftover sale items? There's a pair of polka-dot knickers that would just fit you."

Judith ignored the horrified face Renie was making.

"No thanks, Aunt Ellen, I'm good for clothes. In fact, I should weed out some of my old stuff. I'm calling to ask a favor. Could you have Mayor Boo look up the birth date of someone for me? He's from Big Stove."

"I can do that," Aunt Ellen said. "Sue Boo relies on me to do all sorts of research for her, so I have access to public records. Among other things," she added in a conspiratorial tone. "Give me the name while I go into what I jokingly call my office, but it's really a sewing and crafts room."

"It's Emory Alfred Stokes," Judith replied, and spelled out the first name.

"Hang on for a moment," Aunt Ellen said amid the sound of paper shuffling. "Where did I put my laptop? Oh, here it . . . No, that's a cookie sheet . . . Ah! Patience, Judith. It shouldn't take me long to . . . Yes, here he is. Emory Alfred Stokes, born August fourth, 1907, in Big Stove, Neb—oops! Hold on, one of the balls of yarn I'm using to make an Eskimo sweater for Win just rolled off the table."

"That does make Codger not far from a hundred," Judith whispered to Renie. "Farming must've kept him in good shape."

"Yarn rescued!" Aunt Ellen exclaimed. "Does that part help?"

"Yes," Judith replied. "What do you mean by 'part'?"

"Well . . . Emory Alfred Stokes died February third, 1911. Are you researching a child?"

"No," Judith said as she and Renie stared at each other. "Maybe another member of the family was named in the child's honor. Can you check that?"

"Of course I can," Aunt Ellen asserted self-righteously. "But Big Stove is a very small town, only a few hundred . . . No, there's no other Emory Alfred Stokes in the United States."

Renie leaned into the phone. "How about Canada?"

"Is that you, Serena?" their aunt asked in a vexed voice. "I don't have access to Canadian vital records. You can sort that out. What are you two up to? Why aren't you sightseeing or bargain shopping or visiting shut-ins like Uncle Win and I do when we visit the rest of the family?"

Judith smirked; Renie rolled her eyes. Ellen and Win spent most of their time running around like a couple of chimps in heat, as Auntie Vance always put it. Family members saw them only at appointed times: lunch with Aunt Deb; drinks with Uncle Al; dinner with Auntie Vance and Uncle Vince, unless they missed the ferry from Whoopee Island. Judith and Renie were lucky to get together with them for dessert while listening to Gertrude grumble about why they'd bothered leaving Beatrice in the first place.

"It's some people we met here in Banff," Judith finally said. "As you mentioned earlier, I'm always curious."

"So you are, dear Judith," Aunt Ellen replied with amusement. "I must dash. But be careful. You know what curiosity did to the cat." She rang off.

Renie flopped into a chair. "I'm so exhausted from listening to Aunt Ellen that I forgot why you called her."

"Codger," Judith answered vaguely, and grew thoughtful. "If Emory Alfred Stokes died young, who supposedly was being sent down the river on that bier?"

"Could you ask Adela?"

Judith shook her head. "We can't ask any of them. If this is some sort of scam, I'm guessing they're all in on it." She stood up and paced the room. "There's money involved, I'm sure of that. The farm. That's worth a lot of money. If Codger—and I'll keep calling him that because they do—somehow had control of the farm, that might explain it. Maybe the answer is in Big Stove."

"We're not going there," Renie warned sternly.

"I don't intend to," Judith retorted.

"You'll ask Aunt Ellen to check out Big Stove?"

"No," Judith said. "I've worn out my welcome with Aunt Ellen. I'll do it myself via phone." She sat back down, picked up her cell, and tapped in 411 for Directory Assistance. When the operator came on the line, Judith requested the number of Cornelius aka "Pa" Stokes. Jotting it down on the motel's memo pad, she then asked if there was a listing for Theodore Stokes. After a pause, the operator stated that there was no other listing for anyone with that last name in the area.

"So that tells us the entire family is living with Ma and Pa—that would be Corny and his wife, Delia,"

Judith said, tapping the ballpoint pen against her chin. "I wonder if whoever is caring for the children is staying with them at the farmhouse."

"What wild story will you tell whoever might answer the phone?" Renie asked.

"I'll stick to our original cover—a magazine article. I'll be the reporter. You can be the editor."

"No," Renie said, with a shake of her head. "I don't want the responsibility. Make me your gofer."

"Fine," Judith agreed, tapping in Corny's number. The ring had a tinny sound, as if the telephone equipment belonged to another era. Judith figured it could be a relic if the farm had been handed down through several generations. After ten rings, she disconnected.

"Maybe nobody's staying at the house," she said.

Renie frowned. "Somebody must be around to feed the animals. Didn't I hear a mention of cows? Or chickens. All farms should at least have chickens. Now I really am hungry. It's after noon. Let's go seek food."

"Okay, but let me put on some lipstick. And we really should find out what happened with the Odell twins."

"They're not *your* twins," Renie called after Judith, who had gone into the bathroom.

"Maybe not," Judith responded, "but if they took the family Buick, Adela and Norman are without a car."

"Not your problem either," Renie said as Judith came out of the bathroom. "You just don't want to lose track of your suspects. Speaking of which, why haven't you tried to talk to Ada?"

"I don't know if she *can* talk," Judith replied. "But you're right. I've been remiss. Quiet people are often the noticing type. I'll have a go at Ada after lunch. Where do you . . ." She stopped speaking as her cell rang. "Now, who can this be? Hello?"

The female voice on the other end was unfamiliar. "Who am I calling at this number?" she asked.

Judith stiffened, hesitating to give her name. "May I inquire who wants to know?"

"Someone called me from this number a few minutes ago," the woman said. "If you're selling something, I don't want it."

"Oh!" Recognition dawned on Judith. "My name's Judith McMonigle. I'm a freelance magazine writer."

"Are you selling magazines?" The voice remained suspicious.

"No, I only write for them," Judith fibbed. "I'm on assignment in Banff, Alberta, and I happened to meet some of the Stokes family members. Are you related to them?"

A momentary silence followed. "We can't be," the

woman finally said. "Our relatives went on vacation to Disneyland earlier this week. Jens and I are house-sitting for them."

Startled, Judith glanced at Renie, who had been eavesdropping. "Have you heard from them since they left?"

"No," the woman replied. "They're not much for writing postcards. Or much of anything else, come to think of it."

"No doubt they're busy having fun," Judith said blithely. "At Disneyland, of course. Your first name is . . . ?"

"Doris. Is this for your magazine?"

"I don't know yet," Judith hedged. "It's up to my editor."

"Good. We like to keep ourselves to ourselves. We've got our own problems here in Big Stove. Good-bye now." Doris hung up.

"Not helpful," Judith declared. "She implied that they're related to the Stokeses, though."

"You should've told Doris that she'd be in the article," Renie said. "When did you get a conscience about lying your head off?"

"I never lie!" Judith retorted. "I only tell fibs in my search for truth."

Renie looked thoughtful, puckish. "What?" Judith demanded. "You're up to something."

"I'm considering taking on a responsibility," Renie replied smugly. "Now that I think about it, I want to be your editor. You just flunked your assignment. I heard the word 'problems.' What problems? I'm going to call Doris."

"No!" Judith shrieked. "You can't do that!"

"Watch me." Renie grabbed Judith's cell to see the number. "This could be fun. Hello, Doris?"

It was Judith's turn to listen in. "This is Serena Grover, Ms. McMonigle's editor. I'm afraid she failed to carry out her assignment. What is your full name?"

"What magazine are you talking about?" Doris asked in an annoyed tone.

"*Cornucopia*," Renie replied. "Our readership is made up of persons in the corn industry. Both the edible sweet and the industrial type. May I have your last name?"

"It's Draper," Doris replied. "But we don't own a farm. We're only staying at this house while other family members are away. It's a big responsibility. If you know about raising corn, then you realize it's a huge business here in Nebraska. I have to go now. The chickens need feeding." She rang off.

Renie stared at the cell. "Chickens eat lunch?"

"They peck around all day," Judith said vaguely. The calls to Doris hadn't been very helpful.

"Speaking of food," Renie said, "are we going to lunch or should I fake my own death?"

Judith was still staring at the cobalt-blue drape that covered the room's only window. "I wonder if Doris knew about Codger's last request. Maybe she didn't."

Renie looked exasperated. "Maybe she was hungry. Right now I'm thinking of clobbering you with that lamp on the bureau. Why is the lamp shaped like a beaver?"

"Canadians like beavers. It's a symbol of the fur trade that originally brought settlers to . . ." Judith shook herself. "Okay, okay, you know that as well as I do. I'm trying to think if we learned anything from Doris."

"We didn't learn that she does takeout, and if she does, she's too far away to get it to me before I collapse from starvation." Renie was already at the door. "Good-bye now."

"Ohhh . . ." Judith got up, trying to ignore a twinge in her artificial hip, and fingered the locket-like alarm she wore to summon help if she dislocated. She had only used it once when she'd fallen in the basement and no one else was inside the B&B. The last thing she needed on a vacation was a visit to the ER. "I'm coming," she declared. "You're too ornery to be on your own. The RCMP might arrest you for biting a local resident's arm."

"Sounds good to me," Renie said. "Not the arm, but the arrest. They feed prisoners, don't they?"

"Probably." Judith checked to make sure the door had locked behind them. "What I wonder is if they're getting close to making an arrest."

As they headed for the elevator, Renie shrugged. "The Mounties always get their man, right?"

Judith's dark eyes narrowed. "Yes. But let's hope that if need be, they always get their woman."

Chapter 12

At half past the noon hour, the entire population of Banff and its visitors seemed to be lunching in the commercial area. The cousins ended up back at Wild Flour, where they could order carryout items. Clutching a frittata and coffee, Judith motioned to an empty bench in the Bison Courtyard. Loaded down with two croissants and an omelet, Renie staggered over to join her.

"Wha dwee do affa we ea?" she asked with her mouth full.

"We check in with the Stokeses," Judith replied. "I intend to cull Ada from the herd."

Renie swallowed whatever she'd been eating. "Ada? I thought she didn't talk."

"Maybe she doesn't," Judith said, "but I want to find out if she can."

Renie sighed. "I gather she's challenged, as they say. Then again, who isn't?"

"True," Judith conceded. "But being slow of wit doesn't mean she can't observe. I'm also wondering where the twins have gone. Or if they've finally come back."

"If I were them, I wouldn't." Renie frowned. "We're only going to be here for one more full day. You'd better hurry up and solve this case. We need time to shop."

"I admit I wouldn't mind checking out their woolens," Judith said between bites of the frittata. "Remember how we used to go up to Canada to buy school clothes? Their cashmere sweaters and other woolens were better quality than we had back then. The exchange rate favored us, too. The clan tartans made up into really good-looking pleated skirts that went with . . ." She stopped. "Here comes Sergeant Brewster. Is he looking for us?"

Apparently, he was, as the cousins saw him stride purposefully toward their bench. He smiled faintly and doffed his regulation hat. "I was driving by in my cruiser when I saw you go into Wild Flour. I thought I might find you here. When you've finished your meal, would you mind coming to the station? I have some questions for you."

"Of course," Judith said. "In fact, we have some questions for you."

He nodded once. "My cruiser's just up a few doors. I'll come by and drive you to the station. Five minutes, eh?"

"That's fine," Judith replied. "We'll be done by then."

Brewster nodded again and left the courtyard. Renie polished off the last of her food and glared at her cousin. "He thinks I'm a mute, right?"

"Of course not," Judith retorted. "You spoke to him earlier. I think."

"Maybe *I* should question Ada," Renie snapped. "When it comes to talking or not talking, she and I seem to have a lot in common."

"Coz . . ." Judith's tone had turned plaintive. "I don't mean to take over. Really."

"You're much taller than I am," Renie said solemnly. "Tall people always get more attention. It's a rule of nature." To Judith's relief, she laughed. "I'm used to it. My three kids are taller than I am."

"But they respect you," Judith declared.

"I guess." Renie shrugged. "It's more important that they love me. They can respect Bill and I'm good with that. Let's stand on the curb like a couple of aging hookers. I won't ask you to wiggle your hips, but twirl your purse and show a bit of leg."

"Not funny," Judith muttered. "We have to unload on Brewster and he's not going to like it."

"'We'? You mean I get to talk?"

"You never volunteer. Here he comes."

Except for the sergeant's asking the cousins if they were comfortable, the short drive to the precinct station was made in silence. So was the brief walk to the interview room. Brewster finally asked if they'd care for coffee or tea. They declined.

After they were all seated, Brewster spoke. "Given your reputation, Ms. Flynn, I want to confer with you about any information you may have gleaned since we last spoke. But first I wanted to let you know the crime-scene people from Calgary should arrive later today."

"Do you need us to talk to them?" Judith asked. "We probably wouldn't be of much help since you already know what we saw at the campsite."

"My report should be sufficient," Brewster agreed. "Have you spoken with any of the Stokes family here since this morning?"

"Only Adela Odell," Judith responded.

Brewster waited, but Judith didn't elaborate. "And?" he finally prompted.

"Their twins may've taken the family car on a joy-ride," Judith said with reluctance. "Naturally, Adela was upset."

Brewster's face was impassive. "Well she might be, eh?" he said quietly. "The Buick was found abandoned earlier this morning. It was on a road off the Trans-Canada Highway near the border crossing. Their parents have no idea where the twins have gone. Customs and Immigration officers at the crossing haven't seen them. The Buick showed no signs of damage."

"Then Win and Winnie are probably unharmed," Judith murmured. She switched subjects. "Have you released the victim's name to the public?"

"Our local paper, the *Outlook* is a weekly," Brewster replied. "It won't publish again until this coming Thursday, so there's no rush to make an announcement. Why do you ask?"

"The discrepancy about where the family was headed in the first place," Judith replied, and related Doris Draper's remark about the family going to California. "So how and why did they end up here?"

Brewster stroked his chin. "That's a bit puzzling, eh? We'll contact Ms. Draper. Do you have her number?"

Judith dug in her purse to find her cell and handed

it to the sergeant. "The Big Stove number is on the screen."

"Thank you." He jotted it down. "I'll be in touch with her directly. Anything else?" The tone of his query seemed strained.

Judith shook her head. "Not that I can think of."

"Then I'll drive you back to . . ." He paused. "I assume your car is parked in town, eh?"

Judith had stood up. "You don't need to. We planned on shopping this afternoon. We'll walk."

Two minutes later, the cousins were on the sidewalk. Renie was irate. "'We'll *walk*'? Are you insane? I hate to walk! You know I have flat feet."

"And I have a phony hip," Judith retorted. "Face it, we're both not in mint condition even if . . ."

"What?" Renie asked as they crossed Spray Avenue.

"As we were leaving, I saw Adela walking toward the station. Don't stare, she's going in now. You browse that woolen shop while I wait at the door for her to come out."

"Okay," Renie said. "I'll browse, you pounce."

Good Wools Ltd. was busy with what looked like mostly visitors. Judith had to force herself to keep from pawing the various items on display. She assumed a position next to a wooden rack that held a variety of belts. The pungent smell of leather tickled her nose.

Meanwhile, Renie plundered various display items from sweaters to skirts to what looked like a suede firefighter's hat.

After ten minutes had passed, Judith checked her watch. It was exactly two o'clock. The day was getting away from her. She glanced over her shoulder. Renie had also gotten away, apparently into a dressing room to try on clothes. Turning back to the window, she spotted Sergeant Brewster talking to Adela by the station entrance. Judith hurried to the fitting rooms— there were only two—and called her cousin's name.

"Come on," she said after Renie opened the door a crack. "I'm leaving."

"I'm buying," Renie snapped. "Go away."

There was no time to argue. Judith exited the shop just as a frazzled-looking Adela crossed the street.

"Hi," Judith said in a cheerful voice. "Are you in the woolen market, too?"

Adela grimaced. "Not even close. By any chance, are you going back to the motel? I need a ride."

"Serena's trying on a few items," Judith explained. "Our car's parked near Wild Flour. If you can wait a few minutes, I'll drive you to the motel."

"I'd appreciate it," Adela mumbled. "It's been a bad day. And I thought we'd be on our way back to Ankeny by now. It's a suburb of Des Moines."

"You couldn't have envisioned what would happen with Codger," Judith pointed out. "It's getting a bit warm here under the sun. Would you like to stop for a cool drink?"

Adela seemed to consider the idea but shook her head. "I'd rather go to the motel and get a martini from the bar."

"We can take you there. I'll let my cousin know." She went back inside the store, spotting Renie at the sales counter.

"You abandoned me!" Renie snarled under her breath. "I was forced to spend four hundred and eighty U.S. bucks! If Bill asks, tell him I shoplifted everything."

"It'd serve you right if he blew a gasket," Judith shot back. "Pay for your loot and meet me outside. I've got Adela in tow. As long as you were buying up the place, I should've asked you to get a cardigan for Mother."

Renie looked indignant. "They don't do ugly items in this store. Try Saint Vincent de Paul." With a lift of her short chin, she turned away.

When Judith rejoined Adela, the other woman seemed to have shrunk. Arms crossed as if comforting herself, she huddled in the corner between the store's entrance and one of the two display windows.

"Are you sure you're not sick?" Judith inquired. "Physically, I mean."

Adela shook her head. "I'll tell you after I get my hand around a martini. A double."

"Fair enough," Judith said. The two women stood in silence until Renie emerged, looking like a small, if unruly, Gypsy peddler. Trying on clothes had obviously wreaked havoc with whatever attempt she'd made to tame her wayward chestnut hair.

"Don't say anything," Renie growled. "Let's just *walk*." She spat out the last word, making it sound obscene.

Somehow, Adela ended up in between the cousins. The trio must have looked a bit grim, given the way some of the other pedestrians stared briefly and then looked away. Or maybe, Judith thought, they didn't want to stare because Renie's eyes were cross-eyed from securing the pile of packages by holding them together with her chin.

It took them five minutes to reach the SUV. Renie finally spoke to Adela. "You can sit up front with Judith. I need more space with my purchases. Oof!" She tumbled onto the floor behind the front seat and cussed a bit.

They drove in silence to the motel. It wasn't until

they reached the empty bar that Adela spoke. "Where's the bartender?"

"We served ourselves the last time we were here," Judith explained. "They may be short-staffed. I can mix you a martini. How do you like it?"

Adela seemed dubious. "You're a freelance writer *and* a bartender? Isn't that an odd combination?"

"I tended bar in the evenings at the restaurant my first husband owned," Judith replied, avoiding any reference to being a freelance writer. "It was called The Meat & Mingle." She also omitted the M&M's foreclosure by the IRS. Dan McMonigle hadn't been inclined to pay taxes. Having seen letters from the IRS addressed to him, Judith asked if something was wrong. Dan's response had been to stuff all three warning notices in his mouth and swallow them.

"Writers meet interesting people in bars," Judith said, handing over the martini. "Talking to strangers, especially after a few drinks have loosened their tongues, not only elicits information, but helps a writer in developing characters. So what upset you?"

Adela didn't answer until she'd taken a big sip of her drink. "Not bad," she murmured, and took another sip. "The twins took off. Not that I blame them, but they left the Buick behind. Where the hell can they have gone?" She gulped down more of the martini and her eyes glistened with tears.

"Did you go to the RCMP to report them missing?"

"Yes." Adela pressed her thumb and forefinger on the bridge of her nose as if trying to will her worries away. "Teddy took Norm and me in the pickup, but he didn't want to wait. That tall sergeant told us about finding the Buick. He insisted there was no sign of damage to it or of any . . . violence, but that's cold comfort."

"Where's Norm now?" Judith asked.

"Still at the station. He's waiting until an officer can take him to collect the Buick. I couldn't stand sitting around there. Police stations seem so grim."

"Not," Renie broke in, "as grim as the toolshed Judith's mother lives in." Seeing her cousin's annoyed expression, she shrugged. "Just testing my vocal cords to see if they still work. Carry on."

"Serena knows my family quite well," Judith said a bit stiffly. "We've worked together before. May I be candid?" The other woman nodded faintly. "Who was the murder victim?"

"What kind of a question is *that*?" Adela demanded, drawing back on her barstool.

"A very basic one," Judith replied. "We've learned

that the murdered man may not be Emory Alfred Stokes."

Adela almost choked on her olive. "That's absurd! Of course it was him. Why wouldn't it be?"

"When was the last time you saw Codger?"

Adela had to stop and think. "I was eighteen when I left the farm and never went back. I'm forty-three now." She winced. "Twenty-five years. But Norm and I got together with Corny and Delia a few times in Omaha. Why on earth would you think Codger wasn't . . . Codger? And why would you care?"

"As journalists, my cousin and I have to be accurate, especially about names. We understand his first name is actually Emory."

Adela looked horrified. "You're going to write this up for your magazine?"

"At the very least," Judith said, "our *Cornucopia* editor will want to publish an obit. Codger and the rest of the family must be fairly well known in the world of corn. I can't afford to make mistakes. The family might sue us."

Placing an elbow on the bar, Adela put a hand to her head. "We should never have come here."

"Why did you?"

Adela drained her glass and sighed. "For Pa—my brother Cornelius—and Delia, I suppose." She paused and turned suspicious. "Who told you Codger wasn't Emory Alfred Stokes?"

Judith sat up straighter. "I'm afraid I can't reveal my sources. It'd be unprofessional."

"Rot." Adela slid off her stool. "I'm going to go lie down in our room. I can't stand spending any more time with the rest of the family. Even my brother and his wife seem to have turned weird. Corny and I used to have a few laughs when we were growing up. Suddenly he's turned into a pickle—and a sour one at that."

Judith nodded. "Murder will do that to a person."

Adela didn't comment.

Judith wondered why.

Chapter 13

J udith helped Renie carry her parcels up to the so-
called suite and was surprised to find that although
the beds had been made, the bathroom towels not only
hadn't been replaced, but were piled up in one of the
double sinks. While Renie put her new items in the
Joneses' carryall, Judith dialed the number for housekeeping. After eight rings and no answer, she called the
front desk. The male voice that answered didn't sound
like Niall.

"Sorry," the young man said after Judith revealed
their problem. "We're a bit shorthanded today. I'll see
if I can find someone to send up to your suite."

"Well?" Renie said after Judith disconnected. "Will
they bring fresh towels? You know how fussy Bill is
about his towels. He uses them as part of his neck ther-

apy. Nubbiness counts, too. I'll bet that checking them will be the first thing he does when they get back here tonight."

Judith hadn't gotten past "nubbiness." "How does Bill judge such a thing?"

"He feels the towels," Renie declared solemnly. "Bill knows what's nubby and what's not. It's a gift."

Judith sighed. "If you say so. I wonder what time they'll get here? Maybe we shouldn't make reservations, but rely on which of the restaurants in the Banff Springs Hotel can serve us."

"Sounds like a plan," Renie murmured. "What's our next move . . . or do we have one?"

"We do," Judith replied. "We haven't really talked to Pa and Ma Stokes—Corny and Delia. And I'd like to find out if Ada can talk at all."

"Hoo boy," Renie responded. "Maybe I should go shopping again."

"You can't afford it," Judith said sternly.

"I couldn't afford it the first time," Renie asserted. "I didn't pay for anything. I charged it to my credit card."

Judith shook her head. "You always do. Let's go."

They walked along the river, which seemed benign under the warm August sun. Briefly, Judith could almost imagine they were really on a vacation, free from all their routine cares, free from guests for her and deadlines for Renie, even free from murder.

But the first glimpse of the Stokes encampment crushed the illusion. The scene was made even more doleful by the lack of activity. Family members stood or sat almost motionless, as if posing for an unseen camera. Judith noticed that Codger's tent was gone. A wooden barrel stood in its place. Beer, maybe, even moonshine brought from Big Stove. Nothing about the Stokes family would surprise her.

Pa and Ma Stokes were at the picnic table with Teddy and Martha Lou. A deck of cards and a cribbage board had been shunted aside. Teddy and Martha Lou stood to one side, vacant eyes looking off into the distance while they munched on popcorn out of a huge red-and-white-striped plastic bag. Ada sat on a stool by the big tent, her back turned to the rest of the family.

Renie leaned closer to Judith. "They don't look like they're in the mood for company."

"Maybe we can cheer them up," Judith said, though she sounded doubtful in her own ears.

Corny and Delia were the first to acknowledge the cousins. He raised a red, swollen hand in greeting and said, "How do," in a cheerless voice. His wife merely nodded, her triple chins burrowing into her big bosom. Teddy turned to look at the visitors.

"You write your story yet?" he asked with a frown.

"No," Judith replied. "I won't do that until I'm back in the New York office. I always take time to reflect on my subjects."

Martha Lou's freckled face looked puzzled. "Reflect on what?"

"My approach to the article," Judith replied. "It can get very complicated."

Teddy was still frowning. "You gonna write about *us*?"

"Not by name," Judith said. "I'll want to describe the kind of people who come to Banff and where they're from, especially foreigners from Europe and Asia."

"Oh." Teddy seemed to lose interest.

Martha Lou, however, persevered. "You won't say anything about Codger, will you?"

"Probably not. I'm leaning toward the international angle. What attracts foreigners to this beautiful, rugged part of the world."

"The movie," Martha Lou said. "About the river. That's why we came here."

"So you mentioned," Judith began, but stopped when Teddy yanked at his wife's arm.

"Nobody's bidness 'cept ours, Martha Lou," he asserted, his face turning red. "Shut yer pie hole, okay?"

"Fine!" she snapped, jerking her arm out of Teddy's grasp and stomping over to plop down on the barrel.

Pa Stokes had stood up. "Let's all settle down. These ladies don't mean us no harm. Maybe they'd like some of our cider." He looked down at his wife. "Where'd you put that jug, Delia?"

"In the ice bucket next to your right foot," she replied. "Try not to knock it over."

"Never mind," Judith said, smiling. "We had beverages at the motel. How long do you folks plan to stay on?"

Pa had sat down again. He shot Ma a sharp glance, but she merely shrugged. "Not sure. Cooler up here than in Big Stove this time of year. Guess it depends on . . . things."

"I suppose," Judith said, making her way to the picnic table, "you've heard from Doris and Jens back home?"

"They do all right," Pa replied, taking a tobacco pouch and a sheaf of cigarette papers out of his shirt pocket.

Ma leaned forward, staring at Judith with snapping gray eyes. "Who told you about Doris and Jens?"

Judith realized her gaffe. "I'm not sure," she hedged.

"Maybe whoever mentioned Aunt Sheba taking care of the children."

Teddy, who had parked himself on the end of the table, nodded. "Could be. I ferget." He reached out to bat at a mosquito. "Hey, you seen the blonde from the motel today?"

Something about the question bothered Judith. "A blonde?" she echoed. "Someone who works there?"

"Maybe," Teddy replied. "She was hangin' out here the other day. Aunt Adela thought she was from the motel." He suddenly turned his head in all directions. "Where *is* Aunt Adela? And Uncle Norm? He was gonna help me work on the camp stove. It's busted."

"Never did work worth a damn," Pa muttered, taking a drag on his homemade cigarette. "Hell, nobody and nothin' works worth a damn anymore. Raisin' corn isn't like it used to be. In the old days, it was back-breakin' work, from sowin' to harvesttime. Made a man feel like a man. Now I just sit around and read the commodities reports. Real work done by all this otto-motion."

"*Automation,*" Ma snapped. "I read books, not just those so-called reports. You never try to improve your mind. Why I married you in the first . . ." Her voice trailed off and Judith thought she was about to cry.

Pa, however, remained stoic. He'd rolled a second cigarette and eased his lanky frame off the picnic table's rough wooden seat. "I'll give this one to Ada. She could do with a smoke."

Judith reached out a hand. "I'll take it to her. We haven't met Ada. That's an oversight on our part."

Pa looked so startled that he let Judith take the cigarette. "Why d'ya wanna do that?" he asked, obviously puzzled.

"As journalists," Judith replied, already moving around to the other side of the picnic table, "we have to touch base with everyone involved."

Pa shrugged. "Fine. But she don't talk much."

"Neither do I," Renie asserted, following her cousin. "But I can spell better than Judith does."

"Brat," Judith said under her breath as they approached Ada. "You know damned well you can speak up anytime you feel like it. You just did."

Renie ignored her cousin. Judith saw Ada's thin shoulders tense as they approached. As they came abreast of the young woman, she also noticed that her right hand was tightly clenched.

"Hi, Ada. I'm Judith and this is my cousin Renie. How are you today?"

Ada kept staring straight ahead.

"I see you're keeping out of the direct sun here by the tent," Judith said. "You have quite a nice tan, though. Do you like being outdoors in the fresh air?"

Nothing. Judith took a deep breath. "Are you sad about Codger's passing?"

Still nothing. Judith proffered the handmade cigarette. "Your father rolled this for you."

Only a flicker of Ada's eyes indicated she understood as she held out the hand that wasn't clenched. Judith noticed that it was almost unlined, as if the palm had rarely been put to use.

"Do you need a light?" Judith asked.

Ada kept staring somewhere between the cousins. Maybe she was deaf. In desperation, Judith looked at Renie.

"Hey," Renie finally said after a pause, "how about those Huskers? Think they'll go undefeated this season?"

Ada's head moved in an almost imperceptible negative response. Judith stared, wondering if she could hear, but not speak. "Not with Bill Callahan coaching, right?"

A single emphatic nod answered that question. Judith grabbed Renie's arm and pulled her aside. "What was *that* all about?"

"Football," Renie said. "Bill's been studying his college-football-magazine predictions. What else do Nebraskans care about so strongly except the Cornhuskers? Aunt Ellen and Uncle Win inherited their tickets from his parents. That's one of the few ways fans can get them. Even someone a little . . . slow, like Ada, knows about the Huskers."

Judith shook her head. "Football." She glanced at Ada, who still hadn't budged. "Okay, goofy sports expert, what if Ada isn't as dim as she seems?"

Renie stared up at the sky. "Then maybe she should be the next Nebraska coach."

Judith gave up.

Chapter 14

But Judith wasn't giving in. She still had some un-answered questions. But as soon as they returned to their motel, her cell went off. "Now what?" she muttered, sitting down in an armchair.

"Hey, how's my Jude-Girl?" Joe said in an oddly unctuous voice. "Keeping out of trouble, I hope?"

"Of course," Judith answered, more sharply than she intended. "What time will you and Bill be back?" She glanced at Renie, who shot her a questioning look.

"Well . . ." Joe's chuckle seemed forced. "We didn't have much luck fishing until this morning. Something to do with the river in the middle of August, but now that we're getting to the end of the month, things are looking up."

"Up where?"

"Here. On the river. *This* part of the river, twenty-six miles from Banff." Joe was now talking much faster than his usual soft, mellow drawl. "We'd be fools not to stick around for another day or two. As Bill pointed out, it'd be like throwing our money away."

Judith gritted her teeth, but when she spoke, her voice sounded almost natural. "Of course Renie and I'll be sorry not to see you two sooner, but if you have such a wonderful opportunity to catch a really big mess of fish, you can't pass it up."

Renie gestured with her fingers, as if pointing a gun to her head. Judith suddenly realized that maybe it was just as well the husbands weren't coming back so soon. Their return might put a whammy on the sleuthing.

"Don't worry about us," Judith said. "We can amuse ourselves. I heard there was an outdoor concert close by tonight." It wasn't true, of course, unless she considered the possibility of Ada howling at the moon.

"That sounds really nice," Joe asserted with un-characteristic enthusiasm. Then he lowered his voice, sounding more like himself: "You sure everything's okay?"

"Why wouldn't it be?" Judith retorted. "We've met some interesting people and there are some very intriguing shops. Be sure to tell Bill that Renie has a whole new wardrobe."

"I'll pass on mentioning that," Joe said. "Hey, got to run. Snapper MacDougall—our guide—wants to show us some new lures he's put together. Love you."

"Enjoy." Judith disconnected and looked at a bemused Renie, who'd been gazing out the window.

"Oh, so what?" her cousin said. "They're having a good time. They'd have been bored hanging out here in town. Maybe we'd have been bored, too, if a dead body hadn't turned up. Where do you suppose that body is by now?"

Judith shook her head. "No clue. Literally. I'm still trying to figure out who the body is."

Renie hopped out of the chair in which she'd been curled up while Judith talked to Joe. "Why don't you take a private poll of the survivors and see who each one of them thinks it is?"

"That's up to the Force," Judith said. "That's what the RCMP is called up here."

Renie looked askance. "You think I've never read a mystery set north of the border? Seriously, somebody has to know the victim's ID."

Judith was staring into the bathroom. "The killer probably does," she said in a vague voice. "Why hasn't housekeeping showed up with the towels?"

Renie scowled. "You can't use the ones they didn't collect?"

"That's not the point," Judith snapped. "I'm wondering about Trixie. She worries me."

"Coz!" Renie looked unusually severe. "Stop. You're suffering from your chronic Wounded Bird Empathy. You can't get worked up over everyone you meet who seems to have a problem. Everybody has problems. You hardly know the girl. Trixie probably broke up with her boyfriend."

"That's not a minor crisis for a young girl," Judith argued. "But most girls don't actually pass out over a breakup. Besides, I'm not sure that's the case with Trixie."

"Then what is?"

Judith didn't answer right away. "I don't know. But I think we should figure out what is. Let's find Trixie."

Renie sighed. "I didn't know she was lost."

Judith was already at the door. "If you don't want to come with me, watch TV or design something amazing."

"I can get Canadian TV at home," Renie retorted. "It's part of whatever package Bill chose years ago."

"Big deal," Judith said. "We have the same package . . ." She stopped with her hand on the doorknob. "That means Mother gets it, too. I hope she doesn't watch the Canadian news. She might find out about the murder."

"So? She won't care," Renie asserted. "Unless she thinks you're the victim. Then she'd probably be mad at you for getting killed."

"And I'd never hear the end of it," Judith murmured as they headed to the elevator. "Even beyond the grave."

"Speaking of which," Renie said when they were descending to the main floor, "where do you think the alleged Codger ended up? Why didn't you ask Adela? She might tell you. I'll bet she and Norman are here in the motel."

"I hate to bother them," Judith said as the elevator doors opened. "They must be worried sick about the twins. I'd like to know if they got their car back." She glanced at the clock above the vacant motel desk. "They may be at dinner. Where's whoever should be on duty?"

"Let's find out." Renie slammed her hand down on the bell that sat on the counter.

The door behind the work area opened and a young man who looked as if he was at least part Indian appeared. "Yes?" he said deferentially.

Judith noted that his name tag identified him as Layak Patel. "Are Mr. and Mrs. Odell in their room?"

The young man frowned. "I'm not sure. They were here a while ago, but they may've gone out, eh? I was called away from the desk for a bit."

Judith nodded. "Is Trixie working now?"

"Ah . . ." His dark skin grew darker. "I don't think so."

"That's too bad," Judith said. "I wanted to talk to her. Will she be here tomorrow?"

"I don't know." Layak didn't meet Judith's gaze. "I mean, I usually work the relief shifts, so I don't always know the other employees' schedules. Sorry."

"Never mind," Judith said, smiling. "But we do need clean towels. Flynn and Jones in the adjoining suite."

"I'll bring them up myself," Layak promised. "As soon as everybody checks in. We've got one more party due."

Judith thanked him and practically shoved Renie toward the entrance. "We need to check in with Brewster," she said after they were outside. "He'll know about the Odells' car."

"What about it?" Renie sounded irked. "You think it was carrying contraband maple sugar?"

Judith didn't answer until they were in the SUV. "Despite what we were told, I'd like to know why Win and Winnie abandoned a perfectly good car. Why would they run away from the scene? And where did they go?"

"After meeting the Stokes folks, the twins may've run away *to* home."

"Maybe," Judith allowed, squinting into the early-evening sun. "It's after six. Let's hope Brewster hasn't gone off duty."

There were no vacant parking places within a block of the station. Lynx Street was busy with tourists as well as locals getting off work. Judith could pick out the residents. They kept their eyes straight ahead instead of gawking at the majestic mountains.

"Darn," she said under her breath. "I don't want to walk any more than I have to. We'll park in the RCMP lot."

Renie smirked. "Why not? You've virtually been deputized."

Three minutes later and after one harrowing U-turn at Wolf Street that made Renie grit her teeth, they were in back of the station waiting for an answer to Judith's ring. A young, fair-haired, and very startled Mountie finally opened the door. "Yes?" he said in an uncertain voice.

Judith asked to see Sergeant Brewster. When the young man hesitated, she smiled. "Tell him Mrs. Flynn is here to see him."

The young man nodded, but still looked ill at ease. "Please wait here," he said.

Judith stepped inside, but Renie leaned against the outer wall. "Good-bye," she said with a little wave.

"What do you mean?" Judith demanded, turning around.

"Officer Adolescent didn't say I could come in." She started to pout.

"Oh, for . . . Will you stop acting like you're six?"

Renie abandoned the pout and her brown eyes were angry. "Will *you* stop acting as if I don't exist? What's wrong with you the last few days? I don't mind playing second fiddle, but I thought we were at least in the same orchestra."

Judith bit her lip. "I didn't mean to ignore you. Really. I'm used to being the only one who visits with my guests at the B&B. Yes, Joe helps with breakfast, but he rarely leaves the kitchen. He leaves the socializing to me. I can't help it, even when I'm not in B&B hostess mode."

"You're not now," Renie reminded her. "I don't want to step on your act, but I like being acknowledged, okay?"

Judith sighed. "Okay, I get it—and I'm really sorry." She reached out from the doorway to put her hand on her cousin's arm.

Renie smiled. "Go do your thing. I'm not that keen on hanging out in police stations. You're the one who married a cop." She patted her cousin's hand and smiled. "It's fine. Really."

"You sure?"

"Yes. Go. I actually enjoy being outside, where I can see some of the most spectacular scenery in North America. Or the world, for that matter."

Judith entered the station and made her way into the front office, where she saw Brewster talking on the phone. The younger policeman was no longer in sight.

Judith waited patiently for what seemed like a long time but, according to the big clock, was less than three minutes. The Mountie's black eyes briefly acknowledged her. He was uttering only monosyllabic responses and the nerve in his forehead indicated he was irritated. After almost two minutes had passed, he rang off.

"Yes, Mrs. Flynn?" he said in a tightly controlled tone.

Judith assumed an abject expression, which wasn't hard to do under the circumstances. "I hate to bother you, but I have to ask what happened with the Odells' vehicle. Was it in an accident?"

"No." Brewster's broad shoulders sagged. "See here, Mrs. Flynn, I realize you're a bit of a sleuth and I respect that. The Odell vehicle is in our impound lot, which is at the edge of town. We haven't been able to get in touch with Mr. and Mrs. Odell. They aren't taking calls at the motel, although the desk clerk told us he thought they were in their room."

"I believe they are," Judith said. "I assume you're waiting to tell them about the car so they can collect it."

Brewster frowned. "They can if they have a set of keys. There weren't any in the vehicle. That's why we had to tow it into Banff."

"Oh." Judith paused. "Why would their kids abandon the car but take the keys?" The question came out in a murmur, as if she was asking herself as well as Brewster.

"They're teenagers." His wide mouth hinted at a smile. "Do you have children, Mrs. Flynn?"

Judith smiled. "Yes, a son. Mike's a forest ranger in Maine. He and his family hope to visit us this fall."

"A worthy occupation, eh?" Brewster acknowledged with a nod. "Is there anything I can do for you before I finally get to sign out?"

She offered him a sympathetic smile. "Not unless you have a positive ID on the victim."

"We have to wait for your FBI to respond to our request for identification of the alleged deceased. There may be fingerprints on file. We were able to take some from the tent where he died. But I don't think *they* work on weekends." His expression indicated he would hold her responsible if the agency proved dilatory.

"Of course." Judith was getting irked. First Renie, now Brewster. It was a beautiful summer day in a gorgeous part of the world. Why sour the atmosphere with personal grievances? Then it struck her that a killer had already done just that. "Thank you, Sergeant," she said with a compassionate smile. "Go home."

Chapter 15

Renie was nowhere in sight. Not on the stairs, not by the wall, not in the parking lot. Given how much her cousin hated walking, especially on pavement, Judith was flummoxed. She squinted into the western sun, wondering if someone had given her a ride back to the motel. But who? Judith's trust in most of the people they'd met during their stay in Banff was on shaky ground.

She was still pondering when she heard a horn honk. Nobody was in the parked cruisers. Then her gaze traveled to their SUV rental. Renie was behind the wheel. Judith stalked over to the passenger side and opened the door.

"Well?" Renie said with a puckish expression. "Did you think I'd stay outside in the sun and wilt?

I *do* know how to drive." To prove it, she started the engine. "Where are we going now?"

"You scared me," Judith confessed. "I thought something might've happened to you."

To Judith's relief, Renie laughed. "When you're sleuthing, nothing ever happens to me unless it happens to you, too. Where are we going?"

"*We?*" Judith offered her cousin a tentative smile. "You're sure you're still not irked with me?"

Renie shook her head. "Of course not. You know I never stay mad for long. Especially at you. Besides, I have a short attention span. Now tell me where we're going."

"I'm not sure. On my way out, I noticed a map that shows the impound lot. Maybe we should head there."

"I should ask why," Renie said, waiting for traffic on Lynx Street, "but where is it?"

Judith fretted her lower lip. "Umm . . . take a right. It's near the train tracks. I saw them on the map."

Renie finally found an opening and swung out into traffic. "Now I'll ask why."

"That's where we'll find the Odells' allegedly abandoned Buick," Judith replied. "I gather the RCMP is shorthanded over the weekend with so many tourists in town. They haven't had time to check it out."

"But we do," Renie said. "And how helpful of us.

Your uncanny lockpicking skills will again come in handy."

"I'm rusty," Judith admitted. "It's been a while."

"I trust you. How do we get to the impound lot?"

"It's west of town by the train tracks. Take a left up ahead on Railway Avenue. It can't be far from the station."

"Got it." Renie made a sharp turn that forced a camper with Oregon plates to come to a jarring stop. Moments later they saw a ten-foot-high chain-link fence enclosing at least three or four vehicles. "That's it. Want me to floor it and drive through the fence?"

"No!" Judith cried, terrified that her cousin might actually do just that. "But the gate has a padlock. Those are trickier than the ones on doors and windows. I might have a little problem."

"You can do it, coz," Renie assured her. "Let's go."

They went. Judith studied the padlock before getting out her nail scissors. "Move to my left," she told Renie. "The sun's in my eyes."

"Got it." Renie moved.

"Damn," Judith said under her breath. "You're too short. Hold up your arms."

"Sheesh." Renie shook her head but complied.

Judith struggled at first, then finally managed to

tweak the mechanism just enough to release the lock. Renie lowered her arms to open the gate.

"After you, Super Sleuth," she said with a little bow. "Why didn't we become burglars instead of working for a living?"

"That lock *was* work," Judith declared, looking over her shoulder to make sure no one was watching them. "Let's hope the Odells' Buick is easier to get into."

It was, taking Judith barely a minute to open the driver's side. "Clean," she announced. "I see the front tire looks a bit low. Maybe the twins hit something and it upset them. Let's try the trunk."

They moved to the vehicle's rear. When they lifted the trunk's lid, Judith let out a little shriek and Renie gasped. The first thing that met their startled eyes was a tattered blue blanket.

"I can't look!" Renie cried, turning away.

"Then don't," Judith said sharply. Gritting her teeth and holding her breath, she tugged gently at the fabric's edge. All she could see at first were a pair of running shoes and then a canteen. Judith finally yanked the rest of the blanket away and groaned.

"What?" Renie asked, peeking between her fingers.

Judith sighed. "You can look now, Chicken Liver. Codger's gone."

Renie lowered her hands. "Gone? He's been gone almost since we got here. What are you talking about?"

"See for yourself. It's not gruesome." Judith gestured at the open trunk. "Come on, coz."

Reluctantly, Renie came closer and took a deep breath. Then she looked in the trunk. "Okay. So how did Codger get into the Odells' trunk in the first place? And does the RCMP know he was there?"

"No," Judith replied. "They don't have the keys. The twins made off with them. I wonder if Win and Winnie have shown up in Banff or if they really fled. But why?"

Renie waved away a mosquito. "Maybe they opened the trunk and got scared."

"Of what? A torn blanket? I don't remember seeing any blood on it." Judith frowned. "Or . . ." She bit her lip. "Maybe the family really did send Codger down the Bow River. But that could backfire on the Stokes family if it's found this side of the border."

"Could the twins have been delegated to do the dirty deed by one of the other family members?"

Judith sighed. "Anything's possible with this crazy crew. Why didn't the alleged Codger watch sci-fi movies and insist on being shot off into outer space?"

"I like that," Renie said. "That might even get

Ada's attention. Especially if they did it at halftime of a Cornhusker game."

"Ada," Judith said softly as she closed the trunk. "I still want to talk to her. How do we cull her from the herd?"

Renie's brown eyes lit up. "Tell her you've got footage of the Nebraska team's practice?"

"I wish I did." They started back to the SUV, but paused to padlock the gate. "I'd also like to find out why Doris and Jens Draper told me the Stokeses were originally headed for California."

Renie handed over the SUV's keys to Judith. "If they're like the majority of people," she said after they were in the vehicle, "they have no sense of geography. I read recently that ninety percent of all Americans can't find Canada on a map. They probably think it's in California. They both begin with a *C-A*. Where are we going?"

"Back to the motel," Judith replied, driving away from the train tracks. "I need to unwind. And I want to find out what happened to Trixie. She puzzles me."

"Hmm," Renie murmured. "That's all well and good, but I missed hearing the word 'dinner' in there."

"It's not yet seven," Judith replied. "Let's make a reservation somewhere for seven thirty. The restaurants shouldn't be so busy on a Sunday night. You can do that while I inquire after the troubling Trixie."

"Trixie isn't troubling me," Renie declared.

Judith turned off in the direction of the motel. "She's an emotional disaster. Besides, I want to find out why she visited the Stokes menagerie. There must be a reason."

"Maybe she mistook their campsite for the zoo. Maybe she thought Teddy was a stud." Renie darted Judith a quick glance. "Maybe *some* people are just too damned curious."

"Maybe," Judith said, pulling into a parking spot behind the motel, "you should shut up and focus on finding somewhere we can eat."

Renie grinned. "No maybe there, coz. I'll go inside now. Stay put. It looks like you've got company."

Judith frowned. "Who?"

"The aforementioned Trixie." Renie slid off the car seat and onto the parking area tarmac. "Good luck. Your next person of interest looks higher than a kite."

"Great," Judith said—and groaned.

Trixie was literally reeling around the grassy area next to the narrow strip of plantings by the building. When the cousins exited the SUV, she stumbled and would have fallen if she hadn't grabbed hold of an evergreen shrub.

Judith reached out to take Trixie's left arm. Renie, who had gotten only as far as the door, hurried over to help. She leaned into the girl's back to steady her while Judith took hold of the other arm.

"Can you walk?" Judith finally asked, seeing Trixie's eyes starting to close. "Trixie? Trixie?" she repeated, giving her a little shake.

When no answer came, Judith nodded at the SUV. "Let's haul her inside. There's room for her to lie down on the passenger seat. I think she needs a doctor."

It was a bit of a struggle, though Trixie didn't resist. Her eyes were still open, but she seemed to be staring into space. After the cousins arranged her as comfortably as they could, Renie volunteered to go into the motel.

"They probably have a doctor on call," she said, moving quickly to the rear entrance.

Judith got out of the SUV, but stood by the open door, eyes fastened on Trixie. The girl twitched a couple of times, but otherwise remained quiet. It was difficult for Judith not to speak to her, but she sensed that Trixie's brain was somewhere other than in a stranger's vehicle outside of the Banff Springs Motel.

Three minutes later, Renie reappeared. "Layak called 911. That's the motel's policy for guests or employees who have medical emergencies. Insurance reasons, I suppose. He'll join us as soon as he checks in some new guests."

"I hope your news won't scare them off," Judith said, still keeping watch on Trixie. "What's your guess?"

Renie wrinkled her pug nose. "A drug overdose?"

"Possible," Judith murmured. "But what kind?"

Renie started to respond, but heard sirens in the near distance. "Shouldn't someone from the motel be here to talk to the medics about their employee? If Trixie has to be hospitalized, they'll need her ID."

"You're right." Judith noted that Trixie's eyes were still open, and she was breathing, if somewhat erratically. "Did we ever learn her last name?"

"I don't think so." Renie winced as the sirens grew louder. "I'll go inside and ask Layak while you roll out the welcome wagon for the emergency crew."

"Got it." Renie disappeared inside. A moment later a red-and-white medic van veered around the corner of the motel. Judith waved at the driver, who stopped just inside the parking area. A fire engine pulled up in back of the smaller emergency vehicle. Two husky uniformed men erupted onto the tarmac and hurried to join Judith.

"What have we got here, ma'am?" the taller of the two asked in a calm voice.

Judith explained Trixie's erratic behavior prior to her collapse. "She's a maid at the motel, but hasn't worked here very long. In fact, she seems to be new in town."

The shorter of the EMTs was already checking the girl out. "No visible signs of trauma," he said over his shoulder. "But she should be seen by a pro."

Judith was momentarily distracted by the fire engine's departure. Before she could say anything, Renie virtually flew out of the motel. "O'Hara," she called out, but stopped in her tracks to take in the EMTs and their van. "Ah! Help has arrived. Good."

Judith and Renie stepped back, watching the taller man pause, peering into the SUV at Trixie's motionless body. "Victim's still alive," he announced.

The shorter EMT rolled a gurney from the rear of their vehicle. They were very gentle as they maneuvered the young girl out of the car and onto the heavily padded conveyance.

The shorter man looked at the cousins. "Which of you is coming with her?"

"Not me," Renie replied. "I'm allergic to hospitals. They give me hives."

"I will," Judith said as she discreetly punched Renie in the back, "but only if my cousin comes with me. She can't be left alone. She's a bit . . . mental."

"Ah!" the shorter one exclaimed, darting a look at Renie. whose tongue was lolling on her lower lip. "Yes, I can see that. Get in the back. We're ready to roll."

Once inside, Judith noticed that Trixie still hadn't moved, though her eyelids fluttered once. The shorter EMT was at the wheel, and as soon as he turned the ignition key, the siren went on. As they sped away from the motel, the cousins had to hang on to anything they could get ahold of that wasn't the gurney—or Trixie. Judith tried to overhear whatever information the taller man was radioing in, but the siren drowned out most of his words.

After signing off, he angled around to look at the cousins. "Are you two visitors?"

"Yes," Judith replied. "We're on vacation."

"I figured," he said. "I'm Waldorf. My partner's Statler."

"You're *hotels*?" Renie cried. "Or Muppets?"

Waldorf looked bleak. "We hear that one a lot."

"Darn," Renie said under her breath.

"Where *is* the hospital?" Judith asked.

"Next to RCMP headquarters," Waldorf replied.

Judith remembered seeing the building but hadn't realized what it was. "I know where it is—on Lynx Street."

"Right." He looked at Renie. "I thought you might." He turned around to face the front.

"Oaf," Renie muttered.

Less than a minute later, they pulled into the emergency entrance of the Banff Springs hospital. The exchange between the EMTs and the medical personnel was brief. Before Judith or Renie could ask how they were supposed to get back to the motel, a fortyish man wearing a white jacket leaned into the van.

"Come along, please," he said in a deep voice.

"To . . . where?" Judith asked.

"I'm Medic Roberts," he replied, waving an errant mosquito away from his shaved head. "We need information about the patient."

"But we don't really know her," Judith protested. "She works at the motel where we're staying."

Roberts's blue eyes snapped with impatience. "We'll contact them as well. Please follow me."

Judith glanced at Renie, who was looking relatively benign. The cousins got out of the van and followed the medic through the emergency entrance and into a hallway. Trixie and the gurney had already disappeared. Halfway down the hall, Roberts led them into a small, cluttered office that had room for filing cabinets, a desk, a chair, and a life-sized skeleton. Roberts sat down, picked up a ballpoint pen, and skipped to a blank page in a legal-sized yellow tablet. Then he handed index cards to both cousins and proffered the pen.

"I apologize for the lack of space," he said in a neutral tone. "Can you write your names and permanent addresses, please?"

Judith and Renie complied. After they gave Roberts the cards and his pen, he asked how long they'd known the patient.

"We really don't know her," Judith responded, "except for seeing her on the job at the motel."

Roberts nodded faintly. "Who owns the SUV where the EMTs found her?"

"It's our rental for the trip," Judith said. "We'd just pulled in when Trixie reeled out of the motel's rear entrance. She staggered toward us and collapsed onto the SUV's seat."

"Did she say anything to you?"

Judith shook her head.

Renie finally spoke up. "Nobody ever says anything to me. Can you see me, Medic Roberts? I do exist, if only in my mind."

Roberts's face tightened. "Then tell me if the patient spoke to you."

"I already did. No." Renie folded her arms and leaned back against the wall.

"Very well." Roberts cleared his throat. "Have either of you spoken to her on previous occasions?"

Judith took a deep breath. "Yes, a few times. She struck me as being unhappy, especially about the maid's job she'd just started at the motel. I got the impression she was new to Banff, though I may be wrong."

"Did she strike you as a drifter? That is," Roberts clarified, "the rootless type who moves from place to place?"

Again, Judith had to consider her answer. Hearing a hiss from Renie, she asked her if she'd gotten that impression.

"No," Renie said, mercifully benign for once. "I think she came here for a reason, maybe to be with someone, most likely a man. I'm sure she didn't come to Banff to take a job as a motel maid. She obviously didn't like the work."

"Ah." Roberts looked satisfied with the answer. "Jilted, perhaps. A reason to go off the rails, eh?"

"It's a guess," Judith admitted. "What do you mean by 'going off the rails'?"

His expression grew unreadable. "Is there anything else we should know?"

Judith tried not to wince. "She fainted when she heard that the old man from that campsite by the river had been murdered. We were there. Later she explained that she had a problem with death, having seen so much of it when she worked in a nursing home."

Roberts frowned. "Did she know the family?"

"I have no idea," Judith admitted. "She might have wandered over there to check them out. We did."

"Yes," the medic said thoughtfully. "I've heard about that bunch. But that's up to the RCMP." He put down his pen. "That's all I need from you, ladies. I apologize for the inconvenience."

"We understand," Judith said, smiling. "May we check back with you later to find out about Trixie?"

"Of course," he replied, getting up from his chair. "Enjoy the rest of your stay here in Banff."

"We'd enjoy it more," Renie said, "if we had a ride back to the motel."

Roberts grimaced. "You can call a taxi from the pay phone in the hall. I have to look in on Ms. O'Hara."

"She's doing better than we are," Renie huffed, grasping the doorknob. "The last I saw of her, she had wheels under her. We only have feet." She stalked out into the hall.

Embarrassed, Judith looked at Roberts. "My cousin has fallen arches."

The medic looked askance. "She also has bad manners."

Judith took umbrage. "I have an artificial hip. I don't

like to walk very much either." She left the cluttered little room, but refrained from slamming the door.

Renie was leaning against the wall by a fire extinguisher. "Are you mad at me? Again?"

"No," Judith declared. "You were right. Roberts— or someone—should've offered to take us back to the motel. We're tourists, for heaven's sake! And Canadians usually have excellent manners."

"Maybe," Renie said as they stepped outside, "he's an émigré from the U.S.A. Hey, why aren't we calling a cab?"

"Because we're going next door. The Mounties will give us a ride. I'll tell them about Trixie."

Renie looked puzzled. "She's now a suspect?"

Judith's expression was grim. "Everybody's a suspect."

Chapter 16

The only officer on duty was the fair-haired young man who had let Judith into the building earlier in the day. She hadn't taken in his ID tag at the time, but now she noted that he was Constable Robert Cavendish.

"Excuse me," Judith said with a smile, "is there any way someone could give us a lift back to our motel? We had to accompany a local young woman to the ER."

Cavendish frowned and flexed the fingers on his right hand. "Well . . . that's not a service we provide. There *are* taxis here in Banff."

"Yes," Judith said pleasantly, "but my cousin had a bad experience once with a taxi driver. *Very* bad." She glanced at Renie, who assumed a horror-stricken expression. "Has Sergeant Brewster gone off duty?"

Cavendish nodded. "He signed off at seven thirty. Brewster had already put in overtime this weekend." The young Mountie paused. "We've had an apparent homicide in the last few days. In fact, two of our officers are now at the crime scene. I assure you, it's very unusual for Banff. I'm afraid I can't offer you a ride."

"Great," Renie groaned. "Maybe we'll be the next victims. Is there any way we can file a putative lawsuit?"

Cavendish looked alarmed. "Pardon?"

"Never mind." Renie whirled around to head for the door. "Come on, coz. It's past our dinnertime and I could eat a porcupine, quills and all."

Judith had no choice but to follow her cousin. She paused to thank Cavendish for his time—and to smile at the beleaguered young man. It wasn't his fault that the RCMP had a homicide on their hands.

Renie was already on the sidewalk talking on her cell. "Five minutes," she said as she disconnected. "It's after seven thirty. Let's take a taxi to the restaurant."

"No," Judith said in a firm voice. "That means we'll have to take another taxi to the motel, where we can use our car. We can eat a little later."

"How little?" Renie asked, looking suspicious.

"If the cops are at the Stokes campsite, I want to know why," Judith said. "And before you say anything else, I doubt that young Cavendish would've told us. It won't take long. Trust me."

Renie sighed. "Unfortunately, I do."

The taxi driver delivered them to the motel in less than ten minutes despite some early-evening traffic. Maybe, Judith thought, everybody else in Banff was going to dinner, too.

"So," Renie said, "now we walk to see what madness goes on in Stokesland?"

Judith shot her cousin a wry look. "You want to rent a bicycle?"

Renie didn't respond. They took their time, savoring the sound of the river, the cries of birds in the evergreens, the delicacy of the alpine flowers, and the rawness of the granite mountains surrounding the town like stone walls protecting a medieval castle.

"I spy a Mountie," Renie said as they came within thirty yards of the encampment. "Two of them, in fact."

Judith also saw them. "I wonder if Brewster told them about us."

"You mean about *you*," Renie responded wryly. "I'm not FASTO."

"Let's find out." Judith walked a little faster. She noticed that one of the Mounties seemed to be arguing with Pa Stokes. The other officer was being badgered by Teddy. Adela and Norman Odell stood off to one side, looking worried. Judith decided to tackle them first.

"What's going on?" she asked, gesturing discreetly at the Mounties. "Is it about the twins and your car?"

"No," Adela replied in a subdued voice. "That is, they found the car and it's in the RCMP impound lot. But there's no trace of Win and Winnie." She moved even closer to her husband and touched his arm. "Please, Norm, we've got to ask the police to try to find them. This whole trip is making a wreck out of me."

He patted her hand. "They'll show up. They just got tired of this circus you call your family."

Before Judith or anyone could speak, the older, taller of the Mounties approached them. Judith noticed that the badge on his short-sleeved shirt featured a royal crown and the initials *GRC*.

"Pardon," he said with a faint French accent. "Are you the Américaines?"

"Yes," Judith replied, ignoring Renie's *"oui oui"* at her side. "That is, I'm Judith Flynn and this is my cousin Serena Jones."

"Ah." The tall, dark-haired man's cobalt-blue eyes regarded them with interest. "I am Inspector Claude Colbert from Calgary. Which of you discovered the corpse?"

"Not *moi*," Renie piped up before Judith could answer. "I never discover anything. I'm just here for the excitement."

Colbert's long, lean face remained impassive as his gaze returned to Judith. "Then you, Mrs. Flynn?"

"Yes," Judith replied. "That is, I realized that Mr. Stokes had been stabbed."

The inspector looked thoughtful. "Yes, Sergeant Brewster mentioned you in his report. Perhaps you'd come with me to the station after I've finished here?"

"Again?" Renie all but shrieked. "We were just there."

"Ah . . ." This time Colbert sounded uncertain. "I didn't know that. Perhaps we could talk in my cruiser, eh?" He nodded in the direction of the road that ran some forty yards from the Stokes encampment. "Excuse me, but I must finish my interview with the deceased's family." Touching the brim of his regulation cap, he moved away.

"Darn," Renie murmured. "I wanted to ask him if he has snacks in that cruiser. Or at least some chewing gum. Either there's a bear loose around here or my stomach's growling."

"We can eat after we're done here," Judith said. "I do feel sorry for the Odells. I wonder if the twins are hiding out somewhere. I doubt they've got much money with them."

"Credit cards," Renie murmured. "They're eighteen and old enough to get them."

Judith nodded. "If they use the cards, their whereabouts can be traced. How they got wherever they are is another matter."

"Hitchhiked?" Renie suggested. "Here comes Colbert."

The Mountie touched his cap in recognition, then pointed to the cruiser. "Would you mind?"

"No," Judith asserted before her cousin could say otherwise. "We'll get in the backseat."

Once they were settled in, Colbert removed his cap and swiveled around in the driver's seat. "I confess I only had time to glimpse at Sergeant Brewster's notes about you, Mrs. Flynn."

"Hey," Renie yipped, "how do you know which is Flynn and which is the dim-witted cousin?"

Colbert's aplomb was intact. "Brewster mentioned that Mrs. Flynn was the taller of you ladies. Thus I conclude that you're Mrs. Bones."

"Sheesh!" Renie fell back on the seat and closed her eyes. "I quit."

Judith looked askance. "It's Mrs. *Jones*," she said,

noting that despite Renie's having shut her eyes, her mouth was set in a grim line. "It would be best not to further upset her. My cousin is very sensitive. Being involved in a homicide has profoundly disturbed her."

Colbert nodded, his face sympathetic. "Of course. Perhaps we should take her to your motel before I pose any further . . . distressing questions."

"Oh no," Judith replied a bit too hastily. "She has an amazing coping mechanism when it comes to blocking out unpleasantness of any kind. What do you want to ask me?"

"I understand you found the body," Colbert said, lowering his voice despite Renie being only three feet away. "I'm sure that Sergeant Brewster's notes are thorough and detailed, but with such a traumatic moment, one's memory can play tricks. Is there anything that you may not have mentioned, but has resurfaced by now?"

Judith felt it best to at least pause before answering. "No, I honestly can't." She knew what Renie was thinking: *Seen one corpse, seen 'em all.*

"Very well." The Mountie appeared satisfied. "Can you tell me anything about the bizarre plan to send the body down the Bow River on a raft?"

"It was a bier," Judith responded. "That was Mr. Stokes's last request. Or so his family members told us."

Colbert looked somewhere above Judith's head. "Bizarre," he murmured, now giving the word a French twist. "That explains what the campers found."

"Campers?" Judith echoed.

"Yes," he replied. "Earlier today some campers from Manitoba found what they thought was a fancy sort of raft caught in some trees that were overhanging the river. Did you ever see this bier?"

Judith nodded. "It was a very elegant bier. But has anyone reported finding a . . . body?"

"No." Colbert looked grim. "The family members insist the body has disappeared."

Judith wasn't sure she should mention the telltale blanket in the Odells' trunk. Colbert might find her reputation as FASTO lacking on the other side of the international border. To complicate matters, Adela and Norman were hurrying toward the cruiser.

"Sir!" Adela cried. "Can you take us to headquarters so we can file a missing person's report? We'd also like to get our car."

Colbert opened the door on the driver's side. "Speak to Corporal Jeffries, please. His cruiser is behind that rather large tent. He'll gladly escort you to our offices."

Adela nodded and Norman said thanks. The couple quickly moved away, though Adela grabbed her husband's arm as if she needed support.

"Poor folks," Judith said under her breath. "I don't blame them for being upset."

"Not a very pleasant visit to our country for them," Colbert remarked. "Of course the situation is . . . unusual."

"Takes all kinds," Renie suddenly said, her eyes now open. "Can we go now? I'm so hungry I could eat a chipmunk."

The Mountie's aplomb seemed a trifle shaken. "Well . . . yes, I have no more questions. Thank you for your cooperation."

Renie had already opened the door on her side, but Judith hesitated. "I have a question of my own, Inspector. What brought you down to Banff on a Sunday?"

Colbert's steady gaze shifted ever so slightly. "A request from Customs and Immigration about one of the Stokes party's members. I'm afraid it's confidential."

"I see," Judith said. "I hope this person isn't . . . dangerous."

A faint smile played at Colbert's mouth. "No. No, not at all. Enjoy the rest of your stay, ladies. You've nothing to fear."

Judith and Renie exchanged curious looks. But with a tip of his cap, the inspector got out of the cruiser.

"Guess that means we can eat?" Renie asked hopefully.

Judith nodded a bit vaguely. "Customs and Immigration," she said softly. "I wonder what that's all about."

"It's about time for dinner," Renie asserted in a crabby voice. "Let's go get the car. I say we head to the Banff Springs Hotel. They've got so many restaurants that we shouldn't have to wait. It's almost eight o'clock."

Judith accepted the suggestion without comment. After exiting the cruiser, she tried to see what was going on at the Stokes encampment, where the younger Mountie was still talking to Ma and Pa Stokes. Colbert was standing off to one side, as if observing the interaction. It was tempting to join the inspector or at least get a closer, if discreet, look, but she was afraid Renie might take a bite out of her arm. In fact, her cousin was already heading for the rented SUV.

Ten minutes later, they were at the hotel, where Renie went up to the front desk to ask which restaurant would have the earliest seating for two. The clerk wasn't certain, but suggested the Bow Valley Grill.

"That better be right," Renie muttered, following the directions she'd been given. "If not, I'll come back to the front desk and eat their reservation book."

"It's probably on a computer," Judith pointed out.

"Then I'll eat the computer. Bite the bytes." She

smirked. "That's not bad for thinking on an empty stomach."

Judith didn't comment. When they reached the restaurant, the hostess informed them that they could be seated immediately. Renie squealed with pleasure and practically ran up on the hostess's heels as they followed her to a table.

"We lucked out," she said gleefully as she snatched up a menu.

"Right." Judith's tone was vague.

Renie's brown eyes were riveted on the menu. "Good choices," she murmured. "Meat or seafood. Which appeals to you, coz?"

"What?" Judith hadn't heard her cousin or looked at the menu, but was staring into space.

"Okay," Renie said, putting her menu aside. "What now?"

Finally focusing, Judith sighed. "I'm wondering why we shouldn't be afraid."

"Offhand," Renie said, "I'd say that's a good thing. I'm having the pan-seared trout. I'll make this easy for you. Order the mac 'n' cheese with salmon. It comes with an arugula salad and a charred garlic baguette."

"'Charred'?" Judith suddenly stared at Renie. "Maybe they can't find the body because it was burned."

"Oh, for . . ." Renie shook her head. "Can't you take your mind off of murder while we eat delicious food in a comfortable atmosphere? This *is* a vacation."

Judith sighed. "Maybe for us, but not for the killer. Murder never takes a vacation."

Renie didn't respond. This wasn't the first getaway for the cousins that had included a corpse. "Okay, I get it," she said. "According to Colbert, at least we should feel safe, even if I don't know why."

"Because we aren't part of the Stokes family?" Judith suggested. "That's the only thing I can think of. What about the twins? Are they safe? No wonder Adela's frantic."

"They may be of legal drinking age here, but they're still teenagers. For all we know, Win and Winnie met up with some of their contemporaries and are partying. They seemed bored to me."

Judith was considering the suggestion when their server arrived to take their orders. "That's possible," she allowed after they were alone again. "But still . . ." She shook her head. "It doesn't sound right."

"Stop fussing." Renie sounded borderline severe. "I'd like to eat one meal without a reference to corpses. Okay?"

Judith merely nodded and gazed at the restaurant's calming, tasteful decor. Many of the diners were either readying to leave or had already gone while the cousins were talking. No doubt, Judith thought idly, they'd had seven o'clock reservations. Just after their salads arrived, she remarked that the Bow Valley Grill must stop seating diners at nine, at least on a Sunday night.

Renie agreed. "It's a lot quieter in here now."

For the next minute or two, the cousins attended to their salads. Suddenly Judith gave a start.

Renie stared. "What? Did you swallow an olive pit?"

Judith shook her head. "I heard what sounded like a police siren, but it just stopped."

"So? Traffic violation. No taillights. Over the city's speed limit. Drunk." Renie forked in more potato salad.

"It was only a short burst." Judith tried to hear more sirens, but there weren't any. "Weird."

Renie let out an exaggerated sigh. "The siren was in the town, right? So was the miscreant. You know neither vehicle could get involved in a high-speed chase because of the layout and all the traffic. Relax."

Judith felt foolish. "I guess I'm kind of edgy. We should've ordered drinks, but I didn't want you passing out from starvation."

"That's okay." Renie smiled. "I'm no longer in danger of that. Here come our entrées. They look amazing."

And they were. Judith even managed to put away thoughts of homicide as she put away the salmon mac 'n' cheese. They skipped dessert but ordered Galliano. By the time they left the hotel, it was almost nine thirty. Replete with excellent food and superb drink, they headed back to the motel. To their relief, they found that fresh towels had been provided. In a gracious mood, Judith rang the front desk. Niall answered. She asked if he was to work all night.

"No," he replied. "Nobody works the desk after midnight. We lock up until six in the morning. But guests can come and go any time. But you knew that, eh?"

"I guess I did," Judith responded. "Anyway, I wanted to tell you that we appreciate getting the towels and—"

Niall cut her off. "Hold on. Call on the other line."

Renie saw Judith frown. "What?" she inquired.

Judith shrugged. And waited. Renie headed for the bathroom. She was coming out when Niall returned to the phone.

"Sorry," he said, sounding shaken. "An emergency. A *real* emergency," he added, his voice now cracking.

"What is it?" Judith demanded. "Are you okay?"

"Yes. No. That is . . . someone tried to kill Trixie at the hospital. I have to hang up now."

The line went dead.

Chapter 17

"Why would anyone want to kill Trixie?" a flabbergasted Renie asked, collapsing on the Flynns' bed. "Could she be more harmless?"

Judith also felt a little shaky. "The siren . . . I bet it was for her. The hospital is right by police headquarters."

"Yes," Renie said softly, leaning back against the pillows. "Poor Trixie. First she gets dumped, then somebody tries to kill her. She should've stayed wherever she came from."

"I wonder where that was," Judith murmured, after settling into one of the matching armchairs. "I don't suppose they'd let us talk to her."

Renie looked skeptical. "Tonight?"

Judith shook her head. "I doubt we'd be allowed to see her. I do wonder what the MO was."

"You think someone tried to poison her? I mean," Renie quickly went on, "before she collapsed."

"Not likely." Judith grimaced. "I've had enough experience with poisons to know they don't usually produce hysteria. Do you remember when we were—"

She was interrupted by her cell's ring. Luckily, it was in her purse next to the chair. Judith answered on the second ring.

"Is that you, Judith?" Arlene asked in an anxious voice.

"Yes," Judith replied. "You sound upset. What's wrong?"

"Well . . . it's not exactly *wrong*," Arlene said, "but it's not quite right either. It's your mother. I'm afraid . . ." She stopped; Carl's voice could be heard in the background. "Yes, yes," Arlene said, apparently to her husband. "But it's too soon to call the police. And would you mind turning the channel to something I like, for a change? I'm sick of baseball. They stand around too much. If I wanted to watch statues, I'd go to a museum." With an audible huff, she apparently remembered she was on the phone. "So sorry, Judith, but why must men watch so much baseball? The players do the same thing over and—"

"Arlene!" Judith exclaimed. "What about Mother?"

"Oh. Yes," Arlene said. "Your mother and Aunt Deb went to have supper and play bridge at Sophie Savery's condo on top of the hill. You know Sophie from church. She's the one who sits in the back row and sometimes flosses her teeth. Except I think they're dentures. Why can't she just take them out and soak—"

"Arlene, please," Judith begged, trying to keep calm while Renie rolled over on the bed and winced a lot. "Tell me about Mother."

"That's what I'm doing," Arlene said reasonably. "Sophie picked your mother up at three thirty—she had your aunt Deb in the car—and told me she'd bring both of them home by eight or a little after. But now it's after nine. I called Sophie and no one answers. You can see why I'm worried."

By reflex, Judith glanced at her watch. It was after ten, Alberta being on Mountain Time. "Have you or Carl gone to Sophie's condo to see if they're still there?"

"No," Arlene replied. "I don't know which condo Sophie lives in. There are so many new ones around here and her phone's unlisted. Your mother jotted down her number for me. I called Sophie, but she didn't pick up."

Renie apparently had figured out the gist of Arlene's call and sat up. "Missing mothers?" she whispered.

Judith nodded and spoke into the phone. "Are you at the B&B or your house?"

"We're home," Arlene replied testily. "You know our routine. As soon as everyone has checked in and the social hour is under way, we come back over here. I made sure we were home by seven because my cousin Avery was calling from Winona, Minnesota. They're on Central Time, so it was nine there and he goes to bed at ten. Avery has to get up early to feed his monkey."

"Have you checked to make sure Mother hasn't come home since you've been on the phone?"

"I looked from upstairs just before I called and there wasn't a light on in the toolshed," Arlene said. "It gets dark earlier here now, you know."

"Yes, I do know," Judith conceded. "We've only been gone for a few days."

"It seems much longer." Arlene sounded grim.

"Try calling Sophie again," Judith urged. "She's quite deaf, according to Mother. If she doesn't answer, then—"

"Hold on," Arlene said. "There's someone at the front door. I hope whoever it is hasn't brought us *bad news.*" She emphasized the last two words with what sounded like a touch of relish.

Judith figured that Arlene was in their living room, where she couldn't see the front door. Exchanging curious looks with Renie, she shifted around in the chair. Her artificial hip was reminding her that it had been a long and arduous day. The next thing she heard from Arlene was her muffled voice, apparently talking to Carl.

"Well!" she finally exclaimed. "Guess who that was?"

Judith was in no mood to guess. "Who?"

"Your mother. She brought our mail. Charles mis-delivered it again yesterday. Wasn't that sweet of—"

Judith interrupted. "You mean Mother is safe?"

"Of course," Arlene assured her. "She shouldn't have bothered coming over here after dark, but she told Carl that she was watching one of her favorite TV shows and had to wait until it was over. That's why there wasn't a light on in the toolshed. You know she doesn't like to waste electricity. Carl's walking her back home."

"Good," Judith said in a tired voice. "I'll hang up now. This call is costing you money."

"No, it's not," Arlene declared cheerfully. "I make these calls on your business landline. You do have a business license, Judith. It's here in the kitchen. Anyways, I knew you'd want to know that nothing bad happened to your mother. Night-night." She rang off.

Renie shook her head. "Rankerized again."

Judith nodded vaguely. "Arlene and Carl really are wonderful people. What would I do without them?"

"Good question." Renie stared at Judith. "Well?"

"Well what?"

"Trixie," Renie said. "Something was bothering you before Arlene called. Surely you aren't going to settle in for the night until you find out what happened to her."

Judith didn't respond right away. "You're right." She stood up. "Let's go downstairs to see if Niall can talk to us."

Renie reluctantly got up from the bed. "Can or will?" she asked, following her cousin to the door.

"He'd better," Judith said.

They didn't speak again until they were in the lobby. Niall was behind the desk, looking less than his usual composed self as he sorted through what looked like receipts. He gave a start when Judith called his name.

"What's wrong?" he asked in a tone that suggested most things in his world had gone awry.

Judith leaned against the desk. "Since we were with Trixie when she collapsed, we're concerned about her. Were you serious when you said she'd been attacked?"

Niall shoved the receipts aside and moved closer to the reception desk. "That's what I heard from the nurse who called to find out if Trixie had any family around here. As far as I know, she doesn't. Poor kid." He shook his head.

"Do you know why she became so distraught?"

Niall shook his head. "Not really. I was giving an older couple directions to the golf course. They were both quite deaf and I had to shout. The phone rang just as Trixie came up to the desk, so I told her to answer it. By the time I finished helping the oldsters, she'd hung up and was rushing off somewhere. That was the last I saw of her."

"Did she seem upset?"

"Maybe. I guess." Niall rubbed his jawline. "She's kind of an emotional person, as you might've noticed."

Judith nodded. "Have you checked her belongings? There might be some contact information in there. In fact, she didn't have her purse with her when she collapsed. It's probably in the room."

"Right . . ." Niall paused. "But I can't leave the desk until my shift is over. I'm stuck until I get off at midnight."

"We could do it," Judith volunteered. "If you trust us with the key, of course."

Niall looked dubious. "I trust you, but I really shouldn't. It might get me in trouble if Mr. Barnes found out."

Judith was about to say they'd be very discreet, but Renie had put one elbow on the desk and her gaze was fixed on Niall. "Here's how it comes down, you dear, conscientious, polite Canadian young man. You can stick to the rules, but even if you do, Mrs. Flynn will pick the lock and get inside that room. Trust me. By the way, she's in tight with the Mounties."

Niall gaped at Renie. "But . . . she's not from around here. I don't get it."

"Call them," Renie said, no longer leaning on the desk. "Ask for Inspector Colbert."

Niall sighed. "Okay, let me get the key. It's room . . ."

"Two-oh-nine," Renie interrupted.

Niall blanched. "How do you know that?"

"Because," Renie replied, "it's the only mailbox—or whatever you call those things on the wall—that doesn't have a guest name on it. I, too, can sleuth. Sort of."

Niall handed over the key. "Down the hall on your left," he murmured.

"Thanks," Judith said with a smile. "We won't take long."

Niall didn't respond.

Neither of the cousins spoke until they were inside the room and had turned on the lights. It was obvious that Trixie's housekeeping talents were lacking not only when it came to the guests but also when it came to herself. Clothes, makeup, magazines, CDs, and even food remnants were scattered around the room. A stuffed tiger's head peeked out from under a pillow on the unmade bed.

"Poor Trixie," Judith said under her breath. "Do you see her purse?"

"No," Renie replied. "I'll check the bathroom." A moment later, she reappeared with a hefty imitation leather shoulder bag. "If you're expecting a scary message in lipstick on the mirror over the sink, forget it. That only happens in movies." She handed the bag to Judith. "You do the honors. If this purse is as messed up as the room, I'm not touching anything in it. There might be snakes."

Judith undid the flimsy clasp. "No snakes," she said, looking inside, "but there may be an animal."

Renie made a face. "What kind? Not my nemesis, the common gray squirrel, I hope."

"No." But Judith felt something very soft and faintly furry. "It's a wig. Blond." She held it up for Renie to see. "Rather a nice wig, actually. The curls look natural."

"Trixie *is* a blonde," Renie noted. "Not that shade or style, but still . . ."

"A disguise?" Judith suggested. "But why?"

"Don't ask me. By the way, no sign of drugs in the bathroom, legal or otherwise."

"Check the drawers in here while I go through her purse. I've got her wallet. More of a billfold, really. No pictures, just a few credit cards and her medical coverage information. Ah! Here's her driver's license." Judith stared, then blinked. "It's a Nebraska license. Trixie's from Lincoln. This was issued two years ago. She's twenty-two."

"Their licenses look a lot like ours," Renie noted. "I don't have to be Hercule Poirot to think Trixie knew the Stokes folks before she came to Banff."

"They may be *why* she came here," Judith said before scrutinizing the rest of the contents of the wallet and purse. "Maybe she met them in Big Stove, Nebraska."

"Possible," Renie allowed as she opened and closed drawers. "Nothing of interest. In fact, nothing at all. I'll check the closet." She opened the sliding door to reveal a space only a third the size of the ones in each of the Flynn and Jones suites. "Not much. Jeans, tights, tops, cardigan sweater, and one white dress for, I presume, a hot date."

Judith was still holding the purse. "Maybe we should take this to Trixie tonight. She may need her ID and her Blue Shield card. I assume she'll be released tomorrow morning unless there's something seriously wrong with her."

"Other than being attacked?" Renie said with a droll expression. "You don't really want to go to the hospital, do you? It's after visiting hours."

Judith's face was bland. "We'll drop the purse off at the hospital's front desk."

"We'd better drop off the room key with Niall on the way out."

"You do that while I head for the car. I'll pick you up out front," Judith said. "Tell Niall you need to clear your head. I'd rather he didn't know we left the premises."

"You don't trust him?" Renie asked in surprise.

Judith shrugged. "You know I never trust anybody." She picked up her own purse and removed her wallet. "Put this in that satchel of yours. I'm leaving mine here."

"Dare I ask why?"

"One purse is enough."

Renie didn't ask for an explanation. Sometimes it was better not to know when her cousin was on the trail of a killer.

The earlier evening traffic had dwindled to a few cars all bearing Alberta plates, a couple of delivery trucks, and a California minivan that had a lived-in look.

"Aging hippies," Judith remarked. "I'll bet they've got Janis Joplin on tape and a lot of weed in the compartments."

"No doubt," Renie agreed as they glimpsed the hospital just ahead. "There's a parking place just twenty yards away."

Three minutes later, they were in the hospital and approaching the front desk, where a gray-haired woman was doing a crossword puzzle. Her name tag identified her as Edith Smythe. She looked up with a bored expression. "Yes?"

Judith assumed her most confidential manner. "We were here earlier to see Medic Roberts about a patient who'd just been admitted—Trixie O'Hara. My cousin and I were with her when she collapsed. In the excitement, I ended up with her purse and she must have mine. Perhaps you have it here at your desk? My last name is Flynn."

"No personal items of any kind have been found," Edith replied. "You should contact our lost and found. They open at nine tomorrow."

Judith assumed an air of distress. "Could we wait while you go get it from Medic Roberts's office?"

"I'm afraid I can't leave my position here," Edith

said stiffly. "If you give me your home address, we can post it to you."

Judith grimaced. "We're leaving on a six-week tour of Albania. The post office will be holding our mail." She turned to Renie. "You remember what happened to Uncle Alfred's ashes when the post office had to keep them while Aunt Opal was coming home from her safari."

Renie looked appropriately horrified. "Oh yes! And her grandson Archie insisted he thought the silver case contained marijuana. That's why poor Uncle Alfred was always referred to as Old Smoky from then on."

Judith now wore a mournful expression. "I still can't think of Uncle Alfred without getting upset." She wobbled a bit against the desk. "I need to use the restroom. Is there one close by?"

Edith's stone face seemed to twitch. Or maybe the wobble had caused Judith to wince. But the receptionist finally responded. "The washroom is around the corner and on your right."

When they were out of sight, Renie laughed. "That was one of your more inventive lies. I loved it."

"Thanks," Judith responded. "I should've come up with better names than Alfred and Opal."

"That's okay, coz," Renie assured her. "Edith wouldn't have appreciated anything more exotic. But how do we get from the restrooms to the patient rooms? I don't see a door or a stairway."

"True. But I spy an intercom. You have a deeper voice than I do and you only spoke once at the desk. How about summoning Edith Smythe to the delivery area?"

Renie shook her head. "She won't fall for that at this time of night."

"Yes, she will. The woman's an automaton. She'll follow orders. Make it an emergency delivery."

"Okay. I, too, can follow orders. I can move faster than you can, so start walking." Renie picked up the intercom, waited for Judith to get to the end of the hall, then lowered her voice to a rasp and announced, "Edith Smythe, please collect an emergency item at the delivery entrance."

Renie saw Edith suddenly appear and then disappear. Hurrying to meet Judith, she asked where the receptionist had gone. Judith said she'd taken an elevator going down.

"We'll take an elevator going up," Judith said. "The patient floors are on the second floor. I think Canadians refer to the first floor as the ground floor. Or is that the English way?"

Renie shrugged as the car's doors opened immediately. The cousins kept quiet on the brief ride. Only after they exited did Renie ask how Judith was going to explain their presence.

"I may not have to," she said in a low voice. "I can only see one nurse at a desk up ahead and she's at her computer. The first two rooms are empty. With any luck, we may find Trixie before anybody finds us."

The next two rooms were occupied by men; the third was vacant and an elderly woman was asleep in the fourth. But in the next room on the left, Judith recognized Trixie's tousled blond hair. She was stirring restlessly under a gray hospital blanket.

"She's still alive," Renie whispered. "Count yourself lucky. Not all of your suspects over the years were."

"I'm not sure Trixie's a suspect," Judith said under her breath as they tiptoed into the room. "Trixie?" she called softly. "Trixie?" she repeated a little louder when the young woman fretted at the blanket. "It's me, Mrs. Flynn, with Mrs. Jones."

Trixie gave a start and turned to look at her visitors. "Who?"

"Judith Flynn and Serena Jones from the motel," she replied, keeping her voice down for fear of alerting the on-duty nurse. "I've brought your purse."

"My . . . purse?" Trixie's bleary eyes widened. "Oh!"

Judith set the purse down on the bed. "How do you feel?"

Trixie didn't answer the question, but gingerly touched the purse as if to make sure it was real. "Thank you," she said in a toneless voice.

"Have you seen a doctor?" Judith asked after moving a visitor chair next to the bed and sitting down.

"I think so. She told me her name, but I forget. Jane, maybe. She was really nice." Trixie fumbled with the purse, but finally managed to open it and remove her wallet. "My money . . . I hope it's still . . . yes!" With trembling fingers, she began to count the bills. Three of them fluttered to the floor, where Renie stooped to pick them up.

"Here," she said, holding the bills so that Judith could see they were each a hundred dollars in U.S. currency.

Judith hid her surprise. "Do you know when you'll be released?"

Trixie shook her head as she tossed the bills into her purse without so much as a glance. "They took some tests. Maybe they'll tell me tomorrow. But it's nice here. I don't mind."

"Do you have any family or friends in the area?" Judith asked.

"No." Trixie frowned. "Well . . . maybe, in a way.

But they've been sort of tied up since I got here. Except for . . ." She gritted her teeth. "Anyways, I thought I should get a job while I was waiting."

Judith tried to think of a tactful way to ask why Trixie was carrying around so much cash. Renie, however, was more inclined to disdain tact in general. Unabashed, she spoke up. "How come you've got all those hundred-dollar bills? You could survive for quite a while in Banff without taking on a job."

The blunt query didn't seem to faze Trixie. "I didn't have the money until after I got here." She rubbed at her temples with agitated fingers. "I'm really tired. It's late, isn't it? I want to go to sleep. Thanks for bringing my purse. That was nice of you." She dug deeper under the coverings and closed her eyes.

Renie started for the door, but Judith picked up the purse and put it into the nightstand's drawer. Judging from Trixie's deep breathing, she was already asleep. The cousins made their exit.

When they reached the foyer, Edith Smythe was back at her post. She frowned at them, but Judith wished her a polite good night on the way to the main entrance. The receptionist nodded faintly. Apparently, the intercom-summons ruse had worked.

There were still pedestrians on the sidewalk, so neither cousin spoke until they were in the SUV. "How,"

Renie asked as she buckled up, "did Trixie get all that American cash *after* she got here?"

"From Americans," Judith replied. "Somebody in the Stokes family paid her off."

"The Odells?" Renie suggested. "They're staying at the motel. But would they carry that much cash with them? She's from Nebraska and they're from Iowa. Adela and Norm are the type who use traveler's checks or credit cards."

"You're right," Judith agreed, braking at an arterial on Lynx Street. "Speaking of the Odells, I wonder if they got their car back."

"I wonder if they got their kids back," Renie said in an unusually worried tone. "They may be old enough to drink in Canada, but Win and Winnie are still kids. I remember what our three were like back then and still shudder at some of the dumb stunts they pulled."

Judith smiled wryly. "Yes. After Dan died, I had my own problems raising Mike alone, especially in his teens. By the time Joe and I finally got back together, Mike was virtually a grown-up."

"You did fine," Renie said, seeing the motel sign up ahead. "Are they still planning to come from Maine after the tourist season is over?"

"We hope so." Judith slowed to turn off the street and pull around into the parking lot out back. "He and the family like Maine. Quoddy Head State Park reminds them of home. No real mountains, of course, but . . ." She stopped. "There's the Odells' car. They must've abandoned the rest of Adela's family."

"Good thinking," Renie asserted. "I wonder why they came in the first place. Could Adela be more different from the rest of them?"

Judith had pulled into the only parking space left, some four vehicles down from the Odell sedan. She didn't speak again until they were out of the SUV. "Adela's been away from the farm for over half her life. She went to college and married a man who doesn't strike me as a farmer. In fact, if I had to guess, I'd say Norman is a salesman. The Buick is fairly new. Maybe he sells cars."

Renie laughed. "You do read people. What's Adela's job?"

Judith used her key to open the motel door. "She manages the car company. I think she'd like to manage her weird relatives, but that's a lost cause."

To the cousins' mild surprise, Adela and Norman were about to enter the elevator that was opening its doors. "You're out late, too," Judith said with a friendly smile as they got in with the Odells.

"Yes," Adela replied in a weary voice. "We finally heard from our twins. At least we know they're safe."

"Damned fools," Norman muttered. "They should never have taken off in that car. Couldn't they see the tank was almost empty? We'd only driven it once since we got here and I wasn't going to get gouged for the Canadian imperial gallon price until we were ready to head back home and could fill up on the other side of the border."

The elevator had stopped and the foursome got out. But Judith had an obvious question for the Odells. "Where were Win and Winnie going?"

Adela threw back her head. "Home!" she cried.

Norman put a hand on his wife's arm. "Hey, Del, don't wake up the paying customers. It's almost midnight."

Adela leaned against him. "Sorry. I'm just so upset. I need a drink." She made an effort to compose herself and looked at the cousins. "Do you want to join us? You look like you've put in a long day, too. We've got a jug of Canadian Club in the room."

Judith hesitated, but Renie spoke up. "Why not? We haven't anything better to do since we got dumped by the two frat boys we picked up earlier."

"Coz!" Judith shrieked, then lowered her voice. "She's kidding. Really."

"Darn," Adela said. "I was hoping it was true so you could dish the dirt. It might've taken my mind off of all the negative stuff we've put up with since we got here. Come on, let's hit the sauce."

The Odells' suite was two doors down from the Flynn and Jones accommodations. Unlike the cousins' suites, it didn't have that lived-in look. Maybe, Judith thought, it was because the couple had been forced to spend so much time with their Stokes relations.

"Sit wherever," Adela said with a vague gesture. "Tell Norm what to do with the CC."

Judith and Renie both asked for an inch over ice. With regret, Norman informed them there was no ice. The cousins graciously settled for tap water.

Adela looked at her husband as if waiting for a cue. He shrugged and took a sip from his glass. "I guess," she said, "that's my signal to unload. Oh, we've kept in touch by letters and even some phone calls, at least with my brother, Corny, and his wife, Delia. They have a computer, but only use it for business despite my pleas to send me e-mails. I'm afraid they're a bit rigid about not using high tech on a personal level." She paused to gulp down some of her drink.

Norman snorted. "They sure as hell take advantage of every high-tech method when it comes to raising their damned corn. These days they don't even need hired hands. No wonder they're rolling in money."

"They rarely spend it," Adela put in. "Except for

Codger being generous with our kids, Norm and I never got a dime out of him. I paid my own way through the University of Iowa by working in the school's cafeteria."

Feeling tired after the long day, Judith was nursing her drink. "Did you two meet on campus?"

Norm shook his head. "I went to Drake. We met on a blind date my brother arranged. He was going with Del's roommate. We got married a couple of years after we both graduated."

Judith nodded. "Very smart to get your education first." Wanting to move the conversation back to the twins before falling asleep, she asked if Win and Winnie were enrolled in college.

Norm shook his head. "They both have a yen to join the Peace Corps. Neither of those kids has a clue about a career. They want to see the world."

Adela bridled. "They're seeing it now in Idaho. They hitchhiked to Bonners Ferry. It's a wonder some nut didn't kill them."

Renie finally spoke up. "Are they coming back here?"

"No," Adela said sharply. "We sent them enough money to go home by bus. We told them they could figure it out for themselves since they pulled such a dumb stunt. And," she added in a calmer voice, "they will. They may be foolish, but they're not stupid."

"Why," Judith asked, trying to rally, "did they leave in the first place?"

Adela sighed. "They were creeped out by the whole thing with Codger and that damned bier stunt. He'd been so generous with them that they thought it was gruesome to put him on that bier and send him off . . ." She stopped, drained her glass, and burst into tears.

Norman got up from his chair and put his arm around his wife. "We tried not to let the twins know the poor old guy had been stabbed," he said, "but somebody let the cat out of the bag. That sent Win and Winnie over the edge. Frankly, they were terrified."

Judith asked the obvious question. "Who told them?"

Norman bit his lip before speaking. "Ada."

"Ada?" Judith was shocked. "But she never speaks."

Adela was wiping her eyes. "I know. But I wish she hadn't."

Judith wondered not about *how* the young woman had come to speak but *why*. And yet Adela didn't seem to be wondering about any of the Stokes family's strange behavior. Ada hadn't used words. Or maybe that was because Adela's clan wasn't strange to her. After over forty years, the Stokes Mantra might seem normal. Judith could understand that, but it still struck her as very strange indeed.

Chapter 18

J udith and Renie left the Odells a few minutes later.
They were both so worn out that neither of them
felt like speculating on the events of their very long
day. Instead of entering the Flynns' adjoining suite
and going through the connecting door, Renie took
out her key, mumbled something that sounded like
"ni-ni," and staggered into the Joneses' accommodations. Judith merely nodded. She felt as if she'd talked
herself numb.

The last thing Judith remembered was sitting down
on the bed to undress. The next thing she heard was
the muffled ringing of a phone. Bleary-eyed, she tried
to rouse herself and discovered she'd gone to sleep
with her clothes on. When the ringing persisted, she
grabbed her purse and dug out her cell.

"Yes?" she croaked, forcing her eyes to focus on the digital clock next to the bed. It read 9:49.

"Jude-Girl?" Joe said in an uncertain voice.

"What?" Judith was struggling to sit up. "Joe?"

"Right. Are you okay?"

"Yes. Of course. I'm still half asleep. How are you?"

"Great," he replied. "In fact, that's why I'm calling. Bill and I are having some fantastic luck. Our guide Snapper's incredible. We're going to have to send most of what we've caught to the cannery. So far we've hauled in brown and rainbow trout, cutthroat, and what they call the Bow River bullet. Those babies really fight and you wouldn't believe how high they leap out of the—"

"Joe," Judith interrupted, feeling a bit unsteady as she headed for the bathroom, "why are you calling?"

A brief silence ensued. "Well . . . Bill and I wanted to make sure you and Renie are getting along okay without us. You are, right? I mean, no problems?"

"We're fine," Judith replied, more sharply than she intended. "In fact, like I said, you actually woke me up."

"Wow! My wife sleeping in? This trip must really be relaxing for you."

Judith leaned against the bathroom sink. "You've no idea."

"Then you and Renie wouldn't mind if we stayed

another day? We'd be back in Banff sometime in the early morning."

Judith considered. "I'd have to make sure the motel has room for us," she finally replied. "I'd also have to ask the Rankerses to stay on at the B&B."

"They won't mind," Joe said airily. "There shouldn't be a problem with the motel either. It's Monday."

Joe was probably right about Arlene and Carl, but not about their lodgings. Judith had noticed no decrease in the town's tourists. It was, after all, still August. "I'll let you know if there's a problem," she hedged. "Okay?"

"Sure," Joe said. "Here comes Bill. I'll tell him we can go ahead and let Snapper know he can take us up into one of the lakes around here. Love you." He rang off.

Judith wasn't up to coping with Arlene, but she could call the desk to find out if they had availability for the night. First, however, she'd shower and get dressed. Ten minutes later she used the house phone to see if their suites were still available for that night.

They were, according to the unfamiliar male voice at the other end. Judith didn't ask his name. She'd stop by to introduce herself and Renie before they left for breakfast.

It was ten-fifteen by the time she went into the Jones

suite and wasn't surprised to find her cousin still asleep. Judith put a hand on the shoulder Renie wasn't sleeping on. "Coz," she said softly, "wake up."

There was no response. Judith spoke in a normal voice. "Come on, open your eyes. It's after ten."

Renie moved, but didn't open her eyes. "After ten what?" she muttered.

"Ten minutes for you to get up and get going so we can eat breakfast," Judith said. The lure of food should motivate her cousin.

"Oh." Renie snuffled a bit, rolled over, made some grumping noises, and finally, if slowly, opened her eyes. "Breakfast?" she said. "Did you order from room service?"

"The motel, as you know, doesn't have room service," Judith declared, growing impatient. "Do you know where we are?"

Renie gazed halfheartedly around her. "No, but it looks familiar. Is it Edinburgh?"

"That was several years ago." Judith's patience was ebbing. "Try another part of the U.K."

Renie struggled to sit up. "Maybe I'll figure it out if I see a picture of the queen."

"You better do it fast or I'll leave without you," Judith said, moving toward the connecting door. "I have to make a phone call." She paused just long enough to see Renie toss off the covers.

Arlene answered on the fourth ring. "Hillside Manor," she said in her most gracious voice. "How may I help you?"

Judith identified herself and went straight to the point. "You can help me by staying on another day at the B&B. We've got a problem."

"Foreign countries!" Arlene cried. "Have you been arrested for espionage? Should I call the ambassador?"

"It's not *that* kind of problem," Judith asserted. "It's our husbands. They want to spend another day fishing."

"Why?" Arlene asked. "They can fish around here. We have lots of lakes and rivers and the bay and the— hold on. I think a guest is having a heart attack."

Judith heard Arlene call to someone but couldn't make out the response. In fact, she couldn't tell if the voice was male or female. The next sound was a woman's horrified shriek. Not Arlene, Judith thought, having heard her neighbor shriek before. Often. Other excited voices sounded in the background. Growing anxious, Judith wished Arlene would come back to the phone. When she finally did, the news was not good.

"I have to call 911," she said. "Have a nice day."

Judith stared at her disconnected cell. Briefly, she considered calling her mother, but Gertrude would be in the toolshed and unaware of whatever was going on at the house. Five minutes later, Renie wandered in, looking as if she'd thrown her clothes up in the air and run under them.

"I may be dressed," she mumbled, "but I'm not really awake. Guide me to a restaurant." As if to prove her groggy state, she bumped into the armoire that held the TV. "Oof."

"Let's go," Judith said. It was pointless to tell Renie anything until she'd had her first cup of coffee. They drove in silence until they reached Phil's, which was close to the police station.

"No!" Renie yelped. "I refuse to eat prison food! Take me to the Banff Springs Hotel!"

"Wake up!" Judith snapped. "Phil's is practically in front of us. You loved their pancakes when we were there the other day."

"I did?" Renie blinked a couple of times. "Okay."

Inside the restaurant, they were informed that a table for two was being bussed. It would only take a few minutes before they could be seated.

"It better be," Renie snarled. "I'm about to pass out from . . ." She shut up as she saw Teddy and Martha

Lou coming toward them. Judith wished them a good morning.

"Oh, right," Teddy said, "you folks are still around. You must be enjoyin' yerselves. I wish we was."

Judith exhibited her kindliest smile. "Our reason for coming here is very different from yours. I assume you'll be heading back to Big Stove soon."

"We wish," Martha Lou said, looking petulant. "The ornery Mountie dudes won't let us."

"Why not?" Judith asked.

"Because," Teddy replied, "them cops can't find Codger. 'Course they can't. I bet he's floated halfway to China by now."

Martha Lou latched on to Teddy's arm. "Let's not be yappin' about Codger no more. I'm sorry he's passed, but it's over."

Teddy glared at his wife. "It ain't over until them Mounties say it is. Why do they need poor ol' Codger's body? It was danged well wore out."

Martha Lou shrugged. "These Canucks got some queer rules. Let it be."

Teddy wagged a finger at his wife. "We ain't Canucks and Codger weren't one either. The cops want one of them autotopsy deals to tell how the poor old coot croaked. Stupid. He was old, he croaked. So what if some joker stuck a knife in his back? Probly didn't have a fork to put there to say he's done."

"Was it natural causes?" The question tumbled artlessly out of Judith's mouth.

Teddy and Martha Lou both gaped at Judith. "Hell yes!" he cried. "He was older than one of them dinosaurs."

"How old was he?" Judith asked.

Teddy shrugged. "Really, really, *really* old. Not sure, bein' poor at numbers."

"A hunerd an' one," Martha Lou declared. "I know, 'cause he tol' me once."

Teddy sighed. "Could be. Let's go. The rest of 'em probly wonder where we went. Maybe they think we got done in, too." He nudged his wife. "Move, girl!"

Judith's gaze followed the couple as they left the restaurant. Turning around, she realized that Renie had disappeared. A quick perusal of the establishment revealed that her cousin had already been seated and was studying a menu.

"How," Judith demanded, "did you manage to sneak away like that?"

"While you were blabbing with the Low-IQ Duo, a server beckoned me to an empty table. Since I was about to faint from undernourishment, I decided to save us another hospital run."

"The Mounties aren't letting the Stokes folks leave," Judith announced.

Renie shoved the menu at her cousin. "So?"

"The cops want to find the body for an autopsy."

"Figure out what you want to eat." Renie sounded severe.

Judith set the menu aside. "Pancakes. What else? We're at Phil's." She sighed. "I can't believe how dumb that Stokes pair sounds. They must never have gone to high school."

"Maybe they never went to school at all," Renie said. "Big Stove may not have schools."

Judith merely shook her head as the server appeared to take their orders. After the cousins made their requests, Judith took up where she'd left off. "Pa studies commodities and follows the market. Ma sounds like a normal person. Yes, Ada's got a problem, but the farm has been in the family for . . . what? Three generations?"

"Sounds right," Renie agreed. "What's your point?"

Judith made a face. "I don't know. That's what I'm trying to figure out. It's as if they're putting on an act."

"Whatever's going on, we're not stuck here much longer," Renie pointed out. "After that, you can put Codger and the rest of them in the rearview mirror."

Judith gulped. "Oh, coz! I forgot to tell you! Joe

called to say they're staying at the fish camp another day."

Renie stared. "You *forgot*? We're still stuck here? No!"

"You weren't awake," Judith said. "You don't take in things when you're in a morning fog. Besides, a B&B guest had a heart attack this morning."

"Well." The anger that had started to light up Renie's eyes now ebbed. "I suppose Arlene described the victim as near death. She does love delivering bad news."

"That's not quite fair," Judith said. "I'd put it a little differently. She faces tragedy with . . . detachment."

Renie grinned. "She relishes it. Ah. Here comes food."

"I don't know what happened to the man who collapsed, but I'll have to call back and find out. Arlene called 911. Speaking of medical help, we should see how Trixie's doing this morning. We're right by the hospital."

"I wonder what it's like to go on a vacation and not have to do anything except relax. I hear that's what some people actually do." Renie stuffed a forkful of pancake into her mouth and slowly shook her head.

"You'd be bored," Judith asserted. "Does the extra day screw up your freelance design work?"

"No," Renie replied after swallowing. "I wrapped up everything I had to do before we left and warned my clients not to contact me until after Labor Day. No problem. Some of them are on vacation, too. I'll bet they're not having as much fun as you are with your sleuthing."

Judith paused before biting off the piece of sausage on her fork. "Face it. We don't golf, play tennis, hike, fish, swim, or ride bicycles. Banff is a charming setting in one of the most scenic places in the world. But what else is there to do for people like us?"

"You have a point," Renie allowed. "And a hobby."

Judith frowned. "What?"

"You like to hunt." Renie paused, wearing a sardonic expression. "For killers."

Judith really couldn't argue.

After finishing breakfast, Judith called Arlene at the B&B. There was no answer. She tried the Rankerses' home phone and got their recorded message. Should she check in to see if Gertrude knew what had happened to the ailing guest? But her mother probably hadn't seen Arlene or Carl since they'd delivered her breakfast. The old lady rarely ventured inside the house even when Judith was home. Gertrude may have loathed Dan McMonigle, but she wasn't exactly fond of Joe Flynn. Judith's father had died young and her mother didn't like sharing her only child with anyone else. Nor did she crave the company of other people, except to play cards. There was no sign of senility with the old girl when it came to outwitting the opposition in a bridge game. Judith marveled at her mother's ability to figure out the number of points each player held. So did Gertrude's opponents.

"Struck out, I gather," Renie said after Judith joined her on the sidewalk.

"The Rankerses do have a life besides helping me out at the B&B," Judith reminded her cousin. "Five kids and a bunch of grandkids keep them hopping."

At the hospital, a young man with a shaved head sat in Edith Smythe's place. He wore an affable smile as the cousins approached the desk. Noting his name was Curt Holmby, Judith told him they'd come to see Trixie O'Hara.

Curt nodded and checked his computer screen. "Ms. O'Hara was released almost an hour ago. Eleven is patient checkout time."

Judith tried to conceal her surprise. "Did someone come to give her a ride?"

Curt made a face. "I didn't see her leave. I must have been on break. Are you friends or . . . ?" He left the rest of the question hanging.

"Yes," Judith replied. "As you may know if you saw Trixie's patient information, she's from Nebraska and my aunt Ellen is her godmother. I spoke to my aunt just the other day and she asked how Trixie was getting along since her move to Banff. Aunt Ellen worries about her."

The flow of information seemed to overwhelm Curt. "I suppose I could find out for you. Wouldn't "—he paused to glance at his computer—"you or your aunt know where Ms. O'Hara was living?"

"She's working here at a motel where she's also living," Judith replied. "But there are so many motels in Banff. If you could find out from the nurses who picked her up, that would ease Aunt Ellen's mind. And mine, of course."

"Me too," Renie said in a small, squeaky voice.

Curt agreed to call the nurses' station, rolling his chair away from the desk in an apparent attempt at privacy. Judith and Renie avoided looking at each other. It seemed to be taking Curt a long time to have his question answered. In fact, the young man had begun clicking his ballpoint pen in a show of impatience.

Looking apologetic, he finally turned back to the cousins. "The nurse didn't know. When they went to check on Ms. O'Hara, she was gone. They looked all over the second floor, but there was no sign of her."

Judith didn't hide her distress. "Had she put on her clothes?"

"Ah . . ." Curt was embarrassed. "I didn't ask. I never saw her leave through the main entrance."

"Maybe, as you said before," Judith suggested, "she left while you were on break. Do you know if Ms. O'Hara ate breakfast?"

Curt was shifting from embarrassment to misery. "No. It's not part of my job. I'm sorry, but the nurses would know. Except that Monday through Friday the shift changes at eleven in the morning."

Judith felt helpless. No matter how depleted or upset Trixie might have been, she'd never leave the premises in her hospital gown. "Thanks for your help," she said in a tight voice. "I appreciate your cooperation."

Back outside, Renie asked why they seemed to be heading toward the nearby police station.

Judith paused in mid-step. "So I am," she said in a faintly surprised tone. "Oh, why not? We're almost there."

"Good," Renie responded. "Maybe I'll ask a few questions, like why the Mounties seem more attractive than our police."

"It's the uniforms, even the regulation brown ones," Judith said. "Are you forgetting that Joe was once a cop walking a beat?"

"That was before you met him. By then he was a detective wearing street clothes."

"Whatever," Judith murmured as they entered the precinct station.

Sergeant Brewster was on duty. His face revealed no surprise at seeing the cousins as he wished them a good day. "If you're here to see Inspector Colbert, he returned to Calgary last night."

Judith was only faintly disappointed. "I'm sure you've been brought up to speed on the investigation."

"Yes," Brewster replied. "I'm fully briefed. I've been told the Odell twins' whereabouts have been discovered. But if you have anything to add, let me know, eh?" The suggestion seemed forced.

"Nothing about them," Judith replied, "but Trixie O'Hara has disappeared from the hospital."

Brewster frowned. "Who?"

"The young woman who works at the motel," Judith explained. "She's from Nebraska and there may be a connection between her and the Stokes family. She's been an emotional wreck since she found out Codger was killed."

Brewster seemed skeptical. "Did she suggest she knew these other Nebraskans?"

"Cornhuskers," Renie said. "It's not just the name of the University of Nebraska's football team."

"Sorry," Brewster said coolly. "I follow the other kind of football and not the Canadian version of your game. I'm keen on soccer. It's a much more intellectual sport, eh?"

Renie leaned an elbow on the counter. "What's intellectual about a bunch of scrawny guys running around in ill-made shorts and tacky shirts kicking a funny-looking ball all over the place? Bor-ing!"

Judith gritted her teeth. "Let's not get distracted. Trixie is the reason we're here." She turned back to Brewster. "Trixie O'Hara apparently came to Banff to marry someone. She never mentioned his name, but when she heard of Codger's death, she fainted. She's been an emotional wreck ever since and was hospitalized yesterday. I wonder if . . ." She paused as she wondered if her imagination had taken her for a ride. "Never mind."

"Oh, for . . ." Renie stopped and looked at Brewster, who was suddenly staring at his computer screen. "You know my cousin's reputation for coloring outside the lines when it comes to homicide investigations. If she thinks Trixie is involved in this one, hear her out."

A hint of amusement glinted in the Mountie's eyes as he looked at Renie. "Niall from the Banff Springs Motel has called in to report Ms. O'Hara as missing."

Judith felt relieved. "Good. I mean . . . I didn't want you to think I was an alarmist."

Brewster shook his head. "I wouldn't do that. I do, however, have some new information from the lab in Calgary where we sent blood samples from the homicide scene. The results came less than an hour ago."

"And?" Judith said encouragingly.

"They're not what you'd expect," he said with an expression that seemed either bemused or amused. Judith couldn't tell.

"Yes?" she prodded.

"The blood wasn't from the victim." He paused as if for effect.

"You mean," Judith said, "it might be from whoever stabbed him?"

Brewster shook his head. "It's not human blood. It came from a squirrel."

Renie had let out a shriek. "I knew it! They're the enemy, the evil ones, the plague of humankind!"

Brewster regarded her with concern. "Is she all right?" he asked Judith as Renie staggered around the area by the front desk.

"Yes," Judith assured him. "Or she will be. My cousin and her husband had an unfortunate incident with a squirrel family several years ago. They moved into the Joneses' attic and multiplied. They partied all night. It took some time to find someone to remove them and it was very expensive." To her relief, Judith saw that Renie was regaining her self-control.

"Sorry," she finally said. "The little horrors still plague us. They dig up planters and flowers and small shrubs and someday they'll come with axes and start on the trees . . . Never mind. I'm better now."

"Good," Judith said, then turned back to Brewster. "What do you make of the . . . animal's blood?" She thought it best not to say "squirrel" lest it set Renie off again.

Brewster grimaced. "Without the corpse and the clothing, it's difficult to say. Mr. Stokes could have been stabbed and someone had cleaned up the blood. But why anyone would replace it with the blood of a squirrel is . . . baffling."

Renie had calmed down. "At least there's one less squirrel to plague me."

Judith turned back to Brewster. "Then Codger could've died from natural causes? He was supposed to be at death's door when they brought him here."

Brewster nodded absently. "The family's account of why they came here when the old man was so ill sounded rather strange. But people do get peculiar ideas, especially if they think they're dying, eh?"

"True," Judith conceded. "But we're assuming he *was* dying."

Brewster's phone rang. He turned away to take the call. Apparently, it was a minor highway accident involving an irate local and a combative tourist. When he rang off, Judith remarked that he must be glad when summer ended and the townspeople again had the place to themselves.

"No, no," he insisted. "Banff relies on visitors. Winter brings the skiers and other snow-sports enthusiasts. The Canadian Pacific Railway started all this with its trains and hotels. The CPR remains, of course, though the hotels are now owned privately. This town is geared to pleasing tourists."

"It's beautiful here," Judith said. "My cousin and I visited when we were kids. We loved it then, too. By the way, how long can you keep the Stokes family here?"

Brewster turned dour. "We can't without any evidence. We don't even have a corpse. But it would be in their best interest to stay, eh?"

"Probably." Judith had a sudden thought. "Did you check the Odells' trunk when the car was brought in?"

"Check it?" Brewster looked puzzled. "We went over it, yes. Why do you ask?"

"Oh dear!" Judith was dismayed. "Didn't anyone tell you? I mean, any of the Stokeses . . . I was sure they'd . . . You know that Codger was moved from the tent and taken to the woods by the highway. But when the Odells' car was found, there was a blue blanket in the trunk. What happened to it?"

"There was no blanket in the trunk or anywhere else," he asserted. "Why do you think there was?"

Judith felt foolish. "Well . . . after we told you we found Codger by the road with the blue blanket and then his body disappeared again, I . . . um . . . figured the blanket must've . . . ah . . ."

"My cousin sneaked into the impound lot and broke into the damned car," Renie declared. "The blanket was there then. She's a whiz at picking locks. Go ahead, bust us."

Briefly, Brewster looked flabbergasted, but quickly recovered. "I see. Someone must have removed it. But who and why?"

"You're the detective," Renie said. "Work it out. Even coz here seems stumped."

"I am," Judith admitted. "We can eliminate the twins. They were on the run by then. But something's been bothering me. Why did Inspector Colbert come down here on a Sunday?"

The sergeant's face showed no emotion. "You live in a far more populous country than we do. Thus you have a considerably higher homicide rate than we do. Calgary averages one murder a year. When someone is murdered in Alberta, especially a foreigner, the provincial government takes it very seriously."

Judith was aghast. "I had no idea. I mean, I realize the huge difference in population, but still . . . Of course the inspector would show up. I apologize for the question."

"I accept your apology," Brewster said solemnly. "At least you two Yanks know how to find Canada on a map."

"That," Renie put in, "is only because our husbands were doing the driving."

Brewster actually chuckled. "I don't think so. The inspector told me you both had been to British Columbia twice in the past fifteen years."

"Yes, we have," Judith said. "We live less than a hundred miles from the border."

The sergeant nodded. "Colbert also informed me that each time you'd been in B.C., a murder occurred. That struck him as . . . curious."

"Oh, for . . ." Renie rolled her eyes. "Did Colbert also tell you that Judith helped solve both cases?"

"He did," Brewster replied, turning back to Judith. "If he hadn't known you had a reputation as FASTO, he would've at least reprimanded me for keeping you informed about the situation here."

"I don't flaunt it," Judith said in her most assertive voice. "I wish those so-called fans had never created the Internet site in the first place. If I ever find out who did it, I may sue them for invasion of privacy."

Renie laughed. "You *have* no privacy. We ended up in newspapers and once on TV. Face it, coz, you're a public figure."

"That doesn't mean I have to like it." She turned to Brewster. "Are we done here?"

"I believe so." He smiled faintly. "The RCMP is grateful for your contribution."

"Thanks," Judith said. "Frankly, I've hit a wall on this case. Maybe I should turn in my FASTO card."

The cousins left the building. Back in the SUV, Judith got out her cell. "I've got to call Arlene and find out about the sick guest."

"Maybe," Renie said, "he got snippy with her and she poisoned him at breakfast."

"It wouldn't be the first time that happened," Judith reminded her cousin. "But I wasn't the one who . . . Arlene? How's the man who collapsed?"

"Judith? What man? Have you been drinking?"

"No, I have not," Judith declared. "I'm asking about the guest who had to be treated by the medics."

"Oh, *that* guest!" Arlene laughed. "Such a character! He's a clown."

"You mean he was just goofing off?"

"No, I mean he works for the circus," Arlene said, switching to a serious tone. "Actually retired, but he teaches other people how to be clowns and do pratfalls. So realistic! I almost called 911. He shows them all the tricks of the trade along with how to dress and do their makeup. You should see the face he put on Carl. It scared poor Charles when he delivered the mail this morning."

"You mean Chad?"

"*You* may mean Chad, but I don't. You know I told you that name doesn't fit him."

Judith suppressed a sigh. "Right, right. Were the medics upset about the unnecessary call?"

"Unnecessary?" Arlene sounded puzzled. "Of course not. They treated Charles after he fell off the porch, but it's only a sprain. He should be back on the route by the middle of next week."

Judith realized she was grinding her teeth, but she had to ask: "How's everything else going?"

"Like clockwork," Arlene replied. "After all, Carl and I have filled in for you several times over the years. We're not novices."

"I know," Judith said, trying to calm her nerves. "No cancellations for the next few nights?"

"Full up. Stop fussing, Judith. Do relax and enjoy yourself."

"I'll try. Tell Mother I send my love and thanks for staying on." Judith rang off.

Renie was slumped in the passenger seat. "Don't tell me. I reserve the right not to know."

"Just as well," Judith muttered. "It was vintage Arlene."

"So what do we do next? I'm bored."

Judith took her time to answer. "It's obvious now that Codger wasn't stabbed to death, but someone wanted to make it look like that's how he died. Why?"

"To set somebody up as a killer?"

"That's possible." Judith started the car. "Was Codger really dying? Was he even sick?"

"A cover-up," Renie said. "Maybe he was poisoned."

Judith glanced at her cousin before pulling out into traffic. "That's a possibility. There's a good reason they didn't want his body found. I wonder if whoever it is really did put him on that bier and send him down the river."

"Teddy Stokes told us this morning that they did," Renie reminded her cousin. "Did you believe him?"

"I honestly don't know." She paused. "Somehow, I can't see Adela and Norman being a part of that stunt."

"They weren't," Renie said. "The Stokes crew did it at night while the Odells were asleep back at the motel. Besides, the campground is an open area. Anybody can wander around there. We did."

"True." Judith had turned back in the direction of the motel. "Now that I think about it, why are the Stokeses the only ones camping there? It's August, prime time for campers."

Renie's expression was wry. "Would you want to hang out with that crew on your vacation?"

"No." Judith looked pained as she stopped for a couple of bicyclists to pedal across Wolf Street. "But that's what we seem to be doing, isn't it?"

Renie merely shook her head.

Chapter 19

Five minutes later the cousins were back in the motel parking lot. As Judith removed the ignition key, her cell rang. "Now what?" she muttered, then recognized the number. "Mother. What now?"

"Who sent in the clown?" Gertrude demanded in her raspy voice.

"You mean . . . ? I'm in Banff, Mother. Arlene can explain that. Ask her."

"I don't like pestering Arlene," the old lady retorted. "She's got her hands full taking care of the loony guests you let stay here. Besides, when she and Carl have any free time, we play three-handed pinochle. That's no time for talking. You have to pay attention to your cards. Only your Aunt Deb likes to gab her head off when we play bridge."

Judith shot Renie a beleaguered glance. "So what about the clown?"

"He came out the back door this morning while I was trying to coax Sweetums inside," Gertrude explained. "There was a flock of those little chickadees in the pear tree and I was afraid he'd go after them. Then I looked up to see this creepy clown coming for me! It's a wonder I didn't have a stroke!"

"Uh . . . what did you do then?" Judith asked.

"I shooed the cat inside and told the clown I was calling the cops. Then I hustled my poor old fanny inside and slammed the door."

"Did you actually call the police?"

"No. You know how they are. They take forever to show up. But you'd better start running your guests through the . . . whatever you call it. The system?" She didn't wait for an answer. "Some system! But you ought to know. You married one of those dumb clucks."

"I think the guest actually is a—"

"Never mind," Gertrude interrupted. "Here comes Arlene with a pie. I wonder what kind. You never bring me a whole pie." Judith heard the phone disconnect.

Renie started to open the car door. "Don't bother filling me in. I got the gist. Aunt Gert hates clowns but loves pies."

"You're right. Okay, you take on Teddy and Martha

Lou. I'll handle Ma and Pa. I'll also try to talk to Ada, but that may be a lost cause."

"Sad," Renie murmured after they got out of the SUV. "I wonder if she gets any joy out of life."

"Ada knows about college football." Judith swiped at a mosquito. "Maybe she enjoys watching it. I wonder if I should call Doris again in Big Stove. Why would she say they were headed to California? Did they change their minds after they left or . . ." She stopped as someone called her name.

Niall was running to catch up with the cousins. "Mrs. Flynn! Mrs. Jones! Stop! Please."

Judith turned around. "What's wrong?"

"Jenny's filling in for Trixie," he said, pausing to regain his breath. "She went to make up your suites and they've been trashed. Should we call the police?"

Judith looked at Renie, who nodded. "Yes. Mrs. Jones and I don't have any valuables, but it's an invasion of privacy. I assume you'd do that under any circumstances."

"Oh yes," Niall replied, "but sometimes guests don't want anyone going through their belongings. It doesn't happen often, but some people are . . . strange, eh?"

"I understand," Judith said. "I own a B&B."

Niall's smile was off-kilter. "Then you understand, eh?"

"Ha!" Renie cried. "You wouldn't believe all the weirdos my cousin gets. And not just run-of-the-mill nutcases, but actual psycho—"

"Psychologists like my cousin's husband, Bill," Judith hurriedly put in. "We've had two or three psychology conventions in the city since I opened Hillside Manor."

"That's . . . good for business," Niall said. "Conventions, I mean. Are you coming back to the motel now?"

Judith was torn. Except for their clothes and toiletries, she couldn't imagine anything that a thief would want. Renie, however, felt differently.

"Yes," she said firmly. "I want to make sure nobody stole my cosmetics. I pay a hundred and fifty bucks for my La Mer facial cream. If somebody swiped that, I'll reconsider my stand on the death penalty."

"Coz!" Judith cried. "A hundred and fifty . . . surely you don't spend that much!" She saw Renie's somber expression. "You do?"

"You bet. If you won't go to the motel, I'll go alone."

"I'll come along. If it's still there, I want to see what an outrageously overpriced ounce of face goo looks like. I assume it comes in a solid-gold jar."

Niall had already taken off. In fact, he was almost running back to the motel. Judith frowned. "Why would anyone go through our stuff? It makes no sense."

"Maybe it wasn't just us. Probably not all the rooms have been cleaned yet."

After getting out of the elevator, they parted company and Judith went into her suite. At first glance, the room didn't seem like a shambles, but drawers and cupboards were open, the bedclothes had been pulled back, and it was obvious that the clothes in the closet had been disturbed. As far as Judith could tell, nothing seemed to be missing.

"Weird," she said to Renie after opening the door between the suites. "Everything of mine seems to be here. Is your hotshot face cream still there?"

"Yes," Renie replied, "though whoever did this was thorough. They even went through my purchases. We'll have to ask Niall for someone to put everything in order."

Judith picked up the house phone. As far as Niall knew, none of the other rooms had been disturbed. Jenny was working in the bar, but he'd send her along as soon as she was free.

"You're shorthanded without Trixie," Judith said. "Is the manager going to hire someone soon?"

"Mr. Barnes manages three other motels besides this one," Niall replied. "He lives at the biggest one by the golf course. With the summer tourist season coming to an end, he may wait to replace Trixie. He's . . . careful when it comes to money."

"But isn't Jenny leaving in a couple of weeks for UBC, or does it start later in the fall? I got the impression she was going to Vancouver fairly soon."

"She hasn't given notice," Niall said. "Or maybe Jenny's already told Mr. Barnes. I should ask her."

That, Judith thought, was Niall's problem. But she had another question for him. "Are you notifying the police about our incident here in the suites?"

"Do you think I should?" Niall sounded wary.

Judith exchanged a puzzled look with Renie, who had been trying to lean in on the conversation. "Yes. If nothing else, it's at least malicious mischief. If my cousin and I were inclined to be *fussy*, we'd insist you do that."

Niall didn't respond right away. "Well . . . I'll have to ask Mr. Barnes about it, eh?"

"Please do." Judith hung up.

Renie was smirking. "Nice work. But do you think there's anything not up front about this motel?"

"No," Judith said, "but I'm not sure about some of the people around here. Mainly, I'd like to know what happened to Trixie. She hadn't worked here long enough to get involved in anything sketchy."

"Except to disappear," Renie pointed out.

"Except that," Judith agreed. "And I guess that's enough."

After doing a minimal amount of tidying up personal items, they went down to the desk to ask Niall if he'd called the police. He had, but they were tied up with a serious vehicular accident near Lake Louise. Whoever had answered the phone suggested they come to headquarters and fill out a form. The officer had also asked Niall to caution Mrs. Flynn and Mrs. Jones to leave their suites as they found them. Meanwhile, Jenny had checked the other rooms and confirmed that none of them had been disturbed.

"I'm tired of visiting the RCMP," Renie declared as they headed out of the motel. "Nothing personal, they're great and all that, but they weren't on my list of things to do while on vacation."

"You'd rather hang out with the Stokes gang?" Judith asked in an ironic voice.

"I'd rather never have met them," Renie replied. "I'd also rather not have had to put my La Mer cream in my purse so nobody swipes it."

"Good thinking," Judith said.

"It's going on two o'clock," Renie noted. "Shouldn't we have lunch?"

"You can't be hungry. We didn't finish breakfast

until after eleven. We're going one-on-one with the Stokes family." Judith picked up her step as she headed for the trail along the river. "And don't pout."

"Why would I? I never worry about my clothes getting rumpled. I gave my iron away fifteen years ago."

"Who did you give it to?"

"Anne. As my only daughter, I figured she might as well give it a shot. I'd been using it as a paperweight."

"Has she ever used it?"

"I've never asked," Renie replied indifferently as they approached the Big Stove visitors' encampment. "Egad! It looks as if they're packing up."

Judith stared at the empty place where the family's tent had stood. Only the picnic table remained, but she wondered if it was a permanent fixture. "They can't be leaving. Or can they?"

Renie shrugged. "No habeas corpus. Maybe there's no legal way to keep them here. No Odells, though."

"Maybe they've already gone. They're probably anxious to rejoin the twins."

Ma Stokes was the first to acknowledge the cousins. "Are you from the farewell party?" she asked suspiciously.

Judith shook her head. "We didn't know you were going."

"Well, we are," Ma replied. "As soon as we find Ada."

"She's . . . not here?" Judith tried not to sound alarmed.

Ma glared anyway. "She's gone missing. It's worrisome. Ada can't help missing out in the smarts department."

Renie was heading for Teddy and Martha Lou, who were sharing a bottle of Molson's ale. Judith turned her attention back to Ma. "How long has she been gone?"

"Since before noon." Ma's pudgy face sagged. "It's not like her. Ada always stays close."

"Does she like the river? Or the woods?"

Ma started to shake her head but stopped. "All these mountains scare the dickens out of her. She had to be coaxed from the tent every morning. But once she came out and looked around, she liked the river. She'd never seen one up close before."

Recalling what one of the family had said about Ada's lack of understanding about rivers, Judith considered her next words carefully. "Had anyone explained to her why she should stay away from the Bow?"

"Pa tried, but Ada doesn't always take in things very well." Ma bit her lip. "It'd be like her to go looking for Codger. She knew he loved the river."

Noting that Renie was talking to an agitated Martha Lou, Judith asked Ma if Ada understood what *dead* meant.

"Dubious." Ma pulled a handkerchief out of her sleeve. "We have to find her fast. We're already off to a late start."

"Who's looking for her? Everybody seems to be here."

Ma paused. "They are now, but we all went searching for Ada as soon as we realized she was gone."

"Have you called the RCMP?"

Ma's glare returned. "The cops? No! We had enough of them asking a bunch of questions about Codger. Besides, we're foreigners here. They might think we're up to something. We've never been out of Nebraska before, let alone out of the country."

"Was Ada fond of Codger?"

"Hard to tell. Ada never shows much in the way of emotions. She can't take in what goes on around her."

Judith didn't doubt her. Before she could comment, sirens were heard in the distance. Ma heard them, too, and suddenly looked alarmed.

"Are they coming for us?" she asked in a stricken tone.

"Probably not," Judith said. "There was an accident out on the highway. Someone may have been injured and they're going to the hospital. Why would the police be coming here?"

"Because," Ma said, her eyes narrowing with

suspicion, "we're foreigners. They don't trust us. I'd better talk to Pa." She bustled off to the picnic table, passing Renie on her way.

"Martha Lou's a waste of time," Renie declared to Judith. "Like Yogi Berra, she not only doesn't know anything, but she doesn't even suspect anything."

"No surprise there," Judith said as they walked back to the motel. "Ma insists they're leaving. I wonder if the police know about their plans. Did you see any sign of the Odells?"

Renie shook her head. "Maybe they've already gone. I'm not sure Martha Lou knows they're all about to take off. Teddy was trying to get her to make sure she has everything packed. Should we tell the police?"

"Maybe," Judith said after a pause. "But we don't really know if a crime has been committed."

"Gee," Renie murmured, "that'd mean your vacation's a flop. Joe may figure he wasted money bringing you along."

"He won't care. He's catching fish."

"True." Renie was silent until they reached the motel's rear entrance. "You, of course, would rather catch a killer."

Judith made no comment.

Chapter 20

Judith could hear men's voices coming from the hall near the elevator. She put a finger to her lips and listened. "Brewster?" she whispered.

Renie nodded as Judith motioned at the elevator that was on the first floor. Once inside, they didn't speak until they were on the second floor.

"Are we going to wait for the cops to show up in our suite?" Renie asked.

"Not quite," Judith replied, moving briskly down the hall. "We're going to check Trixie's room first."

"You think she's there?"

"I'd like to think so," Judith replied, "but I have a feeling . . ." She paused to knock. And waited.

"Maybe she's asleep," Renie suggested.

"Let's find out." Judith dug into her purse for the makeshift wire to trip the lock. It took three tries, but she finally heard the magic click. The door swung open. There was no sign of Trixie. "Drat. I hoped she'd be here."

Renie peered into the bathroom. "She hasn't drowned in the shower."

Judith checked the small closet. "Nothing's been disturbed. It's . . ." Something caught her eye in the corner. "Her purse! She must've put it here after she disappeared from the hospital."

"Put it here and left it?" Renie wrinkled her pug nose. "That doesn't make sense. Unless she's somewhere else in the motel."

"*We'd* better be somewhere else right now," Judith said after peeking inside the purse and making sure the contents were intact, including the hundred-dollar bills. Everything seemed to be in order. She put the purse back into the small closet where she'd found it. "Brewster may be checking our suites. Let's go before he thinks *we're* missing."

"What's missing is lunch," Renie grumbled as they moved quickly down the hall.

Judith pretended she hadn't heard. "Check your own suite first. We'll meet in the middle."

"Right." Renie sounded resigned.

Judith almost hit Brewster with the door. "Sorry!" she exclaimed. "I didn't realize . . ."

His expression was wry. "That I'd be finished so fast?"

"Yes." Judith entered the room and closed the door. "I assume you haven't gone over the Jones suite yet."

He shook his head. "Are you sure nothing's missing?"

"Yes." Judith went across the room to open the door between the two suites. "My cousin agrees."

"It won't hurt to be sure," Brewster said as Renie appeared in the doorway. "Excuse me, Mrs. Jones." He moved past her and out of the Flynn suite.

Renie flopped into an armchair. "Did we ever figure out which is Rose and which is Yew?"

Judith had been staring out the window, through which she saw the Odells' car drive away from the motel. "Which is . . . what?" she asked, feeling distracted.

"Never mind. What caught your fancy now?"

"The Odells." Judith turned away from the window. "They just drove off."

Renie shrugged. "So?"

"I'd wondered if they hadn't already left. They weren't at the campsite bidding good-bye to the rest of the Stokeses."

"They probably did that earlier. If Ada hadn't wandered off, the Stokeses would've been on the road a lot sooner."

Brewster returned from the Jones suite. "I already had Constable McCann dust for prints as soon as we got here. He's still downstairs. I'll ask him to come up so he can take yours." The sergeant went over to the house phone.

"Gee," Renie said, "will our husbands become suspects?"

"They have an alibi," Judith replied. "The fish."

"Fish make poor witnesses."

"They make better dinners. Or breakfasts. Right now I'd settle for lunch . . ."

Brewster turned back to the cousins. "McCann will be right up. Are you both sure you had nothing of interest to anyone who might be involved with the Stokes tragedy?"

"Yes," Judith replied. "But have they reported that Ada—the Stokeses' unmarried daughter—as missing?"

Brewster's usually stolid demeanor was jarred. "No. For how long?"

"Since before noon," Judith replied. "And Trixie O'Hara hasn't been found."

Brewster nodded. "Nothing is yet known of her whereabouts."

"Somebody knows," Judith said. "We just found her purse in her room when we went to make sure she wasn't back here. We'd taken it to her at the hospital last night. She seemed quite weak then."

The Mountie now looked downright grim. "It sounds as if McCann has another room to process." A knock was heard at the door. "Here he is now." Brewster moved to let in his junior officer.

Constable McCann looked young enough to pass for a high school student, but his gray eyes were very keen. He acknowledged the introduction to the cousins with a respectful nod. Judith wondered if his superior had passed on her reputation as FASTO. She thought not, since his gaze didn't change as he looked from one cousin to the other.

"This process is rather messy," he said apologetically.

"No problem," Renie asserted. "We're rather messy. You can tell that from the way this room looks."

Judith felt like stepping on her cousin's foot. "Mrs. Jones means in a general sort of way. We aren't the ones who trashed the two suites."

"Of course not," McCann said in a righteous tone as he opened his kit. "Now, if you'll just place . . ."

The process took less than two minutes, but it took almost three times as long for the cousins to clean their hands. McCann had already left by the time they emerged from the bathroom. Judith immediately asked Brewster if he knew of the Stokeses' plan to leave Banff as soon as they tracked down Ada.

"No," he replied, looking startled. "Maybe I should talk to them. The situation is awkward, eh?"

Judith saw no reason for dissembling. "You mean the alleged disappearance of Codger's body?"

"Yes." Brewster frowned. "One of them told me about their plan to send his corpse down the Bow on a bier. I told them that if they carried through with such a stunt, it would be illegal and they'd be guilty of a crime."

"Which one mentioned their plan?"

"The one who's gone missing. Ada Stokes."

Judith was taken aback. It was Renie who spoke first. "The bier is also missing. Have you searched the river?"

"We did, just in case they'd ignored my warning," Brewster replied. "We found the bier caught on a big snag west of town by the Cave and Basin National Historic Site. But we didn't find a body."

Judith wasn't surprised. "I assume the family members would've secured Codger to the bier. Does the river become faster in that area?"

Brewster shook his head. "Not this time of year. We

sent it to the RCMP forensics laboratory in Calgary. As you might imagine, our own lab here is rather limited."

Judith nodded. "Of course. I've been in some small towns over the years where . . . ah . . . I happened to . . . um . . . learn of such facilities."

"I'm sure you have," Brewster said with a glint of humor. "I'll leave you now so I can call on the Stokes family. There may be a way to keep them from leaving the country."

"How?" Judith asked.

Brewster was already at the door. "There are some things I can't tell you, Mrs. Flynn. Let's call them our Canadian Capers, eh?" He nodded to both cousins and left.

"I got to talk!" Renie exclaimed. "Now do I get to eat?"

"Why not?" Judith responded. "Let's go to wherever they serve lunch in the middle of the afternoon."

"High tea! Somebody around here must serve it. Maybe the Banff Springs Hotel?"

"That's an inspired thought," Judith said. "Let's go there and find out. On the way out, let's tell Niall he can send Jenny to clean up the chaos in our suites."

Ten minutes later, the cousins arrived at the hotel. To their delight, the Rundle Lounge served tea all afternoon. Despite it being a weekday, more than half the tables were occupied; Judith and Renie were seated near a window with a mountain view.

"Perfect," Judith murmured as she picked up a menu.

Renie shook herself. "I feel almost civilized. Maybe I should have combed my hair."

"Don't. I wouldn't recognize you." Judith was actually looking beyond her cousin. "Adela and Norm are over at a corner table. I guess they didn't check out after all."

"Try not to spend teatime checking on them, okay? I need a break from sleuthing." Renie focused on the menu. "Goddess Oolong tea for me. Mmm. Some yummy delights included here. White-chocolate-malt éclairs. What a concept!"

"I'll try the Jasmine Gold Dragon tea," Judith said. "It reminds me of home. Or at least of Mother."

"Stop. You know down deep that Aunt Gert really loves you. Which reminds me," Renie went on, "I haven't called my mother today. I hope she isn't worrying herself into a tizzy. She might contact the RCMP and they know where we are."

"At least Arlene hasn't phoned with another disaster," Judith said as their server appeared.

He answered a couple of the cousins' questions

about various items on the menu and moments later another server appeared with their individual pots of tea and a set of timers. "To gauge the steeping process," he intoned somberly. "Each tea requires a different amount of time."

"Sheesh," Renie uttered after he'd gone away. "I didn't know tea was a science. Or is it an art?"

"Take your choice," Judith said. "Maybe both. After all, tea is a Brit thing . . ." She paused and nodded to her left.

The Odells were coming their way. Adela looked anxious; Norman seemed glum.

"We saw you come in," Adela said, dispensing with any sort of greeting. "You're somehow tight with the cops, right? We saw their cruiser outside of the motel when we left to go here. Niall told us they'd come on your behalf. What was that all about?"

"Sit. Please," Judith said, indicating two empty chairs. She waited until the Odells had pulled themselves up to the table for four. "Somebody broke into our rooms."

"No!" Adela looked shocked. Norman remained glum. "Was anything stolen?"

"No," Renie replied, before Judith could answer. "Not even my La Mer."

"Your what?" Adela asked, puzzled.

"My facial cream. It works wonders. Would you believe I'm ninety-two?"

"Not really." Adela's tone was indifferent. "Do you know if any other rooms were invaded?"

Judith shook her head. "Niall told us nobody else had reported a problem. Why did you ask about the police?"

Norman leaned forward. "Why do you think? We didn't want to come here for the stupid bier stunt, but we did it because Codger had been so generous to our kids. Hell, we made them save most of it for college. But they caught the Peace Corps bug. Better to get an education first and then find out what goes on in the rest of the world."

"The Peace Corps would be an education in itself," Judith pointed out. "They could go to college later. Do the twins know what kind of careers they want?"

"Hell, no," Norman replied. "They didn't even know where Canada was until we told them we were going there and showed them on a map. They got excited when they found out they could drink beer up here, though."

"They're still kids," Adela said, "which is why we were so upset when they ran off. I'll admit, they thought the idea of sending Codger down the Bow was gruesome. Norm and I felt the same way, but as it turned out, they put the poor old guy on it while we were at the motel and we missed it."

"Just as well," Norman said, patting his wife's shoulder. "Talk about a damned silly thing to do. What's wrong with a cemetery?"

The cousins took the comment as rhetorical. After all, Judith and Renie had buried Dan McMonigle's ashes on the site of the family cabins.

"How old was Codger?" Judith asked.

Adela and Norman exchanged bemused glances. "Who knows?" she said. "I always thought he was born old."

Norman nodded. "Farmed all his life from the time he was a boy. That was hard back then, not like it is with modern methods." He sat up straight as the server delivered the cousins' orders.

"Codger must've been middle-aged when you and Cornelius were born," Judith said. "Had he waited a long time to get married?"

Adela looked thoughtful. "My father . . ." She stopped, smiling wryly. "I almost never call him that. He preferred 'Codger.' Anyway, he married fairly young the first time. She was a local girl, Marcella, but Codger never talked about her. I didn't know she existed until I was thirteen. It was Halloween and along with some other kids from the town we decided to go to the cemetery and scare ourselves. I saw her tombstone, which said 'Marcella Jane Draper Stokes, beloved wife and companion.' She was only twenty-two. No children listed. I wanted to ask Codger about her, but I didn't have the nerve."

Judith nodded sympathetically. "Did you see any of the other family graves?"

"Yes," Adela replied. "There was an older brother who died not long after Codger was born. When he—my father—turned twenty-one, he legally changed his name to his late brother's. To honor him, you see." She smiled wistfully. "I thought that was rather sweet of him, if out of character."

"He was still young then," Judith remarked after swallowing a bite of smoked salmon. *That,* she thought, *might explain why the name hadn't appeared in Aunt Ellen's search. Maybe Codger had never bothered to follow through on the change.* "What was Codger's original name?"

"I don't know." Adela grimaced. "I never asked him."

Judith nodded. "But he remarried, obviously. Was your mother also a local?"

"No," Adela replied. "She was from Lincoln. He met her at the state fair. Mother was a librarian at the university. She'd gotten her degree there. Athena Pappas was a first-generation Greek. She was beautiful, but delicate. The climate in Nebraska never suited her. Mother died when I was six, but she made me promise to get a college degree. So I did." Adela had related the last sentences without looking at the cousins. Instead, she stared through the window as if she were seeing not the Rockies but Mount Olympus.

"Life on the farm must've been hard on her," Judith said. "You were cheated of a mother's love."

Adela met Judith's gaze. "I was. That's why I never went back to Big Stove."

Norman chuckled. "The place makes me curious, though. If we could go in disguise, I'd like to see it."

"Not a chance," Adela declared with a gentle punch to her husband's upper arm. "I can't wait to get home to Ankeny. Our kids should be there tomorrow. We'd leave now, but . . ." She lowered her head. "Somehow, I can't."

Judith was sympathetic. "I understand. Family ties are hard to break."

Adela stood up. "No, they're not. I did it over twenty years ago. But I believe in justice. If the rest of them think they can leave, that's wrong." She turned to Norman, who was also on his feet. "It's against the law to do what they did with my father. I may never have loved him the way a daughter should, but I respected him." She put her arm through Norm's and they walked away.

Judith turned to Renie. "What do you think now?"

"This quiche is amazing. Even the fruit cup is good. You're way behind with eating."

"Seriously," Judith said. "Adela's on a mission. I wonder if she knows something we don't."

"She probably does," Renie agreed. "She knows what it's like to live in Nebraska and Iowa. We don't."

Judith took a sip of tea before responding. "Get serious. She may have avoided being with the rest of the Stokeses, but she's kept in touch. She's suspicious of someone or something. I'd bet on it."

"Try the white-chocolate éclair. It's a religious experience."

"Okay," Judith said. "You wanted a break from sleuthing. I couldn't expect the Odells would stop by. Now I'll shut up and eat."

Renie nodded approval. She couldn't do anything else since her mouth was stuffed with strawberry swirl cheesecake.

No mention of the Stokes folks was made until the cousins were pulling up in back of the motel. Renie asked if Judith planned to check the status of things at the campground.

"I'm not sure what to do," she replied, shutting off the ignition. "I wish I knew what Adela is planning to do."

"Make threats of some kind?" Renie suggested.

"Maybe. But *what* kind?" Judith paused. "She may know what really happened to Codger."

"You mean before he died or afterward?"

"Either one—or both." Judith started to open the car door but held off as a big black Ford pickup pulled in next to them. "That thing's so wide I'm not sure I can get out on this side next to the blue BMW. My phony hip can't manage the well between the front seats."

"Pull out and re-park," Renie said. "There's room over here."

"Why didn't I think of that?" Judith muttered, retrieving her car keys. "My brain must be dulled from eating so much rich . . . Now what? I think the guy from the pickup is standing right behind the SUV."

"So? Back over him."

Judith kept her eyes on the rearview mirror, started the engine, and honked. He didn't move. All she could see was a blue checked shirt, tan pants, and a broad midsection. She honked again. He stayed put.

"Let me deal with him," Renie said, opening the passenger door.

"No!" Judith cried. "He may be dangerous."

"So am I when I get riled." Renie stepped out of the SUV.

Judith rolled down the window to hear the exchange and watched Renie approach the man, but the nearby traffic drowned out the sound. She caught only a couple of her cousin's words and almost none of what sounded like a low growl in response. But Renie's reaction made her cringe.

"Are you out of your freaking mind?" she shouted. "Why would we trash our own rooms? You're lucky we don't sue you! Now move your big badass truck before I call Sergeant Brewster!"

For a few tense moments, the man didn't change his position or speak. Then he turned away, presumably to walk around the back of the pickup. Renie stomped back to the SUV and leaned in the passenger side. "It's the motel owner, Mr. Barnes. I didn't recognize him at first. When I asked him to move the truck, he accused us of damaging motel property in our suites. He's a real jerk."

"What's he doing now?"

"Moving the blasted pickup, I hope."

Renie had barely gotten out the words when the

truck's engine turned on, reversed, and shot out of the parking space.

Judith opened the driver's-side door and stepped out of the SUV. "What on earth did you *really* say to him?" she asked, fearing the worst.

"You don't want to know," Renie retorted. "Oh, to hell with it. I asked him what had happened to Trixie. That's when he stomped off. Now I suppose you figure he kidnapped her from the hospital."

Judith's dark eyes widened. "Maybe he did. But why?"

Renie shrugged. "She discovered he was cooking the books? But he owns the four motels. He must be making piles of money with a year-round tourist operation."

"Probably," Judith murmured. "But I think Canadians pay even higher taxes than we do. If he really has Trixie stashed away somewhere, that doesn't explain how her purse ended up back in the motel room."

They had gone inside to the elevator. "Why are we here?" Renie asked as they ascended to the second floor.

"I want to make a phone call. I'd also like to see if our rooms have been put back in order," Judith said as they started down the hall.

Both the Flynn and the Jones accommodations had

been restored to their usual pristine state. "Jenny's done her job," Renie announced as she came through the adjoining door.

Judith looked up from her cell phone. "Good. I'm calling Doris."

Renie looked puzzled. "Doris?"

"The relative or whatever she is in Big Stove." Judith tapped in the number. After ten rings there was no answer. "No voice mail. Darn. Not surprising, though." She looked at her watch. "It's after four here. If I remember what Aunt Ellen once told me, they're on Central, not Mountain Time. But some of the western part is."

"Is what?" Renie asked. "On Mountain Time? In Nebraska? Get real."

"Skip it," Judith shot back. "I'm thinking about working people and when they get home. I don't know which time zone Big Stove is in and if they're on Daylight Saving Time."

Renie leaned against the armoire. "Does it matter?"

"I suppose not," Judith admitted. "But does the RCMP know who the victim is?"

"You mean without the corpse?" Renie stood up straight. "Of course not. They can't even find the body. Maybe the Mounties always get their man only when he's still alive."

"I doubt the CIA could figure out this one," Judith said glumly. "I may have to give up my amateur sleuth status."

Renie grinned. "And relinquish being called FATSO?"

"Stop. You know that perverted version of the nickname drives me nuts." Judith stood up. "Let's check in with the current suspects."

"Why not?" Renie murmured, grabbing her big handbag. "What *is* a vacation anyway?" The comment was ignored.

When they got out of the elevator, Judith headed not for the rear door but for the lobby. Behind the front desk, Niall and Jenny were talking in low tones. They both looked wary when the cousins approached. Niall asked if he could help them.

"I want to thank Jenny for straightening our suites," Judith said, smiling. "Mrs. Jones and I are very grateful."

"Not a problem," Jenny said. "It's part of the job."

Renie leaned her elbows on the counter. Judith could tell she had shifted into the corporate mode usually reserved for her graphic design business. "How come?" she asked. "Does it happen fairly often?"

"No!" an aghast Jenny exclaimed. "It's usually the guests who make a big mess. Some people are pigs."

"True enough," Renie agreed, removing her elbows. "Speaking of pigs, what's with your Mr. Barnes? He gave us a bad time in the parking lot just before we came in a little while ago. He'd parked so close to our space that Mrs. Flynn couldn't open the door on her side."

Niall and Jenny exchanged uneasy glances. "The owner's got a lot on his mind," Niall said. "Running four motels keeps him busy. But he's basically a decent boss."

"If you say so," Renie responded. "You might remind him to treat his guests decently, too."

"I'm sorry," Niall said. "Really. It's just that he . . ." The young man winced. Judith wondered if Jenny had kicked him in the shin. "Well . . . with summer running down, Mr. Barnes gets anxious about any kind of lull before the winter sports bring in visitors."

"Okay." Renie literally backed off. "Your turn," she said to Judith, who was smiling at the duo behind the desk.

"I was wondering if you'd heard anything about Trixie since she left the hospital," Judith said. "We went to her room here, but no luck."

Both employees shook their heads. "Maybe," Niall suggested, "she went with her boyfriend."

"Oh?" Judith sounded ingenuous. "Is he someone from around here?"

Again, the pair exchanged quick looks. "Not exactly," Jenny finally replied. "Or so we gathered."

"Trixie never mentioned him by name?" Judith asked.

"Not to me," Jenny said. Niall shook his head again.

"Curious," Judith said lightly. "Forgive me asking so many questions. I own a B&B, which means I'm usually the one on the receiving end. I guess I can't help turning the tables when I go on vacation."

"Not a problem," Jenny said again. "Have a nice evening."

The cousins exited through the front door, then turned onto the path that led to the river, where the mosquitoes were out in force.

"We should arm ourselves with bug repellent," Renie grumbled. "Why don't they sell it at the motel desk?"

"Why didn't we buy some when we were downtown?" Judith retorted.

"Because we were too busy playing detectives?"

"That must be it." Judith peered off into the distance. "I see the VW bus. The Stokes gang must still be here. I wonder if Brewster was able to stop them heading over the border."

"Maybe Calgary can apply pressure," Renie suggested, batting at more mosquitoes. "Didn't Colbert find out something that pertained to the Stokes family?"

"Something he didn't share with us," Judith said with a touch of umbrage. "I hope he shared it with Brewster and the RCMP here in Banff."

"I spy some Stokeses." Renie gestured with her thumb. "I also spy an RCMP patrol car pulling up by the VW bus. This could be fun."

Judith picked up the pace but frowned. "I wonder . . . should we keep our distance?"

"Do you mean, as in *hide*?"

"Sort of." Judith paused. "We'll detour around the evergreen shrubs and come up behind the cruiser."

When the cousins reached the other side of the greenery, they were on a stone path that apparently led to the river. Several other people were using the route for a late-afternoon stroll. Two young women pushed strollers that were so high tech they looked like spacecraft. Three teenagers zoomed past on skateboards, narrowly missing the startled cousins. A dark-skinned woman in a sari restrained a frisky pug that was trying to chase a butterfly.

"Odd," Judith remarked, "that we forget that people live here year-round. Banff has such an otherworldly feeling that it's hard to remember the town has five thousand permanent residents."

Renie agreed. "That's what makes it special to visitors. There's magic all around here in the mountain air."

"And murder," Judith murmured just as the VW bus came into view on their right.

They moved stealthily to the rear of the empty cruiser, which was parked abreast of the bus. Their view of the campsite was narrow, but they could see the picnic table. Ma and Pa were in their usual places. The only others they could make out were Brewster and Teddy Stokes.

"I wonder if they found Ada," Judith whispered.

"I wonder why you're whispering," Renie said in her normal voice. "We can't hear them, so they can't hear us."

"You're right," Judith replied. "But we don't dare move any closer. Why are we here?"

"Don't ask me," Renie shot back. "It was your idea."

"Not a good one." She tried to figure out how they could get closer without being seen but failed. "We might as well . . ." She stopped. "Did you hear a cat?"

Renie listened, but shook her head. "I only hear the river. And a private plane going overhead."

"It must've taken off from . . ." She stopped. "I heard the cat sound again. It's got to be close by or the plane's noise would've drowned it out. Let's be quiet and listen."

Renie started to object but decided to humor her cousin. After a minute or more had passed, both Judith and Renie heard a mewing sound.

"Not a cat," Renie whispered.

Judith nodded. It had been years since Sweetums had made any noises that didn't sound like a growl, but Judith could still distinguish between a feline and a human. She pointed to the VW bus. Renie nodded.

" "Create a distraction," Judith whispered. "Go back the way we came, then enter the campsite the usual way. Tell them you can't find me. Meanwhile, I'll check out the bus. Then you can keep on going and end up back here."

"Sounds complicated," Renie muttered. "Oh well. See you on the flip side."

It surprised Judith to find the bus door unlocked. She was relieved, though, since it saved her some precious time getting inside. Once she was there, she spotted a half-dozen pieces of well-worn luggage, several items of clothing, and a few discarded snack-food bags. But she heard nothing except the faint sound of the river.

Moving cautiously back among the seats, she finally saw a figure huddled under a blue blanket. She was reminded of the blanket that had covered Codger in his tent. And the one that looked suspiciously like it in the Odells' trunk. Judith couldn't help it. She shivered.

The figure under the blanket moved. Judith sucked in her breath. "Trixie?" she said softly.

The young woman raised her blotchy face. "Mrs. . . . ?"

"Flynn," Judith said, leaning on the seat's backrest. "How are you?"

"Tired." Trixie licked dry lips. "I want to go away."

"Can you walk?"

"I don't know. I don't feel so good."

Judith studied Trixie's eyes. They were red and the pupils were dilated. She guessed that the girl had been drugged.

"My cousin and I will get you out of here," Judith assured her. "How did you end up in this VW bus?"

"Is that what it is?" Trixie was struggling to sit up. "I don't remember."

"Take it easy," Judith urged, grabbing the girl's right wrist. "Sit for a few minutes. Mrs. Jones is coming to help."

Trixie nodded as she managed to get upright. Her hospital gown was visible under a tan trench coat that looked as if it had seen better days. Judging from how loosely it hung, it had probably belonged to a man. Trixie's eyes widened as she heard the door open again.

"Oh no!" she gasped, her grip tightening on Judith's hand. "It's one of them!"

Judith glanced over her shoulder. "No, it's my cousin Mrs. Jones. Relax. We'll get you out of here."

"Oh . . . okay." But Trixie sounded dubious.

Once the cousins got the girl on her feet, they were forced to almost drag her out of the VW bus. When they reached the ground, Judith looked out toward the campsite again. She couldn't see Brewster, but Teddy appeared to be arguing with Pa, who turned his back and stalked away.

"My purse!" Trixie cried. "I have to have it. Can you go back into the bus?"

Judith put her free hand to her lips. "Don't let them hear us. Your purse is in your motel room."

Trixie was dubious. "Are you sure?"

"We saw it there earlier. Can you walk just a little bit?"

"Maybe. I'll try." Slowly, Trixie put one foot ahead and then followed with the other. "Sort of."

But as they moved away and out of sight, she gained

momentum. It occurred to Judith that Renie should get the SUV and bring it around to pick them up.

"I thought you'd never ask," Renie shot back. "Keep trudging. I'm on my way."

As her cousin rushed off, Judith again asked Trixie if she recalled how she ended up on the bus.

"No, I don't," Trixie replied. "I remember being in the hospital and I went to sleep and I woke up in that"—she glanced over her shoulder—"VW bus. I didn't know where I was. I didn't even know if I was still in Banff."

"Did you try to get out?"

Trixie shook her head. "I kept waking up, but I'd go back to sleep. Then, not too long before you showed up, I saw a man outside staring at the bus. I got scared. I scrunched down in the seat so he couldn't see me, but he never came inside."

They had reached the street beyond the campsite. Judith asked what the man looked like.

"I couldn't see his face," Trixie replied. "He was fairly tall and not really young. I didn't get a very good look because I wanted to hide."

"I understand," Judith said. "How do you feel now?"

Trixie entwined her fingers. "I'm thirsty. And hungry."

"We'll take you back to your room at the motel so you can get dressed. Then we'll go somewhere for you to have something to eat, okay?"

But Trixie shook her head and twisted her hands. "No! I don't want to go anywhere. Except . . ." Her voice trailed off and she turned away.

"Except where?" Judith asked gently.

"Home," Trixie said. "Except I don't really have one."

Before Judith could ask what she meant, the SUV pulled up. "You can get in the seat behind Renie. There's room for you to lie down if you want."

"Okay," Trixie said, allowing Judith to help her get a foothold and step into the vehicle. "I feel kind of floppy."

Judith got into the passenger seat. "You need food. What would you like to eat?"

Trixie was fumbling with the seat belt. "I don't know. Maybe soup? Beef vegetable?"

"I think they have that at Wild Flour," Judith said. "We'll stop there first. I'll go inside to get it."

Trixie nodded once. Judith wondered what kind of drugs the abductor had given the poor girl.

Luck was with them when a parking space opened up by Wild Flour, and Renie volunteered to go inside. Judith looked in the rear-view mirror, which showed

Trixie's slumped head, and was relieved that at least she was breathing regularly. The drugs must have been wearing off.

Five minutes passed before Renie shot out of Wild Flour and around to the SUV's passenger side. Cradling the container of soup against her midsection, she held a hard roll in her teeth.

"You can't give that roll to Trixie," Judith said as Renie got back behind the wheel. "She's in a weakened condition and you might have germs."

Renie's answer was to take a big bite out of the roll before she started the SUV. "I got it for me," she said after swallowing. "I fancied a snack. And stop sounding like my germaphobe mother."

Judith refused to take the bait. They arrived at the motel ten minutes later, having encountered what passed for rush-hour traffic in a small town. Trixie was asleep.

"We can't carry her," Judith said. "We'll have to wake her up. Maybe Niall can help us."

"Trixie's slim. We can manage." Renie stepped up into the SUV's second row of seats. "Hey, Trixie," she said in a normal voice, "we're home. Wake up."

Trixie shifted slightly, but her eyes remained closed. Renie gave her a little shake and raised her voice: "Trixie! Let's move!"

Trixie moved, but only to rest her chin on her hand. "Mmmm . . ." She smiled ever so slightly.

"We can't drag her all the way from here up to her room," Renie said. "I'll go ask Niall to help."

"Go ahead." Judith leaned against the SUV and waved off a couple of mosquitoes. Looking at Trixie's quiet form, she wondered how the poor girl had gotten into such a mess in the first place. It was obvious that there was some connection to the Stokes family, but what was it? Her driver's license showed that she was from Lincoln, not Big Stove. But Judith didn't know much about Nebraska. Renie, Bill, and their three children had visited Aunt Ellen and Uncle Win almost thirty years ago. Maybe her cousin would know more about the state's geography.

Judith's musings were cut short when Renie reappeared with the motel desk clerk Layak. "Niall's off duty," she said. "But his sub's a gamer."

"Thanks, Layak," Judith said. "You know Trixie, right? She's not well."

"So I heard," he replied, peering into the SUV. "Oh, poor kid! Is she . . . should she . . . ?"

"We got her into the car," Judith explained. "But getting her up to her room daunted us."

"I can do it," Layak said, fingering his chin, "but

it'd be better if she woke up." He suddenly stared at the cousins. "I mean . . . she's not . . . *really* sick?"

"I don't think so," Judith said, "though she should be seen by a doctor. Is there one on call for the local motels?"

Layak shook his head. "The hospital's so close that it's easy to transport sick or injured people to the ER. But my uncle is one of the doctors. He may still be at the clinic. After we get Trixie in her room, I'll call him."

"That's wonderful," Judith said with a grateful smile. "Go ahead and see if you can rouse her. Mrs. Jones and I can help you get her to the room. You know where it is?"

Layak nodded and leaned down to study Trixie. "Breathing's good. Color's not too off. Trixie?" She shifted a bit on the seat but didn't answer.

Shrugging, Layak lifted the girl into a fireman's carry and hauled her out of the SUV. He was slight, but judging from his lack of effort, he was also fit.

Renie was already holding the door open. Once in the elevator, Trixie began to mutter. By the time they reached the second floor, her eyes were open and she screamed.

"Hey," Layak said softly. "It's me, Trixie."

"Oh!" Her body seemed to relax. "I thought it was . . . Never mind."

"Can you stand by yourself?" he asked, setting Trixie on her feet, but still with one arm around her waist. "I have to open the door."

"We'll hold her up," Renie volunteered.

It took only a couple of minutes to get Trixie settled into bed. Layak apologized for leaving but promised to call his uncle as soon as he got to the front desk.

Renie pulled up a chair, sat down, and opened the carton of soup. "You need nourishment," she informed Trixie. "You're going to down this soup or I'll do it for you."

Trixie's eyes widened in horror. "You'd force me?"

"Of course not," Renie replied. "I'd eat it instead. It smells really good."

"That's funny." The hint of a smile played at Trixie's lips. "You're nice. I feel better now. Maybe I can handle the spoon by myself."

"Go ahead," Renie said, handing over both soup and spoon. "Mrs. Flynn is always nice. But I'm not."

"I doubt that." Trixie carefully spooned up some soup. "Mmm-mm! This tastes wonderful!"

Renie got out of the chair and went over where Judith was standing by the closet.

"Good girl," Judith said to Trixie. "You need to regain your strength."

Trixie nodded and kept slurping. The phone rang on the small bureau that also held the TV. Judith answered.

"Mrs. Flynn? Layak here. My uncle will come by in half an hour. His last name is Patel, same as mine."

"We'll be with Trixie." Judith ignored Renie's glare.

"I'm going to my suite," Renie announced, as if she were the town crier. "I need to apply my La Mer." Head held high, she marched out of the room.

Trixie swallowed more soup before speaking. "What's a law mare? Has she got a horse in her room?"

"No. It's face cream." Gingerly, Judith sat down on the bed. "I'm glad you're feeling better. You must've been hungry. Maybe later on you can go out to dinner with us."

But Trixie shook her head. "I'd rather stay here and rest. I seem to have slept a lot lately, but I'm still tired."

"I understand. What did you mean when Layak was helping us and you thought he was someone else?"

Trixie frowned. "I didn't realize it was him. He's nice. Some people aren't."

Judith nodded faintly. "Who did you think it was?"

"Ohhh . . . I'm not sure. I mean," Trixie went

on, with an apologetic expression, "it could've been anyone, even a motel guest. My brain's still not working very well. It's better now. I think."

"You're more like yourself," Judith said. "What's the last thing you recall before you woke up in the VW bus?"

Trixie finished the soup and set the carton on the nightstand. "The nurses at the hospital making rounds. I'm not sure what time that was, though."

"Do you remember breakfast being delivered?"

"Yes." Trixie paused. "I wasn't really hungry and I only drank some orange juice. It tasted kind of weird, so I didn't finish it. Then I guess I went to sleep." She frowned. "I don't remember anything after that except I dreamed that I was moving, like in a car. You and Mrs. Jones looking at me was the next thing I saw."

That made sense to Judith, though in a disturbing kind of way. "Have you *any* idea of who took you from the hospital?"

"No." Trixie fell back onto the pillows. "It's too crazy."

"Did you know where you were when you woke up?"

"I was on that VW bus."

"I mean," Judith pressed on, "where the bus was parked?"

Trixie looked up at the ceiling. "No. Not until we drove away. I realized we weren't far from the motel."

Is she lying? Judith asked herself. Someone had mentioned seeing Trixie at the Stokes encampment. But she couldn't recall who it was.

"Hey," Trixie said, "can you get my purse? I want to see if I look so awful that I might scare the doctor."

"Sure," Judith said, getting up. She opened the closet and blinked twice. The little shelf where she'd replaced the purse was empty. Trying to keep composed, she scoured the meager contents, the walls, the floor, even the ceiling.

"Why are you looking in there?" Trixie asked. "I left my purse in the top left-hand drawer of the bureau."

"You did?" Judith's voice seemed to echo. Feeling uneasy, she went over to the bureau and opened both top drawers. One contained an extra blanket; the other held Trixie's underwear. The big drawer below was empty.

Judith turned to face a curious Trixie. "Not there."

Trixie stared as if she thought Judith wasn't all there either.

Chapter 21

"My money!" Trixie cried. "Somebody stole my money!"

Judith came over to the bed and put an arm around the girl's shoulders. "Don't make yourself sick. Please."

But Trixie was sobbing almost convulsively as she ground her fists into her eyes. "It's all I had! Gone!"

"Trixie!" Judith gave her a little shake. "Listen to me! Please!"

After a few seconds had passed, Trixie began to catch her breath and finally wiped her eyes. She pulled away and stared at Judith. "What?" The question was more like a challenge.

"When we brought your purse to you at the hospital and counted your money, it was all there, right?"

Trixie nodded emphatically.

"I put your purse in the drawer next to the bed," Judith continued. "Did you remove it from there?"

Trixie had to think about it. "No. I was asleep the whole time until . . . somebody took me away."

"Okay," Judith said with a smile of encouragement. "Somebody else did. It was in your room and we found it in the closet. The money was in it. Who do you know in Banff besides the other people who work at the motel?"

"Nobody," Trixie replied promptly. "I haven't been here long enough to meet other people."

"You've met some of the guests," Judith pointed out, not satisfied with the girl's response.

Trixie frowned. "I guess. But just to say hello to or answer questions."

"You know the Odells?"

"Hmmm . . . Are they an older couple from Milwaukee?"

"No," Judith said. "They're from Iowa and the parents of the twins, Win and Winnie."

"I remember seeing the twins." She fingered her chin. "They were stoked about being able to drink cocktails in Banff. But I didn't really talk to them."

"The Odells are related to the Stokes family. Did you know that?"

Trixie shook her head. "Why would I?"

A knock at the door sounded before Judith could reply. "That's probably Dr. Patel." She got up to let him in.

"Ah, you must be Mrs. Flynn," he said with the hint of an accent suggesting Bombay or Calcutta origins. "And the young lady who is feeling unwell must be Miss O'Hara. Let us see if we can find out why she's a bit . . . peaky."

Layak's uncle was approaching middle age, with raven-black hair, warm dark eyes, amazing white teeth, and skin that was just a shade darker than his nephew's.

"It was very kind of Layak to ask you to come here," Judith said.

"He's a good lad." The doctor opened his leather case. "My brother and his wife have done well by themselves as parents. Perhaps you'd be kind enough to step outside while I examine Miss O'Hara?"

"Of course." Judith went into the hall, where she saw Jenny coming out of the Joneses' suite.

"Mrs. Flynn?" Jenny called softly.

Judith moved halfway to meet her. "Is something wrong?"

"No," Jenny replied, "but Mrs. Jones seems as if she might be . . . touchy about certain things."

"She can be," Judith admitted. "What do you mean?"

"I'd already finished with your suite and was almost done with the other one when she came in," Jenny explained. "At first she was fine, but after a couple of minutes she got her cosmetics bag out of a drawer in the bathroom and swore a lot. I asked what was wrong and she told me to butt out. So I left. I don't get it."

Judith didn't either, but wouldn't say so to Jenny. "My cousin can sometimes fly off the handle over some little thing—and get over it just as quickly. Don't be upset. She's really a goodhearted person."

Jenny looked relieved. "Oh, okay. I was afraid she might report me to Mr. Barnes because I hadn't quite finished in her suite. He can be a bit . . . severe."

"Not her style to tattle," Judith said, patting Jenny's arm. "We'll be leaving in a few minutes, so you can finish up then."

"Thanks." Jenny smiled. "I'll be in the room next to Trixie's. How is she? Layak told me she was back here, but not in very good shape."

"Dr. Patel is seeing her now," Judith replied. "Do you know him? He's Layak's uncle."

"I know *of* him. I've only been here since early June. I'd better get busy or I won't finish in time."

Judith wished her well and knocked on the Jones suite's door. Renie answered almost at once.

"Why didn't you just pick the lock?" she demanded in a strained voice.

"What's wrong? You look frazzled."

"I am," Renie said, closing the door. "Come see what I found in my cosmetics bag."

Judith followed Renie to the bathroom, where her cousin removed a faux-leopard-skin bag from the drawer and handed it over. "Go ahead. Open it."

Judith complied—and stared at the wad of hundred-dollar bills. "Trixie's?" she gasped.

"They're not mine," Renie retorted. "If they were, I'd be back at the boutique."

Still carrying the bag, Judith led the way back into the main room and sat down on the bed. "Is this some kind of weird plot or a bad practical joke?"

"Don't ask me," Renie said, still annoyed. "I just came along for the mountain scenery and the fine food."

Both cousins were silent for a few moments. "I'm not sure we should give the money back to Trixie." Seeing Renie's puzzled look, Judith hastened to explain. "It makes her a target. She's had enough trouble already."

"True. The motel must have a safe."

"They probably do," Judith agreed, "but I'm not sure the safe is safe."

"Good point," Renie conceded. "But who can we trust?"

"Us. We'll divvy it up." Judith removed the bills and began to count. "Twelve hundred dollars. We'll each take six hundred. You've got a zippered compartment in your wallet, right?"

"Two of them," Renie said, then looked all around the big room. "Do you think these suites are bugged?"

Judith considered the idea. "No. Why would anybody do that? I mean, nobody here knows us."

Renie grinned. "You mean nobody knows you as FASTO."

"They still don't, except for the Mounties. We registered as Mr. and Mrs. Joseph Flynn and Mr. and Mrs. William Jones. I'll admit we seem to have had quite a bit of contact with the RCMP, but that's only because we chanced upon the Stokes family. Brewster and his colleagues aren't going to blab about our involvement in other investigations."

"What about the other guests?" Renie asked. "I mean, besides the Odells. Could there be somebody else who would know about you as FASTO?"

Judith grimaced. "I never thought of that. Let's find out." She went to the house phone and dialed the front desk. "Layak? It's me, Mrs. Flynn. I have a strange question for you. Did you have any holdovers from the weekend? Besides us and the Odells, I mean."

Layak said he'd have to check and call her back. Judith assured him she'd stay by the phone.

Renie frowned. "Won't he think that's an odd question?"

"If he sounds suspicious, you can assume your guise as a travel magazine editor."

"Great. I have to do all the work." But Renie took the ploy in stride.

Less than three minutes passed before Layak called back. "We only had one other holdover, Mrs. Flynn. A couple from Altona, Manitoba. They didn't plan to stay another night, but Mr. Abernathy fell into a bunker on the golf course Saturday and broke his arm. He was only released today, so they left this afternoon. Mrs. Abernathy has to drive and she said she might kill Mr. Abernathy before they got home. Is that any help?"

"Not for Mr. Abernathy," Judith said. "But it does answer my question. Thanks, Layak."

Judith relayed the Altona couple's minor disaster to her cousin. "I think we can rule them out as suspects. At least of killing Codger. Mrs. Abernathy may be a suspect if Mr. Abernathy goes missing."

"What do you bet most of the patients at the hospital here are tourists?" Renie remarked dryly. "Vacations often have their downside."

"Obviously," Judith agreed in a wry voice. "Let's divvy up the money now."

As soon as they finished, she suggested going back to check in with Trixie—and Dr. Patel, if he was still there.

The doctor, in fact, was coming out of his patient's room. "Ah!" he exclaimed. "Here you are. I administered a mild sedative. Miss O'Hara needs to sleep."

"She hasn't done much else the last twenty-four hours," Renie declared.

"I mean," Dr. Patel said, lowering his voice, "a natural sleep. Does she take recreational drugs?"

Judith shook her head. "I honestly don't know, but did she tell you about being drugged and abducted from the hospital?"

Dr. Patel bowed his head. "She did. It's true?"

"Yes," Judith replied. "In fact, we're heading for the RCMP office now."

"We are?" Renie gasped.

Judith turned to her cousin. "You'd rather stay here and sit with Trixie?"

Renie sighed in resignation. But Dr. Patel looked apprehensive. "I'll tell my nephew to check in on

Miss O'Hara as often as he can. He's a very reliable lad. Meanwhile, I commend both of you for the concern you've shown that poor lass." He sketched a bow and continued down the hall.

"Hey," Renie said after Dr. Patel had gotten into the elevator, "I got commended, too!"

"You should," Judith responded as they started down the hall. "You do your share of . . . whatever we do. Just don't let go of your purse. We don't want to lose Trixie's money."

"I thought you were going to call Doris in Big Stove," Renie said, punching the elevator button.

"I will, but if both she and her husband, Jens, work, they might not be home yet. I'll wait until after seven—which may be eight where she is in Nebraska."

Once inside the elevator, the cousins kept silent. There was no sign of Mr. Barnes's pickup when they reached the parking area. After they got into the SUV, Judith realized with regret that Brewster would probably be off duty. "I don't want to explain all this Trixie debacle to someone I don't know," she said as they made the turn onto Lynx Street.

Renie smiled. "Remember what your former mother-in-law said? Dan's mom insisted that you'd never met a stranger. You might have disagreed with a lot of what she told you, but I won't argue with that statement."

"She'd had a hard life," Judith said. "Dan's father was in the navy and she got pregnant while they were living at Pearl Harbor."

Renie feigned enlightenment. "So that's why the Japanese bombed it."

"Not funny. But she was shipped out and Dan was born in California."

"Right. His dad survived the war, but the marriage bombed," Renie went on. "She never remarried, and Dan grew up fatherless. That was bad for everybody— including you. Dan had no role model as a husband or a father."

Judith nodded absently. "Most people's problems are rooted in the past. That's why I'd like to know more about the Stokeses. I wonder if they ever found Ada?"

"Pull into the RCMP parking lot and find out," Renie said.

To their surprise, Brewster was still on the job. Judging from his beleaguered expression, he wasn't happy about it. Judith sympathized.

"Long hours," she said. "I remember those from when my husband Joe came home very late and sometimes not at all if he was on surveillance."

The sergeant nodded faintly. "Luckily, my wife is understanding about it, but my two little tykes aren't able to take it in yet. How can I help you?"

"It's about Trixie O'Hara, who's employed at our motel." Judith leaned against the counter and related what had happened to the young girl.

Brewster listened to the tale, at first with professional interest, then with perplexity, and finally with incredulity. "You're certain," he said, "she didn't invent some of this?"

Judith hesitated. "Dr. Patel asked if she did drugs. We have no idea, of course, but there was no sign of drugs in her room or in any of her belongings, including her purse. She insists the money was her own."

Renie, who'd been perusing various pamphlets on a shelf by the door, looked up. "The meandering hundred-dollar bills puzzle me most. What's the point? It's like a prank."

"Maybe," Brewster suggested, "it is, eh?"

Judith didn't argue, but changed the subject. "Has Ada Stokes been found?"

"Not yet," he replied. "Given what her mother told us, it's likely that she's hiding somewhere. Apparently, Ada does that when they're at home. She likes getting lost in their cornfield, which I gather is quite vast— close to two thousand acres. Sometimes they couldn't find her and then she'd reappear after two, three days."

Renie gave a little shrug. "If she got hungry, she could eat the corn if it was in season."

"Probably not," Brewster said. "Mr. Stokes told me their corn is for industrial purposes. Ethanol, for example."

Renie made a face. "Inedible corn? That's so wrong."

Judith asked if Brewster's fellow Mounties were looking for Ada.

"They've been informed of her disappearance," he replied, "but she's been gone for only a few hours. We can't initiate an official search until a person has been missing for forty-eight hours. However, in the past we've bent the rule to twenty-four if the person is a child or a visitor."

"Ada is both," Judith asserted. "Besides, she doesn't know how to swim and the family didn't want her to go near the river."

"So they told me," Brewster said grimly. "The only upside is that we won't have to apply official pressure to keep them from leaving until Ada turns up."

"True," Judith responded. "But isn't the missing corpse another reason to keep the family here? I can write a statement that I saw Codger and he was definitely dead."

Brewster looked bemused. "That doesn't mean he didn't die of natural causes. Kidnapping a corpse may be someone's ghoulish idea of humor, eh?"

"It's possible," Judith allowed. "I've always been intrigued by the vagaries of human nature. People react to death and other tragedies in very different ways."

"True." Brewster smiled. "You have a unique understanding of human nature, Mrs. Flynn."

Renie elbowed her cousin. "She was always snoopy. Just be glad she didn't turn into a window peeper."

Judith didn't take offense. She had, upon occasion, peeped into a few windows over the years. But always for a good cause.

After leaving the station, the cousins agreed there was food for thought in Brewster's remark about the hundred-dollar bills.

"Bizarre, at any rate," Renie said when they were back in the SUV.

Judith shrugged. "I suppose you could describe it that way. At least Brewster is sending someone to ask more questions about Trixie's apparent abduction."

"Right. Where to now? It's going on seven and I'm starting to get hungry."

"Well . . . we should go back to the motel and check on Trixie. I hate to leave her alone."

Renie leaned back against the headrest. "Fine. But while we're there, let's figure out where we'll eat and make a seven-thirty reservation."

"Okay," Judith agreed, pulling out onto Lynx Street. "I'm getting hungry, too."

They were back at the motel in five minutes. Trixie was still asleep when they looked in on her. Layak told them he'd only been able to check on her once while the cousins had been gone.

"She looks comfortable," Renie noted. "Let's go eat."

Judith hesitated, but gave in.

"We should try the Banff Park Lodge," Renie suggested. "It's next to the hospital and close to RCMP headquarters on Lynx Street. We could've gone from there and be ordering right now."

"You can't be that hungry," Judith said. "But at least we can find the place. Do they have more than one restaurant?"

"Yes. I saw their brochure while you were chatting up Brewster. They have four restaurants, but I suggest the Crave Mountain Grill. It sounds like hearty food."

"Hearty is good," Judith agreed. "Let's do it and hope we don't need reservations. It's a Monday night, after all."

There was no wait at the grill. The cousins couldn't

resist ordering cocktails called Monkey's Lunch, a smooth concoction of Kahlúa, banana liqueur, and milk. Judith chose the half order of baby back ribs and Renie opted for the mixed grill of pork, beef, and salmon. To make sure Trixie wouldn't starve, they requested a seafood chowder to go. Judith had noticed a microwave oven on a shelf next to the girl's closet. Trixie could warm it up if she slept for a long time.

After they got in the elevator, Renie told Judith she was going back to her suite to call her mother. "It'll keep her from waking me up too early tomorrow. Besides, she's probably sure I'm dead and has called the funeral home."

"Do it," Judith said. "I'll have to check in with Arlene tomorrow—and maybe call Mother."

The cousins parted outside of the Rose and Yew suites. Trixie was still asleep but looked peaceful. Judith noted that the purse was still where they'd left it on the nightstand. Since it was now almost dark, Judith turned on the small lamp next to the bed. She left the chowder container next to the lamp and tiptoed out of the room.

According to her watch, it was exactly nine o'clock. Judith felt as if it should be much later. She was tired, not as much from physical exertion as from mental gymnastics. The Stokeses weren't the usual middle-class kind of people Judith had encountered, either in her day-to-day life or even as a result of coming across a dead body. Like some heretofore unknown insects, there was no easy way to classify them.

But there was no point in dwelling on the Big Stove family. Except that it reminded her to call Doris. Judith tapped the number into her cell. After three rings, a man answered. "Jens?" Judith said.

"Yes. Who is this?" He sounded wary.

"Judith McMonigle," she replied. "Doris and I have been in touch about your relatives. Is she available?"

Silence. After at least thirty seconds, Jens spoke again. "Doris is under the weather. Can you call back tomorrow?"

"I can, but if you could ask her a quick question about—" Judith heard a click followed by the dial tone. "Damn!" she muttered to herself. "He hung up on me."

"Who?" It was Renie, standing in the doorway between the two suites.

"Jens Draper. He said Doris is sick—and cut me off. Why aren't you talking to your mother?"

"Because she's hosting what's left of her PTA group from my grade school years," Renie replied. "I told her I'd call back tomorrow. Remind me. She did ask if I'd bought a heavy muffler. So why the put-off from Jens Draper?"

"I don't know." Judith stood up and wandered over to the window. "I think the Odells are driving around to the parking lot out back. It looks like their Buick."

"Better than driving it into the river," Renie remarked. "Haven't you finished interrogating them?"

"They might know if Ada showed up," Judith said, going to the door. "Let's take an elevator ride. I think they're on the first floor."

"Oh . . ." Renie threw up her hands. "Why not? It beats relaxing in my comfortable suite reading a good book and drinking a nice cold Pepsi. Or not. What's our excuse for just happening to run into them? Again."

"We don't need one," Judith said as they headed for the elevator. "Asking about Ada is real."

"Too bad she isn't," Renie muttered as the car moved down to the first floor.

When they arrived, Judith led Renie beyond the rear entrance. "Pretend we're coming from the bar," she whispered as she glimpsed the Buick's approach.

"Should I slur my words?" Renie asked.

Judith tensed. "Just go to the bar. Mr. Barnes has landed. Really. Go!"

Renie started to balk, but heard his gruff voice, apparently calling out to the Odells. "Fine." She skittered away down the hall.

Judith backed up a few steps to suggest she'd

just come out of the elevator. She could still hear Mr. Barnes, but also Norman Odell. A moment later, the motel owner entered, still blustering. Adela and Norman were on his heels, looking angry.

"I don't give a hyena's hind end about your loony relatives," Barnes shouted. "I don't want the cops coming here . . ." He saw Judith and shut up. "Never mind." Waving an arm as if batting away pesky bugs, he stormed off in the direction of the lobby.

Norman shook his head. "What a jerk!"

Adela linked her arm through his. "Relax. Barnes isn't exactly a paragon of Canadian hospitality. Every place has its clinkers."

He shook his head. "I still think we should have stayed home."

Judith had to ask about the confrontation, but began by mentioning Renie's earlier confrontation with Barnes in the parking lot.

Norman rubbed at the back of his head. "He started in on us about the twins drinking in the bar. He thought they were underage, but Dela had made them bring along their birth certificates for that very reason. Then he griped about why they didn't seem to be staying in their room. Were we the kind of parents who let their children stay out all night doing God-only-knows-what? That really ticked us off, because we were already worried sick about them. The only thing Barnes cares about is that we wouldn't pay for the room if Win and Winnie weren't staying in it."

Adela patted her husband's arm. "Barnes is a real jackass. Then he found out that we're related to the Stokeses. That really made him go nuclear."

"Why?" It was the only thing Judith could think of to say as Renie sidled up to her.

"Barnes thought they were ghouls," Norman replied. "He'd heard about Codger and the bier stunt. So it was wacky, but why did he care? Sure, the Mounties showed up at the campsite, but that had nothing to do with the motel."

"Except that we're staying in it," Adela murmured, and shook her head.

"Barnes is in the wrong business," Judith declared. "By the way, has there been any news about Ada?"

Adela sighed. "No. Of course they're all worried. So are we, for that matter. She seems so . . . helpless."

"Is she?" It was Renie who posed the question.

Norman looked puzzled; Adela seemed embarrassed. But she was the one who responded. "Ada was still a toddler when I left home. In fact, she was named after me. Being a teenager at the time, I didn't know anything about early childhood development. I only recall her as being what I'd describe as 'clingy.' She seemed to crave affection. I guess I thought that was natural for a little kid. Frankly, Corny and his wife seemed like undemonstrative parents."

"What about Codger?" Judith asked. "Was he more affectionate?"

Adela nodded emphatically. "Very. I suppose it was because he didn't have a wife. In fact, I always thought he'd marry a third time, but he didn't. Life on a big farm can be lonely. You're always a long way from your neighbors."

Norman's expression was wry. "Maybe he spent his time daydreaming about Marilyn Monroe. He certainly had a thing for her or he would never have come up with the crazy stunt of being sent down the Bow on a raft."

"A *bier*," Adela remonstrated. "I can't believe the rest of them followed through."

Judith frowned. "Are you sure they did?"

Adela started to speak but paused. "About now I'm not sure of anything."

Judith didn't blame her.

"The Stokes folks can't leave town without Ada," Renie said after they were back in the Flynns' suite.

"The Mounties are making sure they don't," Judith replied. "This may sound like an afterthought, but I wonder if the family had to get a permit to stay on that chunk of land by the river."

"You've got a possible homicide, a missing person, and maybe a kidnapping, but you're wondering about illegal trespassing?" Renie looked genuinely flabbergasted. "Are you insane?"

"No. Think about it." Judith had sat down on the bed. "How long had the Stokeses been there before we showed up? At least overnight, but it could've been longer if they were waiting for Codger to go sticks up. The RCMP could hardly miss seeing them, so why weren't they asked to leave? Banff has an excellent reputation as a tourist destination. Face it, the Stokes camping arrangements are an eyesore. But they must have given the RCMP a good reason for staying there."

"How about the truth?" Renie responded, turning away from the window and sitting down in one of the two matching armchairs. "The Mounties might've been sympathetic."

"Maybe." Judith checked her watch. "It's almost ten. I'm going to peek in on Trixie. Are you coming with me?"

Renie shook her head. "I've seen her before. I'll watch the local ten o'clock news. Maybe we'll be on it."

"We'd better not be," Judith said grimly as she went out the door.

At first glance, Trixie looked as if she hadn't moved since Judith had last seen her. Not having turned on a light, Judith moved closer to the bed. The girl was breathing regularly and looked as if she had barely rumpled the covers. Her purse was where Judith had left it. Nothing seemed to have been disturbed, including the soup on the nightstand. Reassured, Judith tiptoed out of the room and made sure the door was locked behind her.

"All's well," she announced upon entering the Flynns' suite.

Renie switched off the TV. "Are you disappointed?"

"Of course not!" Judith snapped. "I'm not a ghoul."

"Really?" Renie yawned. "Does that mean I can go into my own suite and read a book about espionage during World War Two so I can calm my nerves while on our vacation?"

"Not funny," Judith declared, wishing she didn't sound so grim. "Time is running out to solve this mess."

Renie threw up her hands. "Stop! It's not up to you to solve the stupid case! You're in a foreign country that has one of the best police forces in the world. We're not even sure the alleged victim was murdered.

Heck, we aren't sure who he was. Get a grip on yourself and assume your usual rational approach to what
this may be. *Please.*"

Judith sat down in the other armchair. "Am I an
idiot?" Her voice was weary.

"No," Renie replied quietly. "But what's gone on
here isn't your normal kind of crime. It's almost as
if . . ." She stopped and gazed up at the ceiling. "I feel as
if I were watching some kind of theater of the absurd."

"Maybe we are," Judith said after another pause.
"Maybe that's what we're meant to think. Maybe," she
went on, her voice growing heavy, "it's a charade to
disguise what's really going on with the Stokes folks."

Renie frowned. "Do we want to know?"

"Maybe not," Judith replied. "But I still intend to
find out."

For once, Renie opted for discreet silence.

Chapter 22

Just before ten thirty, Renie kept her word about making an early night of it and went into the Joneses' suite. Judith remained in the armchair, deep in thought. It was eleven thirty in Beatrice, Nebraska. Aunt Ellen never went to bed until after midnight. In fact, Judith wasn't sure if her aunt ever slept. Reaching for her cell, she tapped in the number.

To her surprise, a sleepy-sounding Uncle Win answered. "Judith?" he said in his Midwestern voice that was a cross between a twang and a drawl.

"Yes," she answered. "Did I wake you?"

"No," he replied—and yawned. "Thinking about heading for bed, though."

"Is Aunt Ellen busy?"

"Kind of." He paused. There was never a way to hurry Uncle Win. "She's hanging from the ceiling."

"What?"

"Wallpaper," Win said. "She's redoing the hallway. Should I get her down?"

"I hate to bother her," Judith began, but heard Aunt Ellen shout to her husband.

"Hang on," Win said, though Judith didn't know if he meant her or Aunt Ellen. A sort of scrambling noise occurred at the other end of the line.

"Judith?" Aunt Ellen didn't wait for a response. "Have you ever tried to align red, white, charcoal, and black stripes in your wallpaper?"

"Uh . . . no, I've never put up wallpaper. Renie has, but I don't recall her ever using a pattern with stripes. Wouldn't a floral be easier to work with?"

"The Nebraska football team doesn't wear floral uniforms," Aunt Ellen declared a bit testily. "What were you thinking?"

"Oh. Of course." Judith vaguely recalled an area in their hallway with a glut of Cornhusker memorabilia. "I didn't realize the team had more than two colors."

"They don't," Aunt Ellen replied. "But their fan gear goes beyond red and white. Why are you calling so late? Have you and Renie run out of money?"

"No, I have a question. Do you actually know any-one who lives in Big Stove?"

Aunt Ellen didn't answer right away. No doubt she was considering her vast network of contacts around the state. "I really don't," she finally admitted with a touch of embarrassment. "But Sue Boo might. She and the town's mayor may've met at a conference or some such event. I'll call her in the morning. It won't be early, though. She sleeps in until almost six."

"Okay," Judith said. "I'll wait to hear from you. Re-member, we're an hour behind you here. Thanks."

"No problem. Back to work." Aunt Ellen discon-nected.

Judith remained sitting in the armchair, worrying about Trixie being left alone all night. What if she woke up and was frightened? She knew where to find the cousins. Or she could call on the house phone. Judith was still silently fussing when Renie entered the suite.

"My neighbors on the other side are partying," she announced. "I called Layak to complain, but he didn't pick up. Those loudmouthed sots may keep on with the loud music and the drunken yelling for hours, so I'm bunking in here with you."

"That's fine. But don't talk in your sleep."

"I'll try not to, but you're the one who makes weird

noises," Renie murmured, sitting down on the bed. "Now unload about Aunt Ellen."

Judith related her phone call.

Renie laughed. "If anybody knows someone in a tiny Nebraska town, it'd be our aunt. Why doesn't she run for governor?"

"She doesn't have time," Judith said. "Besides, I think her pal Sue Boo has a lock on public office in Beatrice and maybe the rest of the state."

"Right. Aunt Ellen prefers working behind the scenes."

"Then I suggest we go to sleep. Knowing our aunt, she may call before the sun comes up." Judith put her words into action by crawling under the covers. Renie followed suit.

The prediction proved all too true. The phone rang just before seven. A groggy Judith fumbled for the cell while Renie let out a couple of choice obscenities, burrowed down, and pulled the blanket over her head.

"I hope I'm not interrupting your breakfast," Aunt Ellen began. "I assume you're eating in your room."

"They don't have room service here," Judith replied, still not quite alert.

"You don't bring breakfast with you?" Aunt Ellen sounded aghast. "We always did when we drove out to see you and the rest of the family. The trip took us just two and a half days. We only stopped to sleep because we brought all our meals with us."

"Yes, now it's come back to me," Judith admitted. "You made very good time."

"I also made sandwiches that would keep a couple of days," Aunt Ellen retorted. "We ate them for every meal."

Judith marveled that the sandwiches hadn't spoiled along the way. Her aunt and uncle had been too cheap to get AC in their car. "What did Boo have to tell you about a Big Stove contact?"

"She knows someone there—the postmaster. Unfortunately, he works for the government and won't be in until nine our time." She paused briefly while Judith heard a rustling noise. "His name is Reginald—Reggie—Upton. The number is . . ."

"Wait!" Judith broke in. "I have to grab a pen." Luckily, the motel provided a pen and tablet on the nightstand. "Go ahead."

Ellen rattled off the number. "Are you sure you took that down right?"

Judith repeated the number. Her aunt approved. "You were always better than Renie with numbers, Judith. I'm afraid my goddaughter is a math disaster. Where is she?"

Judith winced. "Still asleep."

"Is she sick?"

"No, she's fine," Judith said. "It's an hour earlier here."

"That still means it's time to be up and doing," Aunt Ellen asserted. "She's wasting the best part of—oh, I have to go. Uncle Win needs me to help pick the paint color to go with the new wallpaper. Do take care." She hung up.

Judith stared at the clock. It was 7:09. Renie was obviously sound asleep. But rousing Renie might lead to the next homicide. Instead, Judith would leave a note telling her cousin to call when she was ready for breakfast.

By seven thirty, she was out the door, down the elevator, and heading for the Stokes encampment. For all Judith knew, the family might have taken off. She'd noted that the Odells' Buick was still parked behind the motel. Maybe they planned on leaving later on.

Judith hadn't gotten beyond the motel parking lot when she heard a soft voice call out: "Mrs. . . . ? Mrs. . . . ?"

Turning around, she saw that the Buick's left rear door was open. "Yes?" she said, moving warily toward the unseen speaker.

"Help me," the voice urged.

Still cautious, Judith approached the car. "Who are you?" she asked, stopping by the left rear fender.

"Ada, Ada Stokes. Help, please?"

"Of course!" Judith looked inside the car where Ada was lying on the backseat. Except for her rumpled slacks and uncombed hair, the young woman appeared unharmed. "Are you sick?"

"No. Just hungry," Ada replied as Judith helped her sit up. "Doesn't this car belong to Dela and Norm Odell?"

"Yes, it does," Judith replied. "Do you want to see them?"

"Honestly, this backseat isn't very comfortable when it comes to sleeping," Ada said, rubbing her eyes. "Sorry, but I couldn't remember your name."

Judith was momentarily speechless. "Judith Flynn. You're not . . . I mean . . ."

Ada laughed, though without mirth. "My crazy relatives love playing games. I've gone along with some of them, including pretending to be a Gypsy foundling and another as Hugh Hefner's illegitimate daughter. But this last one was demeaning. I'm a University of Minnesota grad and a CPA, for God's sake. Who do you think keeps the books and the rest of the family's finances in order?"

Feeling vaguely mesmerized by the revelations, Judith stared at Ada as she got out of the car. Without the slack-jawed, vacant expression, she was quite a good-looking young woman, if on the thin side. The deep-set eyes now showed some spark. Or maybe it was spunk. "Do the Odells realize you're . . . normal?"

Ada brushed herself off. "No. That's how I ended up nodding off in their car. I came over here while everybody else in the family was asleep. Then I figured maybe Dela and Norm were, too. But they were talking about going home today and I wanted them to know I'm normal. I probably should've contacted them years ago, but I never got around to it." She shrugged and shook her head. "Dela hadn't seen me since I was about five or six. I was really shy back then and didn't talk much to grown-ups."

Judith nodded. "I see. But Adela kept in touch with the family. Didn't she realize you were okay?"

"I doubt it," Ada replied. "When Dela called—which wasn't often—Ma or Pa always talked about the farm. I swear that all they know is *corn*. Dela wrote letters, too, but I can't imagine Ma would respond with anything except about the farm and Pa's arthritis and her bunions."

"But you still live at home?"

"No. I live and work in North Platte," Ada replied.

"It's about thirty miles from Big Stove. Of course, I respect family ties and all that, but I need my own space." She paused, her gaze looking off in the direction of the Stokes encampment. "I wonder if the gang's still there."

"I was going to check that out," Judith replied. "Do you want to join me?"

"No thanks," Ada said. "I want to eat breakfast. I'll walk to town and forage."

"I could drive you," Judith volunteered.

Ada smiled. "That's kind of you, but I'll walk. I've missed my morning workouts at the gym during this zany trip. I've vowed not to turn into a lump like my mother. 1 still don't know why I agreed to go along, but . . . well, they *are* family."

Judith nodded. "Yes, kinship's important. My cousin and I are both only children, but we grew up together, so we're more like sisters. I admire you for your fitness regime. That's smart. I've struggled with weight all my life."

"You're tall," Ada said. "Which is good. I'm only average and that makes a difference. Thanks for the wake-up call. If you see the Odells, tell them I'd like to talk to them before they leave, okay? I want them to know that I'm fine. They've got two teenagers and some-day they'll probably get married. Genes are important."

"Of course." Judith paused. "I am so sorry about your grandfather's passing. I gather he was a very special person."

Ada's expression changed, but she quickly recovered. "That's very kind of you. Thanks so much. Enjoy the rest of your vacation." She turned around and jogged away toward the town's center.

Judith watched the young woman disappear around a corner. She liked Ada, especially the intelligent, candid version. But, as Bill Jones was wont to say, "Something's off."

She was still brooding when Renie stumbled out into the parking area. "Are you insane?" she yelled. "I thought you'd been kidnapped!"

"Pipe down," Judith said. "You'll wake up everybody."

"Good. *You* woke *me* up. I heard you close the door. What's going on?"

Judith explained about finding Ada in the Odells' car—and the discovery that the young woman had apparently been forced to perpetrate a hoax. "But that's not the strangest part," she added. "Her reaction to Codger's death was odd."

"How?" Renie asked. "Did she applaud?"

"No." Judith again considered Ada's manner. "The

best word I can come up with is 'indifferent.' By the way, your T-shirt's on backward."

"The UW's Husky mascot wants to see where he's been, not where he's going."

"No wonder they went two and nine last season," Judith muttered. "I assume you want to eat breakfast."

"That or one of your arms," Renie said. "Let's go."

"Fine," Judith agreed. "I was going to see if the Stokeses are still here, since Ada didn't say otherwise."

On the way into town, Judith thought they might spot Ada, but there was no sign of her on the streets or at a restaurant called Tooloulou's, where they found a parking place by the entrance on Caribou Street. They also found a lineup of other hungry people.

The wait wasn't long, however, but Renie was still grumbling after they were seated. "Some of these people don't look like tourists. Why don't the locals eat at home?"

"You and Bill eat breakfast out sometimes," Judith reminded her cousin.

Renie merely sniffed. "We rarely have to wait."

"But you get to have breakfast out," Judith said. "Owning a B&B means Joe and I can't do that."

"Stop trying to make me feel guilty," Renie said, gazing beyond her cousin. "Here comes Mr. Barnes with, I assume, Mrs. Barnes. It looks like they've already eaten. I'll hide behind the menu."

The couple passed by without so much as a glance. "You can come out now," Judith said. "They're gone."

Renie put down the menu just as a server appeared. She ordered apple cinnamon French toast with ham and an egg over easy. Judith decided to have the same.

The server had just gone off when Judith's cell rang. She heard her mother's gravelly voice at the other end.

"Why aren't you here yet?" the old lady demanded.

"We aren't due home for at least a couple of days," Judith replied after mouthing the word "Mother" to Renie. "Didn't Arlene tell you the husbands decided to extend their fishing expedition?"

"Those lunkheads did that?" Gertrude sounded aghast. "How can they make any decisions? They don't have a brain between them."

"Are you sure Arlene or Carl didn't let you know?"

"Oh, you know Arlene," her mother said in what passed for an affectionate tone—at least for Gertrude. "She gets so caught up in how hard she's working while you're off gallivanting that things slip her mind."

It crossed Judith's mind that Arlene didn't have to work any harder at the B&B than she herself did. But the thought was best left unsaid. "We'll be home before the weekend," she promised.

"I should live so long," her mother grumbled. "You forget how old I—oh, here comes Carl with some cinnamon rolls Arlene made. That woman likes to bake, unlike *some* people I know." Gertrude hung up.

Renie was looking sympathetic. "I'd better check in with my mother later today. She's probably fussing her head off."

"Aunt Deb does that when you're at home," Judith reminded her.

"Too true." Renie paused as their orders arrived. "Mmm. Whipped cream on top of the French toast. Brilliant."

Judith was about to take her first taste when her cell rang again. "What now? If Mother's on another rant . . . Hello?"

"Hey, Jude-Girl," Joe Flynn's mellow voice said into her ear, "is my favorite wife already up and doing?"

"Renie and I are having breakfast," Judith replied, sensing her husband was going to tell her something she didn't want to hear. "What's up?"

"Guess I'd better make this quick since you're eating. Our guide, Snapper, insists we have to see the Athabasca Glacier in Jasper National Park. We'll do that tonight, but we won't leave here until the morning. Don't worry, we'll still get home in plenty of time. Everything okay with you?"

"I'm not sure we can keep our motel room another night," Judith said. "Besides, I've already imposed on the Rankerses for longer than they expected to run the B&B."

Joe seemed to force a chuckle. "They love it. You know how Arlene revels in meeting new people so she can hear all their dirty little secrets."

"That's not fair to her," Judith asserted. "She likes people, she enjoys learning about them, she—"

"Come on," Joe interrupted, no longer mellow. "Arlene loves to dig the dirt. All of you women do. Or are you and Renie tired of shopping and eating in nice restaurants and relaxing by the pool?"

"Apparently you didn't notice there is no pool at the motel," Judith retorted. "We only went shopping once. And even decent restaurant food gets to be a drag—not to mention an expense."

"Are you running low on cash?" Joe asked, almost sounding as if he cared.

"Not quite, but I will be. The extra motel expense isn't cheap. If, in fact, we can't keep our suite another night at the Banff Springs Motel, Renie and I won't like sleeping in the SUV."

Joe laughed. "Dubious. Renie would evict starving orphans to sleep in a comfortable bed. You'll be fine. Unless," he added, lowering his voice to the mellow tone Judith always found hard to resist, "you miss me that much."

Judith sighed. "Of course I miss you. It's just that it's inconvenient, not only for Renie and me, but for Arlene and Carl to change their own routine and . . ."

"Hey, got to run," Joe broke in again. "Bill says Snapper's ready to roll. We can't keep our guide waiting. He's the punctual type. Love you." He disconnected.

Renie looked up from her half-devoured French toast. "They're still fishing, I gather."

Judith nodded. "And seeing the Athabasca Glacier."

"We saw it once," Renie said. "It's receding, you know."

"Not fast enough," Judith retorted. "Maybe Joe empathizes since his hairline is doing the same thing."

Renie laughed. "So's Bill's. I'll bet you're glad we aren't leaving so soon. I've never yet seen you walk away from an unsolved mystery."

Judith grimaced. "I admit it'd bother me. I'm going to call the Big Stove postmaster at nine our time."

"What about Doris?" Renie asked. "Maybe she's recovered enough to talk on the phone."

"That's possible. I think I will call her. But before we do anything else, I want to check on Trixie. Do you know who's working the desk this morning?"

"Niall's back. He was on the phone when I peeked into the front office."

Judith gave a nod. "I'm beginning to feel as if I live here."

Renie took her last bite of French toast. "Don't tell anybody. Canada has a very low homicide rate. You might hex the whole country."

"Not funny," Judith retorted, placing her napkin on the table.

"I wasn't trying for humor," Renie said solemnly.

Judith didn't respond. There were times like this one when she felt as if Renie could be right when she called her cousin a magnet for murder.

Chapter 23

After arriving at the motel, the cousins went directly up to Trixie's room. Judith knocked on the door. There was no response.

"Maybe she's still asleep," Renie said.

"Maybe." Judith knocked again and called out, "Trixie?"

"Mrs. Flynn?" The voice was faint, but steady. "Wait a sec."

It seemed like a lot more than that to Judith and Renie when a pale, almost gaunt Trixie opened the door. "I just woke up a little while ago," she said, stepping aside. "I still feel weak."

"You need to eat," Judith declared. "Do you feel like getting dressed?"

Trixie shook her head. "Not quite yet. In fact, I'd

better sit down." She made her slow way to the bed and sat down but didn't get under the covers. "What's wrong with me? I mean, Dr. Patel didn't really say. Am I dying?"

"No," Judith assured her. "Someone apparently gave you a drug that knocked you out. Do you have any idea who'd do something like that?"

Trixie shook her head. "The only thing I can think of is . . . Where's my purse?"

Judith pointed to the nightstand. "Try the drawer. Dr. Patel may've put it there for safekeeping."

Sure enough, the purse was right on top of some toiletry items. Trixie fumbled a bit before hugging the purse to her breast. "Thank goodness!" she exclaimed, shutting her eyes and smiling. "Now everything will be okay."

"You must be hungry," Judith said. "Do you feel like getting dressed or should we get you something from Wild Flour?"

"Um . . ." Trixie frowned. "I don't know. Maybe I should try to get dressed and see if I can go back to work. I don't want to get fired. Oh!" Her eyes grew big. "My money! I must make sure it's here." She snatched up her purse.

"Wait," Judith urged. "We have your money." She turned to Renie. "Get out your half of it."

"What . . . ?" Trixie looked disturbed. "Why does she have some of my money?"

"I've got the rest of it," Judith assured her, and went on to explain how the other hundred-dollar bills had ended up in Renie's makeup kit.

Trixie remained aghast as both cousins counted out the money. "That's crazy," she gasped. "Who steals money and then doesn't keep it?"

"I don't know," Judith admitted. "But maybe you do, Trixie. Who was the man you came here to marry?"

Trixie bowed her head. "I can't tell you."

"You're going to have to tell the police," Judith said, "so you might as well tell us."

Head still down, Trixie seemed to shiver. "It was an older man. His name was John."

"Did he have a last name?"

Trixie nodded, but didn't look up. "It was Jones."

Renie practically fell out of the chair she'd been sitting in. "*Jones?* That's my last name!"

"So?" Trixie finally looked up. "A lot of people are named Jones. Besides, it doesn't matter what his name is. He's dead."

Judith's efforts to get more information failed. Trixie wanted to be left alone for a while. The return of her money was all very well, but it brought back too many memories of her hopes to marry a kind, generous, yet older man. The cousins left her to mourn.

"Okay," Renie said after they were back in the Flynns' suite. "Who was the old coot? Codger?"

Judith sighed. "That's my best guess. Trixie passed out when she heard Codger was dead, which indicates she knew him. If he really was murdered, she'd be the last person to do him in. Unless he reneged on the offer and the money was a payoff."

"How about payback?" Renie said. "Maybe she wanted more."

"This case is the most confusing we've ever encountered." Judith got up from the chair she'd been sitting in and took the cell out of her purse. "I'm calling Doris in Big Stove. Let's hope she's home and up to talking on the phone."

"Don't forget to call the Big Stove postmaster," Renie reminded her.

"I won't. I . . . Hello, Doris. Are you feeling better today?"

"A little," she replied, sounding weak. "Who is this?"

"Mrs. McMonigle. The magazine person. I understand you've been ill. Are you improved today?"

"A little," Doris replied. "But I stayed home from work."

"Very wise," Judith commented. "People are often compelled to rush back to the job and then they have a relapse."

"It isn't just that," Doris said. "We had some bad news a few days ago. Very upsetting. I really should hang up now. I'm expecting a long-distance call from relatives."

"The travelers?" Judith asked artlessly.

Doris sniffled. "Yes. I wish they'd never taken that trip! I had such a bad feeling about it. I really must go."

"Oh dear!" Judith cried. "Did someone . . . die?"

"No, no," Doris replied in a choked voice. "But Grandpa disappeared not long after they left here. We all thought he'd love Disneyland. Even if he didn't go on the rides, we knew he'd get pleasure out of watching the children on them. He's not senile, but still . . . There's someone at the door. I must see who it is." The line went dead.

Renie looked bemused. "Did I hear the dreaded word 'grandpa'?"

"Yes." Judith sighed. "He never got to Disneyland."

"Hold it." Renie sat down in the other armchair. "Who's kidding who?"

"I wish I knew," Judith said. "Maybe the Stokeses lied to Doris and Jens about where they were going. But why?"

Renie frowned. "They wouldn't approve of the barrel stunt?"

"That's possible. I wouldn't blame them."

"Maybe the postmaster can enlighten you. It's a small town. He'd know most of the locals."

"I wrote down his name and number somewhere," Judith muttered, digging through her purse. "Here it is—Reginald Upton, also known as Reggie." She checked her watch. "It's after ten in Big Stove, so he should be on the job."

But an impatient female voice informed Judith that Mr. Upton was on vacation. "Even postal workers have to get time off. Call back after Labor Day."

"She hung up on me," Judith said, faintly dismayed.

"You expected good service from the post office? Don't you remember some of the mailmen we used to have years ago, especially the one who read all of the family's magazines on his lunch hour and the issues arrived three days late smeared with mustard, ketchup, and God only knows what else?"

"I've been trying to forget," Judith said. "I'm having enough trouble with our new one, Chad."

"We had one last winter who came so late that he wore a miner's hat with a lamp on it. At least we could see where he was when he got to our part of the hill."

Renie paused, looking speculatively at her cousin. "Well? What's our next move? Securing a place under a roof for tonight, I hope?"

Judith looked contrite. "I forgot. I'll call the front desk now." She picked up the house phone.

Niall had bad news. "We're booked," he said with what sounded like regret. "I guess a lot of visitors wanted to stay this week instead of coping with all the Yanks who show up for the long Labor Day weekend."

"I get it," Judith said, giving Renie a negative shake of the head. "What about Mr. Barnes's three other motels? Are they also full?"

"I'm afraid so," Niall replied. "We've already had to turn away a few tourists."

Judith thanked Niall and hung up. "Want to camp out with the Stokes folks?"

"Sure," Renie responded with a dour expression. "Then I can have even more fun by shaving my head with a cheese grater."

"There are other motels," Judith pointed out.

Renie looked unconvinced. "If only our idiot husbands hadn't screwed up in the first place. We could have spent all our time in luxurious splendor at the Banff Springs Hotel. Of course, you would have missed out on encountering the latest corpse."

Judith felt uncharacteristically glum. "This is a discouraging way to end our vacation. No lodging and no solution to our mystery. I feel like a big flop."

"You don't even know if there *is* a mystery," Renie asserted. "Codger was ancient and probably died of natural causes. The knives were just a very bad joke."

"Some joke," Judith muttered. "What was the point?"

"An insurance scam?" Renie suggested.

"Maybe." Judith stood up. "Let's get out of here for a while. Checkout time isn't until noon. It won't take more than ten minutes to clear out our belongings. We can have a look at the golf course."

"We don't play golf," Renie said.

"So? It's one of the sights we haven't seen."

"Golf courses all look alike. They have greens and tees and roughs and . . ."

"Move," Judith interrupted. "I don't want to argue about golf courses."

"Fine," Renie said, heading into the hall. "How about tennis courts? They have tennis courts—"

"Stop!" Judith cried as the elevator door closed. "You're driving me crazy!"

"That cuts both ways," Renie responded.

They both stopped talking after they exited the elevator and went through the lobby. Niall was on the phone, but he acknowledged the cousins with a nod.

Outside, Judith noticed that a few streaked cirrus clouds moved slowly against the vast blue sky. She could always remember a few of the more common cloud names. One of her fellow librarians had been married to a local TV weatherman and she often pointed out the different formations.

Closer at hand, Judith saw Martha Lou appear from around the shrubbery. She called out to the cousins.

"You seen Teddy?" Martha Lou slowed her step, breathing hard. Her pretty freckled face was very red.

"No," Judith replied. "Was he supposed to be coming this way?"

Martha Lou reached into her low-cut polyester top and pulled out a wad of Kleenex from her cleavage. "Yes! If he ain't showed up yet, he will, damn his cheatin' hide!" She dabbed at her eyes with the tissues.

"Are you going to ask your aunt and uncle if they've seen him?" Judith asked. "I think they're still at the motel, though they may have gone out."

"Dela and Norm won't know nothin'," Martha Lou asserted. "How could they? It just happened." She stuffed the Kleenex wad back into her cleavage. "But I'll look for that two-timin' rat there anyway." She brushed past the cousins and hustled off to the motel.

Renie smiled wryly. "What's that all about?"

"No clue," Judith admitted as they reached the SUV. "Did Teddy come on to one of the motel guests?"

Renie shook her head. "I haven't seen a female at the motel who'd appeal to Teddy except maybe Jennifer."

"Most of the guests seem middle-aged or even older. Like us."

"Yes, the twins are the only young ones I've noticed, but they're back home in Ankeny." Judith shrugged. "It's not our problem."

Traffic was heavy in Banff that morning. It took almost ten minutes to reach the golf course. Renie was first to espy the clubhouse. "Want to inspect it? Maybe they serve a midmorning snack."

"You can't possibly be hungry so soon," Judith said. "It's not quite ten thirty. Besides, we should probably go back to the motel and find out if there are any vacancies in town. Some motels keep a room open for guests who have an emergency."

"Not having a bed *is* an emergency," Renie declared.

Judith sighed as they retraced their route. "You're right. I just had to get outside for a few minutes. I'm frustrated. I still have to call Arlene and deliver the bad news. They may have their own family plans coming up with the long weekend."

"Very close-knit," Renie remarked. "That's great. I wish my offspring were nearby."

"I feel the same way about Mike and his family," Judith said. "Maybe we should've gone to Maine to visit them instead of coming here and . . ." She stopped, staring at a car that had just passed them. "That blue BMW . . . where have I seen it before?"

"There was one parked next to us at the motel yesterday," Renie reminded her. "What about it?"

"I could swear Teddy was driving it. Or one like it. But the only vehicle we saw by their camp was the VW bus. It definitely had that lived-in look. I assumed all of the Stokes family rode here in it."

"They probably did," Renie said. "Are you sure you saw Teddy? That car was going fairly fast."

"It looked like him. But I could be wrong." They'd reached the motel. "Let's go in the back way. I'd like to see if that BMW is still there."

Renie scowled. "There are probably a half dozen . . . never mind. I can't squelch your curiosity."

There was no sign of the blue BMW behind the motel. Judith decided to ask Niall about the owner. He was on the phone, but held up a finger to signal for the cousins to wait. After a few more words, he hung up.

"That was Mr. Barnes," he said. "I can't interrupt the boss. Are you checking out now?" His expression was apologetic.

Judith looked at Renie, who merely shrugged.

"We might as well," Judith said. "But I'd like to make sure Trixie's okay. Have you seen her this morning?"

"No," Niall replied ruefully. "Jenny and I have been busy. Do you want a passkey to her room?"

Judith refrained from saying she didn't need it. "Yes, thanks."

Niall opened a drawer and handed over the key. "You can drop it off on your way out, eh? I'm really sorry about not being able to accommodate you and Mrs. Jones tonight."

"That's not your fault," Judith said.

"Right," Renie put in. "Blame it on our husbands. They can't stop fishing and admiring glaciers. We both intend to file for divorce when we get home."

Seeing Niall's startled face, Judith told him her cousin was kidding. "By the way, who owns the blue BMW that's been parked out back?"

"Nobody," Niall replied. "It's Trixie's rental. It has Alberta plates because she rented it after she got here. I think she came to Banff by bus."

"From Nebraska?" Judith said.

Niall shook his head. "She mentioned Winnipeg. I guess that's not all that far from Nebraska, is it?"

Judith wondered if Canadians were as vague about

geography as Americans. "Both places are sort of in the middle," she said. "Should we settle up with our bill now?"

Niall told them they could. After the paperwork was finished and the cousins prayed that their credit-card charges would be approved, they went up to Trixie's room. Judith knocked, but got no response.

"She's probably still asleep," she said, using the passkey.

"Who do you think drugged her?" Renie asked.

"Honestly? I can't imagine." Judith opened the door. And gasped.

There was no sign of Trixie—not in the bed, not in the room, not in the bathroom or the closet. Her clothes and other personal belongings were gone. Except for the rumpled bed and the soup container, it was as if Trixie O'Hara had never existed. Judith said as much.

Renie merely shook her head. "Maybe she didn't."

Chapter 24

Back in the Flynns' suite, the cousins sat down to conjecture. Judith started by recalling that they'd seen Trixie's wallet with the Nebraska driver's license. Yes, it could be phony. There were do-it-yourself Internet sites for creating a new identity.

"The problem," Judith said, "is why Trixie would do that. She doesn't strike me as the criminal type."

"Unless the ditz bit's a put-on," Renie remarked. "Gold diggers and scam artists often start young."

Judith ran a hand through her graying hair. "Maybe I'm too old for this bunch of craziness."

"No, you're not," Renie insisted with a shake of her head. "Let's keep to the latest weirdness. Why would Teddy Stokes be driving Trixie's rental car?"

Judith considered the question. "The only reason I can think of is that Trixie was in it."

Renie's eyes grew round. "In the trunk?"

"No. She may still have been asleep or at least groggy. Trixie may've been slouched down in the passenger seat. I barely glimpsed Teddy."

"But . . ." Renie paused. "The Other Woman?"

"That thought just crossed my mind," Judith said. "Trixie comes here to marry an old man. Let's assume it could be Codger. He dies. Teddy somehow meets Trixie. Remember, someone mentioned seeing her at the Stokes encampment. He likes what he sees, he's tired of Martha Lou, he may be fed up with raising corn. Am I making sense?"

"As much as anything around here does," Renie replied. "But leaving the farm would mean leaving Codger's inheritance. Or would it? Adela left the farm ages ago, so I'm assuming Corny and his wife would inherit everything. They're in their fifties, which means it could be a long wait for them to be out of the picture, especially given Codger's longevity."

"But his wives didn't live long," Judith noted. "Nobody can predict that sort of thing."

"True. Look at your own father. He died in his forties."

Judith stood up. "Let's get out of here. We can load up the car and have an early lunch while we go through the AAA tour books and try to find some lodgings."

"Lunch is always a good idea," Renie said. "We can do it up right at one of the restaurants in the Banff Springs Hotel."

Judith winced. "I'm getting kind of low on money."

Renie grinned. "Who isn't? I'm down to eight bucks. American, of course, since we never changed our money. Let's go out in style. We can card it."

Having made their farewells to Niall and Jenny, the cousins went directly to the parking area. The Odells were just getting into their Buick, but Adela paused to say hello. Judith asked if they were checking out.

"No, unfortunately," Adela replied. "We planned to, but Corny called to say they had another crisis. We're going to get some expensive Canadian gas for the car first in case we can make our getaway later today."

For fear of sounding too nosy, Judith hesitated. But she decided it wasn't fair not to let the Odells know that the motel was booked for the night. "We have to find another place to stay," she added.

Adela made a face. "Darn! It's too bad we didn't keep the twins' room. But we'd already paid for it before we found out they wanted to go home. Our own reservation is open-ended."

"Lucky you," Judith said with a rueful little smile. "What's the Stokes crisis this time?"

"I didn't ask," Adela responded. "We'll find out when we get there. By the way, thanks for being so understanding about all the horrors. I'm sorry you got mixed up with our loony relatives. Now you know why I stayed away from Big Stove for so long."

Renie waved a dismissive hand. "No problem. We've got some loonies of our own. Most families do."

"I suppose," Adela murmured. "Maybe mine aren't as crazy as they act. Good luck finding another room."

"Thanks," Judith said. "Oh—by the way, did the crisis involve Ada?"

Adela looked curious. "You mean about her going missing? That's old news."

Judith shook her head. "She spent part of the night in your car. Ada wanted to talk to you."

Adela gasped and Norm scowled. "What about?" he asked. "That girl doesn't make any sense."

Judith wasn't sure she should blow Ada's cover, but Renie had no such qualms. "Ada's probably the smartest one of the bunch. Present company excepted, of course," she added with a wry expression.

Norm looked flabbergasted. "What the hell are you talking about?"

Renie shrugged. "Ask Ada."

"We sure as hell will," he bellowed, grabbing his wife's arm. "Let's go!"

The Odells hustled themselves into their car and roared out of the parking lot.

"I'd kind of like to be there when Ada reveals all," Renie said as she and Judith got into the SUV.

"So would I," Judith agreed, "but it *is* a private family moment."

Renie laughed. "You want to hide behind the VW bus and listen in?"

Judith didn't answer right away. "No. But I'm wondering what Adela meant when she referred to how her family acts. Especially since Ada told me they like to pretend all sorts of weird things. So how much of what's going on with that crew *is* an act, besides Ada?"

"A corpse being sent on a bier down the Bow River seems fairly theatrical to me," Renie said as they drove away from the motel. "Blame it all on Marilyn Monroe. She dazzled a lot of people besides Codger."

Again, Judith was briefly silent. "That white dress and blond wig in Trixie's closet. Did Trixie intend to dress up as Marilyn to make sure the old coot would marry her?"

"I wouldn't put anything past anyone involved in this caper," Renie declared. "We don't even know if Codger existed. At least here in Banff."

Judith nodded vaguely. "I wonder how the RCMP is coming along with their investigation."

"What's to investigate?" Renie retorted. "They can't prove Codger didn't die a natural death—even if he did exist. Heck, they can't even prove Codger is Codger."

"True." Judith braked for a teenager who had swerved in front of them on his bicycle. "If the old guy really was stabbed in the back, he would've bled out where I could see it. Maybe we should stop at RCMP headquarters on the way back from lunch."

"You think they can put us up for the night?"

"Hardly," Judith replied as they drove through the hotel's porte cochere. "But I'd like to hear Brewster's take on the Stokes stunt with the alleged Codger."

After a parking valet hurried to meet them, they entered the Banff Springs Hotel's handsome two-story lobby. To Judith's surprise, Renie headed for the front desk.

"What are you doing?" Judith asked her cousin, who was waiting for the desk clerks to finish dealing with departing guests.

"You'll see," Renie whispered. "You've taught me a lot about lying over the years."

"I never lie," Judith whispered back. "I only tell fibs for a good cause . . ." She had to stop. One of the desk clerks had turned to Renie.

"I've just arrived in town," she said, fanning her face with her hand. "There's been a family tragedy here and I've no place to stay. Is it possible you have a vacant room at least for one night?"

The clerk, who was a fair-haired young man with a ruddy face, exhibited concern. "A death?" He saw Renie nod solemnly. "I'm sorry. Yes, we always keep at least one room available for . . . emergencies." His eyes flickered over Judith. "Is it just for you or . . . ?" He raised his eyebrows.

"That's my maid," Renie said with a vague gesture. "I couldn't cope without her. She's so good at scrubbing."

"Of course." He handed Renie a form. "Your luggage?" he asked when she was done.

"The valet may've already parked my SUV. I'll have someone fetch my bags later. Now I'd like to lie down for a bit. Grief is so stressful."

"I understand," the desk clerk said in a tone that would have done an undertaker proud.

Judith had backed off a bit. "Well? I don't know whether to congratulate you or kick you. What made you think they'd have a room in reserve?"

"High-end hotels always do," Renie replied as they headed for the elevators. "Hey, if your mother ever dies, you could use the toolshed as your emergency reserve room."

"Ha! Mother's so ornery she'd come back to haunt it. Now we'll have to collect our luggage from the parking lot after we have lunch. Don't you dare suggest that your maid can do that for you. And," Judith went on as the elevator door opened, "how are we going to pay for this?"

"Good question," Renie muttered. "Why don't we let our goofy husbands figure that out when they show up tomorrow to collect us?"

"That's the best idea you've had since you lied to the desk clerk," Judith responded as they got out of the elevator on the third floor.

Renie checked the key's room number. "This way," she said, turning left. "I only got one key because you don't need one. You're the maid and she picks locks. We can go back to get our luggage after we eat lunch. I'm famished."

As they expected, the room was tastefully furnished with a view of the mountains. There were two beds, both standard size.

"Good," Renie said. "We won't have to fight over the covers. You always need too many blankets. Let's head for the . . ." She paused to study a brochure on the desk next to the window. "How about the Rundle Lounge? We know their food is really good."

"Fine with me," Judith agreed.

By the time they reached the lounge, it was still a

few minutes before noon. There was no lineup though half of the tables were already occupied.

"Feels like home," Renie said after they'd been seated in white high-backed chairs. "This lounge is big. Take a look outside to admire the view in daylight."

Judith had already seen the balcony that went around the big room. Straight ahead, she saw a window in an archway and the green grounds outside. "Lovely. It's a shame we couldn't have stayed here as we planned in the first place. But it turned out just as well, since the extra days would've put us in the poor house."

"I think I'm already there." Renie perused the menu. "Ah! Smoked salmon sandwich, fries, and a salad. Sounds good to me. I can never eat enough smoked salmon."

"I'm going old school," Judith said. "A beef burger with Gouda on a brioche."

"That sounds more like nouveau French Canadian to me. And it definitely calls for a glass of beer."

"You don't like beer," Judith reminded her cousin. "But I might do that."

"Go ahead." Renie checked the menu. "Why not? How can I resist a Grizzly Paw Powder Hound Blonde ale?"

Judith shuddered. "I can. Okay, I'll stick to Moose-head ale. It should be tamer than your Grizzly."

After giving their orders to a bubbly redhead named Fay who wore braces on her teeth, Judith noticed that the lounge was beginning to fill up. An elderly man was being seated at the table next to them. She wondered if he was waiting for his wife. Apparently, his server wondered the same thing. But the man shook his head and the unneeded place setting was removed.

Judith smiled wryly. "I never mind seeing an old woman—a lot older than we are—sitting alone as much as I do an old man. That's unfair, I suppose."

"Not if she's like Aunt Gert," Renie said. "But you're right—women cope better than men when they're on their own. Even my worrywart mother does quite well. She's always having people stop by to chat and have tea."

"I wonder if we should ask him to join us," Judith said softly. "I suppose that would be cheeky."

"For all you know, his wife's out playing golf."

"That's possible," Judith allowed. "Or he may be visiting here with his children and grandchildren, who are doing something that didn't appeal to him."

Their orders arrived. Judith couldn't resist asking Fay about the elderly man.

"A lovely old fellow," she replied softly with a dimpled smile. "He's been staying here for a week. He's a Yank, but he doesn't seem to know anyone here. He never leaves the hotel grounds. I guess he just enjoys the scenery."

"That's nice," Judith said. "I mean, it really is. Maybe this was a favorite vacation place for his family."

Fay nodded. "We get a lot of return visitors, even from abroad. Three, four generations, I'm told. Enjoy your meal."

Renie took a sip of her beer. "This Grizzly Paw's not bad. Try your Elkhead."

"It's *Moosehead*," Judith declared. "I've had it before. I think they sell it at Falstaff's Grocery on the hill."

"Probably." Renie darted a glance at the elderly man. "He's not having beer, but wine instead. Classy kind of guy. I'll bet he never stranded his wife while he took extra days to go fishing and she was forced to spend all of her money."

"You want to put a move on him?" Judith asked wryly.

"No thanks," Renie replied, enthusiastically attacking her smoked salmon sandwich. "Ahmtufundobll."

Judith translated that mouthful to mean that she loved her husband. Then she looked at the old guy sitting at the next table. He was eating slowly, savoring every bite. She hoped that if he'd had a wife, she'd been good to him.

Judith didn't know the half of it.

Chapter 25

After Renie's Visa card was approved, they headed for RCMP headquarters. Sergeant Brewster greeted them with a wary smile.

"I hope you don't have a crime to report," he said.

Judith decided to approach the Mountie obliquely. "We wondered what's going on with the Stokes investigation."

Brewster's smile disappeared. "We're not sure that it's an actual investigation. The only reason they're still here is because of some technicalities that are being sorted out by Inspector Colbert in Calgary."

"Technicalities?" Renie echoed. "Such as what?"

Brewster's tan face seemed to darken. "It's complicated. They arrived late at night to set up their encampment. We didn't know about it until last Thursday afternoon. That vacant strip of land belongs to George Barnes, who owns the motel you've been staying in. He plans to develop the site—maybe a pool or tennis courts. We contacted him and he stopped by to see what was going on. After speaking to Cornelius Stokes, Mr. Barnes decided there was no reason they couldn't stay for a few days as long as they didn't cause trouble."

"But they did," Judith declared. "Even if Codger Stokes wasn't stabbed to death, you and your other officers had to investigate what appeared to be a possible homicide."

Brewster grimaced. "True. Colbert called on Mr. Barnes, but he told the inspector that homicide or natural causes, the family's loss was still hard to cope with. They should take time to mourn, eh?"

"*Mourn?*" Renie practically shrieked. "Frankly, they seemed almost cavalier. Who did they fool with their sad-sack act?"

"Mr. Barnes," Brewster replied doggedly. "I told you that already."

Judith felt she'd better speak up before Renie blew a gasket. "I assume money didn't pass hands."

Brewster shrugged. "That would be between the Stokes family and Barnes. It's not a crime to rent your own land."

Judith suppressed a sigh. "Right. But there's something else I should mention. I don't want to be an alarmist, but Trixie O'Hara—the motel maid—disappeared from her room this morning. She's been quite ill, as you may know. Has anyone notified you that she's missing?"

"No." Brewster uttered the word without any expression. "Maybe she didn't feel up to working."

"She was unwell when we saw her last night," Judith said. "It's possible that she's been abducted by one of the Stokes family members. We saw Teddy Stokes drive off in a rush earlier today and Trixie may have been with him."

Brewster sighed heavily. "Why didn't you report this earlier?"

"We should have. Except . . ." Judith bit her lip. She didn't want to expose the skein of thought that was unraveling in her head. "Trixie has an odd history in Banff, especially for somebody who hasn't been here very long. I don't want to butt in, though it wouldn't hurt to see if she's at the campsite. My cousin and I found her the other day passed out in the family's VW bus."

"I'll send someone over there," the sergeant said in a resigned voice. "Is there anything else I ought to know?"

There probably was, Judith thought, but she held

back. "Not really, but we figured we should stop by now before we leave town."

"You're heading home?" Brewster sounded hopeful.

"Tomorrow morning," Judith said. "Thanks for keeping my cousin and me stay apprised of what's been going on with the case."

Brewster's smile seemed sincere. "Our pleasure. It's rare to have a famous amateur detective helping us."

Judith suspected the Mountie might be kidding. But at least he hadn't called her FATSO.

Banff's downtown was still buzzing with tourist traffic, both vehicular and pedestrian. Judith counted license plates from six different Canadian provinces, eight U.S. states, and one from Costa Rica.

Renie wasn't intrigued by the sightings. "Why," she asked in a plaintive tone, "do I sense that we're going to make yet another call on the wretched Stokes folks? Am I supposed to claim we're still working on the *Cornucopia* article?"

"Good idea," Judith said, brightening. "We'll tell them it's an in-depth series."

"More like an in-death series," Renie muttered glumly.

"Okay, so I'm concerned about Trixie." Judith braked for a family of five at a crosswalk.

"Maybe you ought to give Brewster time to check

out the Stokes menagerie," Renie suggested. "I got the impression he's a bit overwhelmed by your sleuthing."

"Nonsense!" Judith snapped. "He's a typical man and he doesn't like it when a woman—and in this case, an older tourist from across the border—gets involved with his job." She stopped again, this time at an arterial. "Fine, we'll hold off checking out the current suspects."

Instead of continuing to the Stokes campsite, Judith turned the SUV around the corner and drove in the opposite direction. Renie kept quiet. She sensed where her cousin was going.

"The old guy, right?"

"Yes, yes," Judith replied impatiently. "I'm curious. I'm remembering what Doris told me about her family going to California and how Grandpa took off. I have a feeling that he can tell us something we should know."

Renie nodded. "I guessed as much."

"I thought you might," Judith said in a more normal tone of voice. "We've always been good at reading each other's mind. Like sisters. Maybe better than a lot of sisters."

"True." Renie stared at the rugged mountain crags that surrounded the town. "Oddly enough, I'm going to miss this place, despite going broke. It's such spectacular scenery. A lot more primitive than our part of the world."

Judith didn't argue. Instead of heading for the hotel entrance's porte cochere, she turned in the direction of the Banff Springs golf course. "I suspect parking's free here. It better be. I'm tired of tipping people."

After they got out of the SUV, the cousins looked in every direction for the elderly man they'd seen in the Rundle Lounge. There was no sign of him.

"The old guy should be around here somewhere," Judith muttered, shielding her eyes from the sun. "He didn't look as if he could walk very far."

Renie had turned to look at the hotel. "I see him coming out of the Banff Springs' rear entrance. He's heading this way. Slowly. Why don't we go get a snack while we wait for him to get here?"

"Not funny," Judith said, though she smiled. "We could offer him a ride."

"For twenty yards? He may be feeble, but he's not nuts." Renie had turned back to face her cousin. "Are we going to stay here or offer him a joyride?"

"I hadn't thought of that," Judith replied. "But why not? He must get bored sitting around the hotel all day."

Renie grimaced. "So we get busted for elder-napping?"

"We're too old for that charge to apply. Harassment,

maybe." Judith considered her approach to their prey. "Who could he remind us of that we actually know?"

"He's as old as your mother. Why not ask if he'd like to date her?"

Judith shot Renie a dark look. "I've been feeling sorry for him being all alone, but I've no intention of ruining the rest of his life."

"Good point," Renie murmured as the old man came within ten feet of them.

"Hello," Judith all but shouted. "Lovely day, isn't it?"

The oldster hesitated and narrowed his gray eyes at the cousins. "I may be up in years, but I'm not deaf. Who are you?"

"Tourists," Judith replied in a normal tone. "And you?"

"The name's Smith," he answered, stopping a couple of feet away from them. "John Smith. Are you two planning on staying anonymous?"

Judith kept smiling. "No. This is my cousin Mrs. Jones, and I'm—"

He interrupted her. "Don't kid a kidder. You two got *real* names?"

"That *is* her real name," Judith replied. "I'm Mrs. Flynn." She turned to Renie. "Show him your driver's license, coz."

John Smith waved a gnarled hand. "Never mind,

never mind. It doesn't matter." He stumbled slightly, but managed to circumvent the cousins and went on his cautious way.

"Gosh," Renie said in feigned shock, "you just flunked warm and friendly camaraderie with a stranger. Isn't that a first?"

"Hardly." Judith turned just enough to watch John Smith's slow progress toward the golf course. "I suspect he may keep going as long as we're still here. Let's go back into the hotel."

"I thought we were going to bid farewell to the Stokes zoo," Renie said as they headed for the rear entrance.

"We are," Judith replied, opening the door. "I want to find out if John Smith registered as . . . John Smith."

It took over five minutes before anyone behind the front desk was free. Finally, a faintly harried-looking young woman with short ash-blond hair offered her best effort of a smile and asked if she could help the cousins.

"Yes, thank you," Judith replied, noting that the desk clerk's name tag identified her as Caitlin. "Mrs. Jones and I are staying here tonight. We work for a magazine and have been interviewing guests in Banff. A few moments ago we talked to an older man who's staying here. He stated that his name is John

Smith. We need to verify that, as it struck us as possibly not his real name. Would you mind checking your registry?"

Caitlin hesitated, but acquiesced. It didn't take long. "Yes," she said, and then lowered her voice. "That's the name he gave us. He paid cash in advance, so we had no reason to question if that was his real name. We have celebrities who come here under false names, of course."

"Yes." Judith nodded and smiled. "I suppose he could be one of them. That is, being so elderly, he might not be recognized by his former fans. Did he say where he lived?"

"He did." Caitlin uttered a small, discreet laugh. "It was a funny-sounding place in the States." She paused, still amused. "Big Stove, Nebraska."

Bingo! Judith managed to keep a straight face. "Very unusual. Our magazine's readers have probably never heard of it. Thank you, Caitlin."

As they went back to the rear entrance and got into the SUV, Renie nudged Judith. "*Cornucopia*'s readers would love to hear about Big Stove. Have you forgotten that its audience is made up of people in the sweet and industrial corn business?"

"I'd forgotten it was a magazine until I just told that fib," Judith admitted.

"As its editor, I find that disheartening. Any ideas about where we should have our last dinner in Banff?"

"Good grief!" Judith cried. "It's not even four o'clock. Remind me again around six."

"Are we really having another chin-wag with the Stokeses?"

"Yes." Judith was driving the route that would, in fact, take them back to the far end of the encampment. "Call me crazy, but if the corpse wasn't Codger, why did they go to so much trouble with the bier?"

"Did they?" Renie's question was artless.

Judith didn't say anything while they waited for two women and at least a dozen preschool children to cross the street. "Day care, I bet," she said softly before speaking in her normal voice. "You're right. We don't know that really happened. We only know the old guy was dead. But how he got that way and who he really was is another matter."

"But," Renie said resignedly, "we're going to find out."

"I hope so," Judith replied with a tinge of pessimism. "But we only have until tomorrow morning to do it. The clock is ticking."

She hoped that her brain was, too.

Chapter 26

As the cousins approached the campsite from the street, Judith could see an RCMP cruiser parked at the curb. "Now what?" she muttered. "Can you spot Brewster anywhere?"

"Not with all that shrubbery," Renie replied. "You can pull in behind the cop car where it says No Parking."

"The last thing I need is a ticket. I'll make a U-turn up ahead and park across the street. If Brewster—or another Mountie—is with the Stokes crew, I probably won't get busted."

After parking the SUV, the cousins jaywalked across the street. Judith's rationale was that there were no other cops in sight and Brewster was preoccupied with the Stokes family at the campsite.

They spotted Brewster, but he was accompanied by Constable MacRae. They were directing their attention to what appeared to be the entire Stokes family, including the Odells.

"Damn!" Judith said softly as they stood by the shrubbery. "Can you hear what they're saying?"

Renie shook her head. "If we hid in these shrubs, maybe we could."

"The shrubs aren't tall enough," Judith said. "I can't really bend down with my phony hip. We'll just have to barge right in."

Renie emitted a low groan but didn't argue.

MacRae was the first to notice the cousins. His ruddy face was puzzled as he stepped away to confront them. "Pardon me, but this is an official investigation. I have to ask you to leave the area."

Judith was stymied. Apparently, Brewster hadn't informed his fellow officer of the cousins' sleuthing. Renie, however, smiled and shook her finger at him. "Now, now, Constable MacRae," she said in an unusually pleasant voice, "I don't think your superior would like that." She moved closer to the Mountie and whispered in his ear.

MacRae jumped a bit. "Seriously?" He stared at Judith and his face turned almost crimson. "I'm sorry,

I've been off for the last few days. I had no idea. Oh my!" He goggled at Judith. "Is it true there's a FASTO comic book about you?"

"Not yet released for publication," Judith replied with a kindly smile, despite being horrified at the mere idea. "Maybe after the first of the year. Would you mind telling us what's going on here?"

But Brewster had seen the cousins and he gestured at them. Whatever he'd been saying to the Stokes family had left them with a variety of reactions: Pa's stoicism, Ma's irritation, Teddy's sheepishness, Martha Lou's consternation, Ada's indignation, and the Odells' mutual dismay. Only Trixie seemed oddly at ease. But then Judith realized she wasn't part of the family. Or was she?

MacRae regained his aplomb. "It's a very queer case. I'll let Sergeant Brewster explain it to you."

But his fellow officer was reluctant. "Before I can tell you anything, I have to contact Inspector Colbert." Brewster removed his hat and ran a hand through his thick hair. "It's a confounding situation."

"Yes," Judith agreed. "Shall we join you at the office in half an hour?"

Brewster hesitated. "I suppose you could. I have to find out what the inspector thinks, eh?" He put his hat back on and motioned for MacRae to follow him away from the encampment.

"Our turn," Judith said under her breath as she moved toward the now-glum family gathered at the picnic table. She considered speaking first to Pa, but decided Ada was a better choice. "What did your family tell the Mounties?"

Ada's eyes flashed at her kinfolk. "The truth."

"I thought so." Judith saw what looked like alarm in Ada's eyes. "Don't worry, I won't press you. I'll let Brewster tell me."

"Maybe he won't," Ada said.

Judith shrugged. "It doesn't matter." She smiled kindly at the young woman. "I already know."

Renie stalked off, apparently heading for the SUV. Judith knew she was irked about not confiding in her cousin that she'd come to understand what was going on with the case, but it had only been in the last hour that everything had started to come together. And there were still some gaps.

Still, Judith hesitated. Maybe she should first talk to Ma and Pa. *No,* she thought, *they still won't tell me the truth.* She headed for the shrubbery.

Renie was sitting in the passenger seat looking miffed. "Well?" she said when Judith slid into the SUV.

"I wasn't sure until now," Judith replied, only fibbing by three-quarters of an hour, but still feeling remorse. She'd almost always been candid with her cousin. "Okay, so it was a little longer, but not by much. It was John Smith who enlightened me."

Renie stared. "John Smith? How?"

"Because I think he's the real Codger."

"Well." Renie thought about it for a moment or two. "I admit I had to wonder. But why stick around?"

"That's why we're going back to see Brewster. I have a feeling only he can tell us who Codger—the dead one—really is."

Renie decided not to query her cousin further. She sensed when the sleuthing wheels were turning in Judith's brain. Before Judith could turn the ignition key, a female voice called to them. A sheepish-looking Ada was hurrying to the SUV.

"I want to apologize," she said, leaning into the open window on the driver's side. "I never wanted any part of this charade. Neither did Dela and Norm. I'm not going to try to explain why Ma and Pa did this and the rest of them went along with it, because it makes no difference now that they've been found out. Anyway, I'm sorry if they caused you any problems."

"I suppose we could guess," Judith said.

Ada made a dismissive gesture. "Don't bother. It's over. At least I hope so. Once we get back to Big Stove,

I hope we can forget any of this happened." She whirled around and rushed back through the shrubbery.

Renie gave Judith a quirky look. "Okay, FASTO, tell me this—why was Trixie looking so pleased with herself?"

"Because," Judith replied in an ironic tone, "she got what she came for, even if it wasn't what she expected. She's found a man with money."

Renie was faintly aghast. "Teddy?"

"It's not Codger," Judith replied. "I'm calling Doris Draper. I think she can answer my question."

Renie noted the time on the SUV's clock: 4:25. "Won't she be at work?"

"I'll leave a message she can't refuse to answer," Judith said, tapping in the number. As expected, the call went to voice mail. "Judith McMonigle here. We met the elder Mr. Stokes. Why did you tell me the family was going to California? Please call me and explain that or my editor won't include your family's farm in the magazine article. Thank you for your cooperation."

"Wow," Renie said softly. "That was a really big fib. I might lose my editor's job at *Cornucopia*."

Judith smiled. "I think your job is safe since . . ." She paused as a pickup truck pulled up alongside of them and stopped. "Now what? I can't pull out."

"It's Mr. Barnes," Renie said, twisting in the seat to get a better view. "He's getting out of the truck. Maybe he doesn't think we really know how to drive."

Judith saw him coming to her side of the SUV and reluctantly rolled down the window. "Yes?" she said as he wedged his burly body between the two vehicles.

"Where's my damned maid?" he shouted. "Trixie O'Hara's disappeared! I'm told you two were the last ones to see her at the motel."

"We probably were," Judith replied calmly. "She's been ill, you know. We left her sleeping last night."

Barnes's scowl deepened. "The room's empty. I even checked the bathroom. Everything's cleared out. I hear you two spent quite a bit of time with her. She'd already been in the hospital a day or so. I can't keep an employee who either gets sick or runs away. Come on, you must have some idea where she went."

Judith debated whether to tell him the truth or fib. She decided on something in between. "Why don't you ask those people who are camping on the property beyond the motel?"

"That crowd? Pah!" He made a disparaging gesture. "I'd rather talk to a bunch of donkeys. And somebody should tell that freckle-faced broad to stay way from my motel!"

Judith assumed he meant Martha Lou. "Your motel, your call," she said. "But they're close enough to the motel that they may've seen Trixie leave."

Barnes rubbed the side of his bald head. "Well . . . maybe I'll give it a shot." He turned away and went back to the pickup.

Renie laughed. "I'd almost like to be there when he confronts the Stokes folks. But that's probably a bad idea. Where to now?"

Judith didn't respond right away. Her brain was coping with a sudden insight. "I wonder if Martha Lou is responsible for the meandering money. It sounds like the kind of weird thing she might do."

"Malicious mischief," Renie murmured. "At least she didn't steal it."

"True." But Judith's brain was moving in a different direction. "I hate to do it, but we have to talk to Sergeant Brewster about a more pressing matter."

At a little after four thirty, the rush hour hadn't yet started. Judith pulled in behind the police station. They found Brewster and MacRae behind the counter, though the younger Mountie was on the phone. Judith approached the senior officer with a deferential expression. Brewster, in turn, looked on guard. "Yes?" he said after a moment's hesitation.

"There's something I have to know before we head

home," Judith began, and took a deep breath. "Who was the dead man called Codger?"

Brewster raised his hands in a helpless gesture. "We don't know. What little DNA we could get from the tent turned out to be a John Doe."

Judith nodded. "That's what I thought. But the family insists otherwise, right?"

Briefly, Brewster avoided her eyes. "Yes."

Judith nodded again. "Would you think I was out of line if I suggested the man they sent down the river may have been dead before they came to Banff?"

The sergeant looked jarred. So did MacRae, who had gotten off the phone. "Pardon?" said Brewster.

"You never saw the body." Judith paused. "Of course, the poor old man couldn't be identified as anybody but a John Doe. I doubt that the Stokeses knew who he was."

Brewster grimaced. "You mean . . . the ridiculous plan to send . . . the body down the river was a hoax?"

Judith shook her head. "No. The body may eventually be found along the river or else it washed out to sea. The whole sorry idea was a cover-up for something else, but I'm not exactly sure what. I'm waiting for a phone call from Big Stove."

"I see." But Brewster didn't really look satisfied. "You will let me know if you find out, eh?"

"I promise," Judith replied with a smile, then turned around and realized that Renie wasn't anywhere in sight. Apparently, her cousin hadn't followed her inside the RCMP headquarters. Judith hurried out the back way to the parking lot.

"Hi," Renie greeted her from where she was standing next to the SUV. "Are you done solving the case for the Mounties?"

Judith expelled a sigh. "Are you mad at me?"

"No." Renie laughed. "I knew what you were going to tell them. Unlike you, I *can* take a break from sleuthing."

Relieved, Judith opened the door on the driver's side. She'd barely slipped behind the wheel when her cell phone rang. "Now what?" she murmured. "Hello?"

The female voice was faint. "Doris?" Judith said.

"Mrs. McMonigle?" The volume rose slightly at the other end of the line. "It's me, Doris. You called?"

"I did," Judith said before continuing in a brisk, businesslike voice: "At *Cornucopia,* we strive for accuracy and honesty." She ignored Renie, who was rolling her eyes. "You told me that your relatives were going to California. Was that a lie?"

A sharp intake of breath was heard at the other end of the line. "No. That is, they told me they were going to Disneyland. But I found out it wasn't true. Instead, they went to Canada."

Judith exchanged glances with Renie, who was leaning in to hear the conversation. "To Banff in Alberta?"

"Yes." Doris's sigh was audible. "Then . . ." She couldn't seem to continue. "Grandpa Stokes disappeared somewhere outside of Spearfish, South Dakota. They looked all over for him, but he'd . . . just . . . disappeared." Doris began to sniffle and snuffle.

"I gather the family gave up trying to find him?" Judith asked after a pause to let Doris get herself under control.

"Umm . . ." Doris cleared her throat. "Yes. It started to get dark. They thought they were near the Badlands. Cornelius—my uncle—felt that area might be dangerous and if Grandpa—Codger—had wandered off there, they'd never find him. Instead, they kept going north. I guess they thought Grandpa—Codger—would've liked that. He'd talked about a river he wanted to see up there."

Judith bit her lip and looked at Renie, who shook her head in a disdainful way. "You shouldn't give up on your grandfather," Judith said. "He may've wanted to do some exploring on his own. Given his nickname, I suspect he's a strong-minded old guy."

"Well . . . that's true," Doris replied. "Anything's

possible, I guess. Thanks for the encouraging words. I'll tell my husband that when he gets home."

After exchanging good-byes, Judith put a hand on her forehead. "Whew! Doris bought it. I wonder if Codger will go home after the rest of the family does."

Renie shrugged. "I wouldn't. He'd be better off to stay here and apply for Canadian citizenship."

"He should live so long."

"He's working on it," Renie noted. "My money's on him."

"Well . . ." Judith frowned. "Money. This whole caper must be about money."

"Aunt Ellen told you that most big corn farmers are rich."

"Right," Judith agreed, "but that doesn't mean their children and grandchildren are, too. The Stokeses live together on the farm. They're provided for, but that doesn't mean any of them have money of their own."

"A tight rein," Renie murmured. "So what's your latest zany plan?"

Judith sighed. "I don't have one. But we can't sit here in the RCMP parking lot." She paused. "Maybe a sneak attack would work."

Renie held her head. "Good grief. So we can get busted by Brewster for assault?"

"We need an accomplice," Judith said, backing the

SUV out of its parking place. "Someone Trixie trusts. Jenny or Niall or . . ." She paused, braking for a group of young people who were dressed in Bavarian costumes.

"A band?" Renie suggested.

Judith was lost in thought. "What?"

"Never mind. Just keep plotting."

"I don't like going back to the motel," Judith said. "I'd rather not run into Mr. Barnes. It's after five. I wonder who's on duty. I'll call and find out. No, I've got to get out of this parking lot first. You call."

Renie groaned. "I get stuck with all the dog work." But she dug out the cell from her purse. "What's the number?"

"Look at your bill," Judith said, pulling into traffic behind a camper with a Texas license plate.

Renie rummaged some more in her giant purse and found the receipt, then tapped in the number. A breathless Jenny answered.

"Hi," Renie said in an unusually chipper tone. "Former guest Serena Jones here. Are you coming off duty, by any chance?"

"I am," Jenny replied, sounding wary. "Is there something I can do for you?"

"It's Mrs. Flynn who needs you," Renie said. "Could you meet us behind the motel in five minutes?"

"Well . . . I guess I could. Is something wrong?"

"Not exactly," Renie said with an ironic glance at Judith. "My cousin will tell you when we get there. We're just leaving RCMP headquarters. See you."

Judith grimaced. "Did you have to say that about the cops?"

"Why not? At least Jenny knows we haven't been busted. Look out for the skateboarder."

The skateboarder was avoided. Renie glanced up at the two gondola cars above the town. One was going up and the other was coming down. "Hey," she said, "why don't we top off our visit with a gondola ride before we have dinner?"

"You can't afford it and neither can I," Judith shot back as she turned off Lynx Street. "I'm getting low on funds, too. Besides, you've forgotten how I got sick and threw up on the Ferris wheel at Playland. Dad had to make them stop the ride so he could haul me off."

Renie looked thoughtful. "Hmm. How come he didn't ask me to go along?"

"You were probably already sick," Judith responded. "You had even more allergies than I did, especially to food. I never missed as much school as you . . ." She paused as they approached the motel. "There's Mr. Barnes pulling out from the parking lot. Good, we won't have to run into him again."

"Too bad you can't run over him," Renie remarked. "He's probably going to another one of the motels he owns."

"Maybe Barnes is checking out the Stokes gang," Judith said. "I wonder if he charged them to park on his property. I wouldn't put it past him."

"He should charge them. They can afford it." Renie gazed up at the mountains looming above them. "Am I looking up at Mount Revelstoke or Mount Eisenhower?"

"How do I know?" Judith shot back. "I'm lucky I can identify some of the mountains at home."

They'd reached the motel. Judith drove around to the rear entrance, but didn't pull into a parking place. Jenny was pacing back and forth on the walkway when she recognized the SUV and came over to the driver's side. Judith rolled down the window.

"I'll make this quick," she said. "How well do you know Trixie?"

Jenny frowned. "Not all that well. She only started work here a little over a week ago and then she got sick. Why do you ask?"

"Because she may be in danger," Judith replied. "That Stokes bunch at the camp behind the motel made off with her. Probably twice, in fact. Did she ever mention them to you?"

"Well . . . not exactly," Jenny said. "Aren't the Odells related to the campers?"

Judith nodded. "Mrs. Odell is. But I think Mr. and Mrs. Odell are decent people. Did they ever mention an old man who's staying at the Banff Springs Hotel?"

"Not to me," Jenny replied. "I did overhear them talking about her crazy relatives, though. Mrs. Odell sounded as if they were trying to scam somebody. But I don't know who."

"What about Mr. Barnes?" Judith shielded her eyes from the sun that was shining through the windshield. "Did he say anything about the Stokes family?"

Jenny shook her head. "Niall did tell me that Mr. Barnes went to see them, though. They'd set themselves up on his property."

"Did he insist they pay him?"

"I don't know. Really." Jenny's expression was apologetic. "He might have. I guess he's entitled to it, since he owns the land, eh?"

"Right." Judith smiled. "You'll be heading back to Vancouver soon. Good luck with your studies."

"Thanks." Jenny made a face. "I was promised a bonus from Mr. Barnes, but Niall says it won't happen. He insists Barnes is the original Scrooge, living in one of his other motels, the Banff Springs Edelweiss."

Renie had been quiet long enough. "How does Mrs. Barnes feel about living in a motel?"

"There is no Mrs. Barnes," Jenny replied. "He lives with his sister, who's also his accountant. She's as greedy as he is when it comes to money." Jenny took a quick look around her. "I should go. Some new arrivals need my parking space. Have a safe trip home." She hurried off to her car.

"Well," Judith said with a wry expression. "Now that I think about it, when we saw them at the restaurant, Ms. Barnes looked as unpleasant as he does. It must run in the family."

"Speaking of restaurants," Renie said, "now that you flunked getting Jenny to be your spy, why—"

"I merely wanted to get her take on Trixie," Judith interrupted. "She didn't seem to have one."

"Don't fib to me," Renie retorted. "You also wanted her to snoop around the Stokes folks. She'd probably say no. I'll say the same if you suggest it to me, okay?"

Judith knew when she couldn't push her cousin too hard. "Okay, I won't. Yes, we should have dinner. It's early enough that we can probably get seated at a place that doesn't cost an arm and a leg."

Renie leaned back in the seat. "That was easy." *Too easy,* she thought, and wondered what Judith had on her always curious mind.

Chapter 27

Judith found a parking place a few doors from Melissa's Missteak, a restaurant Renie had noticed in her guidebook. Somewhat to Judith's dismay, it was also on Lynx Street and thus not that far from the police station.

"And you wanted to get away from sleuthing?" Judith said as they got out of the SUV. "Why not invite Brewster to join us?"

"He has a family," Renie said, all but skipping on the sidewalk. "You'll like this place. It's been around forever and the locals call it Mel's. It's got a second floor where the patrons can play darts."

"Let's hope they're not aiming them at other customers," Judith grumbled. "Slow down. You're going too fast."

"I'm excited," Renie said over her shoulder. "It's very popular and I don't want to wait in line. It's a good thing we're early."

Once inside, Judith was impressed by the old yet handsome interior of the Tudor-style brick building. There was no one waiting. In fact, the tables appeared to be not quite half occupied. She suspected that the locals preferred to dine later at Mel's.

After they were seated, Renie wagged a finger at her cousin. "No sleuthing allowed. We're done with solving mysteries. When we go back to the hotel, I'm going to pack, watch mindless TV, and make an early night of it. The husbands will probably show up at some ungodly hour like nine o'clock."

"Fine," Judith said, opening the menu and stifling a shriek. "This place is expensive," she declared. "You're broke and I can't afford to treat you. Are you insane?"

Renie shrugged. "No, but this is our last big meal in Banff. Stop fussing. I called and had the limit raised on my credit card. I'll pay for both our dinners. It's our last fling."

Judith sighed—and smiled. "You don't have to."

"I know." Renie paused, studying the menu. "But I want to. You've done most of the driving. It's payback time. Now let's talk about how we'll have to pretend we're utterly fascinated by the fishing adventures Bill and Joe have had without us."

The menu was extensive, so it took some time to decide what to order. Mel's featured Alberta beef. "It's our last chance," Judith declared. "I'm going for the ten-ounce rib-eye steak."

Renie slapped her menu on the table. "Me too. Along with the Caesar salad and a baked potato with topping."

As they savored their meals, the cousins managed to avoid the subject that was on their minds—or at least on Judith's. She couldn't help wondering if the Stokes family were still at their campsite or if they'd been greenlighted to leave. She worried about Trixie, despite the smile she'd last seen on the girl's face. Nor could she forget the old man at the Banff Springs Hotel.

Halfway through her apple pie with a cheddar cheese wedge and Renie's New York–style cheesecake, she had to unload, though she tried to keep her voice casual. "I suppose if the Stokes bunch are heading home, they won't leave until morning."

Renie shrugged. "Who knows with that crew? Do you want to be on the road with them?"

"They'd take a different route once they got on the Trans-Canada Highway." Judith's expression was apologetic. "Okay, we changed the subject. Are you happy now?" She saw Renie nod and keep on eating.

Renie shrugged. "Probably."

Judith shut up.

When they got back to the SUV, Judith resumed her place behind the wheel. "You're still going to make an early night of it?" she asked Renie.

"Yes. You know I can't function in the morning. I'm not going to have breakfast either. I'll wait for our mid-morning coffee stop. Bill will insist on doing that. If you want to eat, you can go without me."

"I won't do that," Judith said. "We can pick up doughnuts or something on the way back to the hotel."

"Good idea." Renie yawned. But she checked her guidebook and then the digital clock on the dashboard. It showed 6:55. "Most of the bakeries are closed, but the Good Earth Coffeehouse has pastries. It's on Banff Avenue between Moose and Elk."

"Animals or streets?" Judith asked.

"Streets." Renie yawned again.

Twenty minutes later, they were back in the hotel room with a half-dozen cinnamon rolls. Judith stood by the window, considering her options.

"I suppose I should get everything ready too," she

said, more to herself than to Renie, who was laying out her fold-over suitcase on the floor.

"What?" Renie asked. "You're talking into your socks."

"I ate too much," Judith confessed, settling into a cushy green-and-black-striped armchair. "I'm going to sit for a few minutes before I start packing."

"Go for it," Renie said. "Drat. I can't fit all my purchases into this thing."

"Hmm," Judith murmured. And the next thing she knew the room was almost dark and Renie was sound asleep in one of the two beds. She'd been awakened by the sound of a siren. Or maybe she'd been dreaming about a fire. Startled, she struggled to stand up and looked out the window. But she saw only the now-deserted golf course.

Peering at her watch, she noted that it was only nine thirty. Maybe she should pack, too. But when she cautiously walked over to the closet, she discovered it was empty. As her eyes adjusted to the semidarkness, Judith saw her own open suitcase already filled with her belongings. Obviously, Renie had done her packing for her except for a few toilet articles. She smiled at her sleeping cousin and went into the bathroom.

Looking in the mirror, Judith realized that her dark eyes looked wide-awake. *I'll never get to sleep after taking such a long nap,* she thought to herself. She put on some lipstick and decided to go down to the lobby. After all, people-watching was one of her favorite hobbies.

Finding a comfortable chair was no problem, though the handsome, two-tiered lobby was fairly busy. The other guests had an international flavor: women in saris, at least three Asian families who were speaking in unfamiliar tongues, a foursome with the two men in clerical garb and their wives in decorous frocks. Anglican, she decided. A little girl with curly blond hair broke away from her parents and had to be chased down before she left the premises. Judith smiled, thinking of Mike at that same adventuresome, heedless age.

Judith watched the family head for the elevators with the protesting little imp and her two older brothers. But after they disappeared, she turned away and saw a grim-looking Sergeant Brewster striding up to the front desk. He spoke briefly to one of the clerks before heading to what appeared to be an office door.

Curiosity got the best of Judith. She stood up from the chair and casually walked to the main entrance. Stepping outside, she again heard a siren wail in the distance. Brewster's cruiser was parked right at the bottom of the stairs. He'd exit the same way he came in, so Judith would wait for him. She wasn't leaving

Banff without hearing what had brought the RCMP to the hotel.

Judith didn't have to wait long. No more than five minutes passed before Brewster emerged, his stride longer and quicker as he headed down the stone steps.

"Sergeant!" Judith called after him. "What's happened?"

Brewster turned to look at her. He didn't seem pleased to see her. Or maybe he wasn't pleased by what he had to tell her. The sergeant came back to the stairs and lowered his voice. "You'll find out soon enough through the hotel grapevine, eh?" He saw her nod. "An elderly man was assaulted with some kind of weapon between the golf course and the hotel. A nine-iron, I'm guessing. He suffered a severe head wound and is on his way to the hospital. I'm sorry, I can't tell you his name."

Judith regarded Brewster with sad dark brown eyes. "That's all right. I can guess. It's John Smith."

The sergeant's eyebrows lifted. Then he shrugged. "Of course you'd know. You're FASTO, eh?" He hurried down to his cruiser.

Judith was torn. She couldn't go back to the room and just sit around. She certainly wouldn't be able to go to sleep for a while either. Pacing a bit, she finally went back through the hotel lobby and out to the parking lot. Maybe she'd brought her purse with her because deep down she knew she had to find out if the Stokes family was still in Banff.

No parking valet was in sight. She crossed over to the lot, but it was getting darker, which made it harder to find the rented SUV. In fact, it appeared that almost half the guests had driven SUVs to the hotel. After about five minutes of searching, Judith found the one with Washington license plates—and Renie's guidebook on the passenger seat.

She got behind the wheel and headed for the street next to the campground where she and Renie had parked when they'd sneaked onto the site and found Trixie in the VW bus. At this time of night, she was able to pull up next to the curb by the encampment. Sure enough, she could see the VW bus's outline beyond the shrubbery. Briefly, she considered getting out of the SUV to find out if the Stokes gang was heading home in the morning, but before she could make up her mind, she saw a huddled figure coming out of the shrubs. She leaned across the seat, recognizing Trixie, who was furtively looking in every direction of the street and sidewalk.

Judith rolled down the window and softly called Trixie's name. The girl seemed to shrink into herself as she froze in place. "Who . . . ?" The single word sounded like a sigh of relief. She stumbled over to the SUV as Judith unlocked the passenger door.

"Are you sick?" Judith asked after Trixie had settled into the seat and lain back on the headrest.

"No," Trixie answered faintly, running her hands up and down the white pleated dress Judith had seen in the motel closet. "Just . . . scared. Why did I ever come here? It's been a nightmare."

Judith had pulled away from the curb. "Do you want to go back to the motel?"

Trixie's head shot up. "No! I'll never go back there! I hate that place! It's even worse than being with the Stokes loonies. That man who . . ." She shook herself. "Never mind. Maybe all men are a pain."

"Well . . ." Judith was driving aimlessly to give Trixie time to collect herself. "What about Teddy? I thought he wanted to marry you."

"He's creepy," Trixie said in a more normal tone. "The whole family is creepy, at least the ones who live on that farm in Big Stove."

Judith didn't say anything for almost a minute. She realized they were going in the direction of the Banff Springs Hotel. Dare she suggest that Trixie spend the night with her and Renie? At least her cousin was asleep. Maybe she wouldn't know they had company until she woke up in the morning. And if Renie was her usual barely conscious self, she probably still wouldn't notice they had a guest. Judith finally asked Trixie what had happened to all of her belongings.

"Everything's at the campsite," the girl answered glumly. "Except my purse." She fingered the small faux-leather shoulder bag. "And my money. They didn't steal that."

"Good," Judith said. "How come you're wearing that nice white dress? Was the family having a farewell party?"

Trixie shook her head. "It was Teddy's idea. His grandpa Codger was crazy about Marilyn Monroe. It's like the one she wore in those pictures of her standing over an air vent with her skirt blowing way up. Teddy insisted I wear it today. I guess it was his lame idea of a joke."

They were approaching the hotel. "You can stay with my cousin and me tonight, Trixie. Unfortunately, we're leaving in the morning. Our husbands are coming back from their fishing trip to pick us up."

"I'm leaving, too," Trixie said. "I'm heading back home to Lincoln, Nebraska. I can't believe those Stokes creeps are from the same state. They give us all a bad name."

"I'm glad you're leaving," Judith said as they approached the hotel's porte cochere. "Do you have relatives and friends in . . ." The SUV suddenly slowed down—and stopped. "What on . . . ?" She scanned the dashboard. The fuel gauge was on E. "Damn! I forgot to get gas today! I'll have to call Triple A or . . . Triple C . . . or whatever it is in Canada to rescue me."

"That's okay," Trixie said. "I'll wait with you."

"No," Judith responded. "You have to tell the front desk that I need help." She paused to dig in her purse and take out the room key. "Then you can go up to our room and spend the night. Just be quiet so you don't wake up Mrs. Jones. You can sleep in the empty bed."

Trixie frowned. "That's not fair to you and your cousin. I'll sleep on the floor. That's what I did at the campsite."

"This is different." Judith patted Trixie's arm after handing over the room key. "Just go. I'm blocking traffic."

"Okay." Trixie's smile was tremulous. "You're really a nice person, Mrs. Flynn. Your cousin is sort of nice, too. In her own way. I think."

Trixie hesitated briefly, then got out of the SUV and scooted through the porte cochere. There was already another vehicle behind Judith. With a heavy sigh, she opened her door and stepped onto the pavement.

It was now dark, but Judith could see the pickup's

driver coming toward her. She recognized Mr. Barnes even before he spoke.

"What are you doing here?" he asked gruffly.

"I ran out of gas," Judith replied.

"Oh?" He sounded suspicious. "You'd better go inside. It's not smart to hang out here this time of night."

"By the Banff Springs Hotel?" Judith attempted a smile. "It strikes me as a safe place."

"Go inside," he all but barked. "Now!"

Fighting for composure, Judith shrugged. "Fine. Maybe I can catch up with Trixie." She reached into the car to grab her purse.

Barnes had moved up behind her. "What about Trixie? Where the hell is she?"

Judith twisted around to look up at him. "In the hotel. Why do you want to know?"

"You don't get to ask questions, Mrs. Smart Mouth Amateur Sleuth!" He grabbed Judith's arm. "I'm not letting go until you tell me where Trixie is!"

"She's not in the trunk," Judith retorted, trying not to wince from Barnes's rough grasp. "If you want to talk to her, wait until tomorrow."

He shook his head in an almost violent manner. "I want her back now," he growled, trying to keep his voice low. "You're going to take me to her unless you want your freaking arm busted!"

Judith's eyes peered at her surroundings. Not only was it dark, but no one else seemed to be in the parking area. Surely someone should be coming or going at only a little before ten o'clock. Her free hand touched her breast. "Okay," she finally said. "Let go of my arm and I'll take you to see Trixie. Why do you want to talk to her?"

"I told you, none of your damned business!" He yanked at Judith's arm, dragging her toward the rear of the hotel rather than through the porte cochere.

"Hold on!" Judith shouted. "I can't go fast. I've got an artificial hip. I could dislocate!"

"Pipe down!" Barnes hissed, but he hesitated, his voice still a low growl. "You could *what*?"

"You heard me," Judith said in a normal tone. "I know something about you."

Barnes leaned closer. "What the hell do you mean?"

Judith lifted her chin. "You're not Canadian."

"So what?" He seemed genuinely puzzled. "Lots of Americans move to Canada. Remember Nam and all the young guys who came up here to keep from getting their butts shot off in freaking Asia? I was one of 'em."

"I did wonder," Judith said, now speaking in a more normal tone.

Barnes was still leaning in on Judith and had narrowed his eyes. "You ran me through the system?"

Judith attempted a shrug but couldn't manage it with her adversary's hand clamped on her arm. "I didn't need to. You mentioned that I'm an amateur sleuth. How did you know that?"

"The cops. Who else?" He nudged Judith's thigh with his knees. "Move. We're going inside. Once we get there, you do what I say. Got it?"

Before Judith could speak, the sound of a siren could be heard. Barnes didn't seem to notice. "Come on, move, woman!"

"I can't," Judith protested. "My hip!" Her free hand clutched at the good side, but Barnes wouldn't know the difference.

"Okay, okay," Barnes muttered, reaching around Judith to open the hotel's rear door. "You go first. Move!" He gave her a rough nudge. Judith awkwardly crossed the threshold. The sirens were much closer.

"What the hell?" Barnes bellowed as Judith felt several drops of water splash onto her slacks.

As his hand fell away, Judith slammed the door behind her. The first person she saw was a startled busboy carrying what looked like a load of garbage.

"Ma'am!" he exclaimed. "Are you all right?"

"I am now," she replied, hearing the sirens behind

the hotel. "But don't open the door. There's a crazy person out there."

The fair-haired young man was big-eyed. "Are the Mounties here?" He looked excited and worried at the same time. "Has anyone been hurt?"

"No, but I understand an elderly guest was injured earlier . . ." She stopped, seeing Renie heading their way. She was wearing a jacket over her short summer nightgown and looked grim. "Excuse me," Judith said. "I must talk to my cousin."

Renie waved away the busboy and addressed Judith. "Well? Did I save your life or not?"

"You did," Judith replied. "I couldn't believe it. I thought you'd still be asleep."

"How could I sleep through Trixie falling over my suitcase and wailing like a banshee? Somehow she skinned her knee. Don't worry, she's fine."

Judith nodded halfheartedly. "Having escaped from what seemed like a near-death experience, I need to collapse. How did you know I was outside with Barnes?"

Renie shrugged. "Where else would you be? Trixie told me you ran out of gas. When you didn't show up right away, I looked outside—and there you were, being menaced by Big Bad Barnes. I emptied the fruit bowl on the credenza, filled it up with water, and dumped it out the window. Do you think the cops have busted him?"

"If not now, they will," Judith said as they crossed the lobby with its handsome two-story stone arches. "It turns out someone tried to kill John Smith. I figure it was Barnes, though I'm not quite sure why."

Renie, who was ignoring stares from some of the other guests, made a face. "Now that I've had a nap, I'm kind of hungry. Why don't we find a place where we can talk about it and I can get a snack?"

"Not in your nightgown, you ditz! Show a little class!" Judith picked up her step and headed for the elevators. "Call room service."

Judith still felt shaky when they entered their room. *Post-traumatic stress disorder,* she thought to herself. No wonder. Flopping down on the bed, she noticed that Renie had left the light on between the two double beds. There was no sign of Trixie in either of them and the bathroom door was open—and the room vacant.

Renie was at the credenza, putting the fruit back into the bowl she'd used to dump water on Barnes. "Oh no!" she cried, scanning the room. "Trixie's gone! She left a note."

Judith was beyond shock. "Well? Read it to me."

Renie sat down next to Judith. "'Teddy called me to say they heard about the poor old man who got hit on the head and is in a bad way. He seems to be all alone with no one to take care of him, so I'm going to help him recover. Thanks for being so nice to me. Have a good trip home. XXXOOO Trixie.'"

Judith sat with her chin on her fist. "I'm usually good with my insights about people. But I flunked on Trixie. She's not really the helpless type. In fact, she's an opportunist. My evil side almost makes me wish she ends up with all of the money. *If* John Smith is Codger, of course. The whole bunch should be put on a bier and sent out to sea."

"We're leaving in the morning. Does what happens to any of them matter?" Renie asked in a droll voice.

Judith shook her head. "Not anymore. You're right, we're done here. Order your snack and something for me. Getting menaced by Mr. Barnes has given me an appetite."

"Gosh," Renie said innocently, "I thought you'd be used to being endangered by now."

Judith just stared at her cousin.

Chapter 28

The cell phone rang at 7:34. Judith was getting dressed while Renie rolled around in the other double bed and groaned a lot. After fumbling with the cell, she heard Joe's overly chipper voice at the other end.

"How's my darling girl this morning?" he asked.

"Fine," Judith all but snapped. "I left you a message last night reminding you we're at the Banff Springs Hotel. Did you get it? Are you outside waiting for us?"

"Not quite," Joe replied, not so chipper. "Bill's doing his exercises and I'm waiting to sign off for the fish we're sending on home to the cannery. It's sort of complicated. International rules and all that."

Judith locked gazes with Renie, who had stopped

groaning and was sitting up in the bed. "So when will you get here?"

"Ten, ten thirty? It's hard to predict," Joe replied. "You and Renie can have a big, leisurely breakfast at your first-class hotel. You aren't bored with the wonders of Banff by now, are you?"

"We're fine." Judith's tone was still terse. "We'll see you when we see you. I have to get dressed now. Good-bye."

Renie grimaced. "What now?"

Judith explained. "We'll be lucky if they get here by noon."

By a little after eight, they were both dressed and ready to head out for breakfast when Sergeant Brewster called Judith. He said he was in the lobby and could he see them for a few minutes? She told him to come up to the room.

"He's coming here?" Renie looked flabbergasted, but suddenly grinned. "I'm calling room service." She picked up the house phone and placed the orders. "You'll note I kept it simple—eggs, sausage, and toast. Coffee, of course, and an extra cup for Brewster."

"Fine," Judith said. "He probably ate before coming to work."

The tired-looking sergeant arrived barely two minutes later. Judith figured he'd probably worked long hours investigating the assault on the alleged John Smith—and on Judith. She invited him to sit down and said that coffee was on the way. Brewster looked grateful and thanked her.

"Thank Mrs. Jones," Judith responded, having caught Renie's baleful look.

The Mountie gave her a weary smile and expressed his appreciation before turning back to Judith. "I understand you had an encounter with George Barnes last night. We received an alert from you shortly before ten o'clock, but the officer on patrol talked to a busboy who'd seen you come in and assured him that you were safely inside the hotel."

"I was," Judith confirmed. "How did you find out that my alert involved Mr. Barnes?"

"We didn't know that at the time," Brewster replied, "but we were looking for him. We got the fingerprint results back from the golf club that was used to put Mr. Smith in hospital. They matched those of George Barnes."

"Ah!" Judith exclaimed. "How lucky that you had his fingerprints on file."

Brewster nodded. "He'd had to be fingerprinted to get his liquor license for the motels. Tell me, were you suspicious of him all along?"

Judith considered the question, but Renie spoke up

first. "You bet we were. He was a real jerk. I'd already had a row with him in the motel parking lot. A motel owner who disses a guest has to be an idiot or a crook." She stood up as a knock sounded at the door. "Breakfast," she murmured, and raced off to let in whoever was delivering the food.

Judith asked Brewster if the RCMP had ever investigated the business operations of Barnes's motels. The Force hadn't, he replied, drawing back his feet as the breakfast trolley was rolled into the room. "There were never any serious complaints from guests. He and his sister had moved here from the States about thirty-five years ago. They bought out the motel where they now live, and then acquired a second one by the ski lifts. He built the other two about six years ago. In fact, I doubt that his younger employees know he's not Canadian."

"Coz knew," Renie said, removing lids and filling up her plate.

Brewster gazed curiously at Judith. "How did you figure that out, Mrs. Flynn?"

"His speech," Judith replied. "He used the phrase 'in the hospital' instead of 'in hospital.' And he never said 'eh?' Those were giveaways."

Brewster actually chuckled. "You're a canny one,

Mrs. Flynn. Did you also know that George Barnes wasn't his real name?"

"I didn't," Judith admitted. "What was it?"

"Barnard Georges." He paused. "He was born and raised in Big Stove, Nebraska. I only found that out this morning. Quite a coincidence, eh?"

Judith noticed the irony in Brewster's tone. "No relation to the Stokes family, I assume?"

"There is, in fact," the sergeant replied. "Mrs. Cornelius Stokes was Delia Georges before she married. A cousin, whose immediate family didn't get along with Barnes's branch. There had been a quarrel over property ownership years ago."

Judith hadn't yet uncovered her own breakfast, but Renie was wolfing down hers. That didn't prevent her from speaking up. "Did the Thokth folkth know about Barnth before dey got here?" she asked with her mouth full.

Brewster shook his head. "They had no idea. Neither did he, until they arrived. In fact, if he had known who they were, he probably wouldn't have allowed them to camp on his property. When he figured it out, I suspect he tried some kind of con to extort a large sum of money before they left Banff."

Judith almost dropped the spoon she'd used to add

sugar to her coffee. "The knives in poor Codger's back!" she cried. "I'll bet Barnes wanted to make the old man's death look like murder! That explains why the family kept moving the body. They were afraid Barnes might actually succeed in framing them as killers."

Brewster nodded. "Mr. and Mrs. Stokes really are simple farmers. They'd never traveled much before and certainly not to Canada. Mr. Stokes's sister, Mrs. Odell, and her husband are more sophisticated. But they hadn't seen the rest of her relatives in a very long time except for her brother Cornelius and his wife, who'd met them in Lincoln once or twice. The Odells didn't know what to believe about their relatives, especially the plan to honor the head of the family's peculiar request about being sent down the Bow on a bier."

"But they were serious about it," Judith said. She looked at the Mountie. "You told me such a stunt was against the law. Will there be charges?"

Brewster shook his head. "We can't prove they did it. No one has discovered a body along the river. There's a lot of wilderness in the area that doesn't have easy access."

"Yes," Judith said thoughtfully. "And John Smith? Will he recover from the attack?"

"He may," the sergeant said. "The doctor I spoke

with thought he must have a very rugged constitution to reach such an advanced age. He told one of the orderlies that he was a hundred and two."

Renie laughed. "He almost looked it. But we saw him eat. He's got a good appetite. Did you ever find out his real name or why or how he got here in the first place?"

"He refused to tell us," Brewster replied, looking bemused. "But Barnes insisted his victim was part of the Stokes entourage. We hoped we could get confirmation from the family, but they'd already left. We'll go through channels to figure it all out."

Judith considered telling him that they could ask Trixie. But the RCMP would figure that out for themselves when she showed up at the old man's bedside. "Who'll run the motels with Barnes under arrest?"

"Ms. Barnes, his sister. She's not under arrest. Yet." Brewster took a final sip of coffee and stood up. His gaze took in the packed luggage. "You *are* leaving today, eh?"

"Yes," Judith replied, noticing he looked faintly relieved. "Our husbands are picking us up in a couple of hours. So the Stokeses were allowed to leave?"

Brewster shrugged. "We were on shaky ground to ask them to stay in the first place. They're American citizens and our guests. Banff, after all, depends in large part on tourism." His eyes glinted a bit. "You understand that as well, eh, Mrs. Flynn?" Seeing that Judith did, he tipped his regulation hat and was gone.

By a little before ten, Judith and Renie had headed for the lobby, checked out, and proceeded to the entrance near the porte cochere. They already had asked the nearby BP station to bring a gas refill. The SUV had been brought around to the porte cochere and they had stowed their luggage and their purchases inside.

It was another gorgeous summer morning in Banff. The thick stands of tall evergreens, the majestic, craggy mountains, the blue ripples of the Bow River, and the snug little town with its hint of Bavaria had won Judith's heart.

"I almost hate to leave," she said softly. "It's even better the second or third time around."

"It is," Renie agreed. "Banff has to be one of the most beautiful settings I've ever seen."

"Maybe we can come back again someday." Judith sounded wistful.

She'd barely uttered the words when Snapper's pickup with its logo of a big fish came into view. "Here come Joe and Bill," Renie said. "Maybe we can make Revelstoke by late afternoon."

The husbands climbed out of the truck while Snapper started to unload their gear along with a large chest that no doubt held some of their most recent catches. The rest of the fish would have been sent to the local cannery back home that Joe had spoken of. The husbands and their wives reunited halfway between the pickup and the hotel.

"Hey," Joe said, after soundly kissing Judith, "you look terrific! You and Renie must have gotten to really relax on this trip."

Judith caught her cousin's eye as Bill seemed reluctant to let go of his wife. "We did. I even took a nap yesterday." It was true, though she wouldn't admit it had been in the evening before almost getting killed.

Joe's green eyes—magic eyes, Judith had always called them—studied her face. "Seriously, you weren't too bored?"

"Of course not!" Judith exclaimed with a big smile. "Would I lie to you?"

"Well . . ." He turned serious. "No, I don't think you ever have. But how would I know?"

Judith shrugged. "I guess you wouldn't."

Snapper had finished his task and joined the foursome. "These two are some pretty fine fishermen," he declared. "You ladies ought to be proud of them.

You're going to have some tasty meals when you get back home, eh?" He turned to Joe and Bill, shaking their hands.

"Our pleasure," Joe said. "Thanks again."

"Mine as well," Snapper assured them, and started back to his pickup. "See you next year, eh?"

Judith and Renie stared at each other. Then they glared at Joe and Bill.

"He's kidding," Joe finally said, with a grin that looked a bit forced.

"Right," Bill agreed, rubbing at the back of his neck. "Canadian humor, eh?"

The cousins weren't laughing. But once they were in the SUV and on the road, their mood improved. Judith finally got to the point at which she could ask Joe if he and Bill were serious about a repeat next summer.

Joe, who was at the wheel, shrugged. "Snapper tried to talk us into it, so we told him we'd think about it. When you're there on the river and the fish are biting, you really get stoked. But you and Renie had fun, right?"

"Yes," Judith replied. "In fact, you could say we got Stoked, too."

Joe nodded and smiled. Judith smiled back. There were some things that husbands never needed to know.

About the Author

MARY RICHARDSON DAHEIM is a Seattle native with a communications degree from the University of Washington. Realizing at an early age that getting published in books with real covers might elude her for years, she worked on daily newspapers and in public relations to help avoid her creditors. She lives in her hometown in a century-old house not unlike Hillside Manor, except for the body count. Daheim is also the author of the Alpine mystery series. She is the mother of three daughters and has three grandchildren.

www.marydaheimauthor.com
www.facebook.com/mary.daheim

HARPER LUXE

THE NEW LUXURY IN READING

We hope you enjoyed reading
our new, comfortable print size and found it
an experience you would like to repeat.

Well – you're in luck!

HarperLuxe offers the finest in fiction and
nonfiction books in this same larger print size and
paperback format. Light and easy to read, HarperLuxe
paperbacks are for book lovers who want to see
what they are reading without the strain.

For a full listing of titles and
new releases to come, please visit our website:

www.HarperLuxe.com